twisted RIVALRY

DEVON McCORMACK

TWISTED RIVALRY

Copyright © 2024 Devon McCormack
Hardcover Edition

Cover Design by Murphy Rae
Editing by Keren Reed
Proofing by Lyrical Lines, Lori Parks, and Judy's Proofreading

This is a work of fiction. Names, characters, places, and incidents either are the product of author imagination or are used fictitiously, and any resemblance to actual persons, living or dead, business establishments, events, or locales is entirely coincidental. All products and brand names mentioned are registered trademarks of their respective holders/companies.

This book is licensed to the original purchaser only. Duplication or distribution via any means is illegal and a violation of international copyright law, subject to criminal prosecution and upon conviction, fines, and/or imprisonment. Any eBook format cannot be legally loaned or given to others. No part of this book may be reproduced or transmitted in any form or by any means, electronic or mechanical, including photocopying, recording, or by any information storage and retrieval system, without the written permission of the Publisher, except where permitted by law.

TRIGGER WARNING: *This book includes the following content, which may be triggering for some readers.*

- Discussions about intrafamilial child abuse, including sexual coercion and assault perpetuated by someone who is not a main character (non-MC). The book also contains very brief flashbacks of abusive situations, but details of the abuse are not graphic or fixated upon.
- Discussions about non-MC suicides, which occur prior to the start of the book.
- Self-harm of a non-MC, including cutting.
- Depictions of manipulation, stalking, surveillance, gaslighting, and trauma-bonded relationships with non-MCs.
- Depictions of characters who have unresolved trauma that would necessitate therapy in a real-world setting.

CONTENT WARNING

While *Twisted Rivalry* is a steamy romance, it features content that may be triggering for some readers. The trigger warning contains spoilers, so it's included on the copyright page of this book, where it can be easily located but also as easily avoided. Because of the nature of these triggers, they are as specific as possible to protect those individuals who may struggle with the content of this novel.

1

RYAN

SWEAT CLINGS TO the inside of my arms as I trim the hedges, keeping at a decent speed. I've got plenty of work to get to today, so I started with the easiest task on my list. When I take a moment to catch my breath, I wipe the sweat from my brow and enjoy a cool breeze. I close my eyes, absorb it fully, and intentionally store it in my memory so I can summon it as my work becomes more challenging throughout the day.

I use this as a mini break, taking a swig of water from the tumbler affixed to my work belt. I'm about to continue trimming when I hear my brother's voice coming from the side of the house. Even a good twenty yards away, I know his voice like my own. Even if he hadn't been speaking, I would have felt him in my bones before seeing him.

Simon rounds the corner, a guest at his side.

I have the faintest of hopes: is this the extra help I've been pleading with him for? I know better. I've been asking for help since Kenneth moved on, and Simon hasn't so much as posted an ad to hire someone who could make the workload more tolerable for me and the two other workhands. It's more likely a new lawyer working on the trust, or some business acquaintance he's trying to impress by offering them a tour of the estate. Maybe he wants to introduce them to me to show how I'm little more than the help now. It's not something I mind Simon using me for, since anyone who would feel superior to me because of the life I've chosen, I wouldn't respect them anyway.

I press the trigger on the trimmer and slice away at the lengthy branches around the hedge as Simon and his guest draw near. I glance their way once again before zeroing in on his guest.

I know that face.

No, not… It can't be…

But how…what…

As they approach, it's as if they're moving in slow motion. That unmistakable face can't be real, just a phantom haunting me.

I've short-circuited, struggling not to be sucked into the past, until they're just a few yards away. It's easier then to see it's a different face, but the similarities are uncanny—the shape, the curvature of his jawline. Hell, even his eyebrows seem to be the right thickness. His hair's the right shade of dark brown, but thinner, and the bangs are longer than the ones I remember.

If I didn't know better, I'd swear it was him. I'm surprised I haven't dropped the trimmer during my distracted inspection.

"Good morning, Ryan," Simon says.

Conflicting feelings war within me. I haven't taken my eyes off that face, but I can see Simon's mischievous smirk in my periphery. There was a time when we were connected so deeply, I'd have been able to pull thoughts from his mind, know exactly what he's thinking right now, but Simon severed that connection long ago, so now I'm left struggling to read what lies behind that cunning expression.

"Aren't you going to greet me?" Simon asks.

I relax the trimmer at my side and approach him. When I lean in to kiss his cheek, he turns, and my lips hit his mouth. He offers a gentle peck, and I take it, knowing it's best to just give him what he wants, especially if I want him to explain why the hell this guy's here.

I turn to his guest, close enough now to see that even the subtle gray hue in his blue eyes looks just right. Disturbingly so.

"These hedges are looking great," Simon observes.

I nod, but just want him to tell me what fucked-up game this is.

"Come on, Ryan. Be polite and say hello to our newest employee."

"Employee?"

"You said you needed help around the yard. Mr. Finley is here to assist you in whatever way you may need."

"Assist?" Simon's attempt at an explanation only confuses me more.

Mr. Finley steps toward me, extending his hand, and I pull back instinctively. He's not Kieran, and he's clearly older, but…wouldn't Kieran be older too?

"You can call me Jonas," Kieran's ghost says, keeping his hand out.

Simon's grin overtakes his face. I've often wondered if I look that villainous when I smile. After all, we share the same face—something Jonas is noticing since he glances between us, maybe trying to find some identifying feature that will set us apart in his mind.

"You didn't mention I would be working for your twin," the look-alike tells Simon.

"My brother has a bad habit of leaving out pertinent information." I can't disguise the bitterness in my tone.

"Maybe I just like surprises," Simon replies, then returns his attention to Jonas. "I figured you could take the day to get settled in, and start tomorrow?"

I open my mouth to object, but nothing comes out. If I could, I don't even know what I'd say, but probably something accusatory toward my bastard of a brother.

I need to get into this with him, but not in front of his poor victim. "It's nice to meet you, Jonas," I say curtly. "I should get back to work."

I fire up the trimmer and hear Simon say, "He's busy right now," before offering to give him a tour of the yard and introduce him to the other workhands.

Once they're a safe distance away, I glance at Jonas's profile.

It's the same face—how is it the same face?

Where did Simon find this guy?

My nerves are so on edge, hands stiff on the trimmer, gut clenched. Feels like I might vomit. Fortunately, I manage to keep it together until they return to the house.

Normally, my work helps me escape the past, but not today. Jonas's face brings back a torrent of memories I struggle against, my rage at Simon intensifying over the next hour until I can't contain it any longer. I head inside to confront my brother about what must be some kind of perverse joke.

I find him in his office, his fingers clicking away on his laptop.

I wonder if he's really in the middle of an engrossing email or if he started faking as soon as he heard my footsteps coming down the hall.

"What the fuck is this?" I ask, approaching him like I might have when we were kids, after he'd pulled some mischievous prank or cheated during Monopoly.

He grins before glancing up. He looks so damned pleased with himself, as though he's planned this so perfectly, he knew exactly how I'd react—and of course he would. Who would know me better than my twin brother?

"Yes, Ryan?" he asks, simpering, looking even more mischievous than when he approached me with the stranger with Kieran's face.

"You know what you did."

"I got you the help you asked for, didn't I?"

"Millions of people in the world you could have found, but you found him?"

"I thought it'd be a comforting face."

Rage sears like a hot poker stabbing into my chest. "Simon, I let you have your way around the house. I let you do whatever you want. But I won't let you have this."

"It's my house, Ryan. My money to do what I want with, and I let *you* stay."

That isn't true. I can stay here because of the provisions in Father's trust, but I don't bring that up. I can't get sucked into Simon's red herrings. There's only one thing on my mind now: "Please let him know we won't need his services. If this was your way to screw me out of extra help, then Morgan, Forsyth, and I can get along just fine. There. You win."

Because he fucking loves to win.

Simon looks to the bay window like he's considering what I've said before he pushes to his feet and starts around the desk. "Ryan, I don't think you want me to do that. In fact, I *know* you don't want me to do that."

Why would he say that? "Are you suggesting I want him here because he looks like Kieran?"

He finally makes eye contact, an evil smirk playing across his lips. "Why? Is that how you feel?"

I don't even know how to respond to that, but he doesn't give me time.

"That's not what I was suggesting at all, Ryan. You don't want him to leave because the poor guy needs the money. He's in dire straits. Lien on his house. Sick sister. I offered to cover the lien for him, and 10K can go a long way for the summer. Maybe help take care of some past-due medical bills."

"Sick sister?" I don't try to hide my suspicion.

"Acute lymphoblastic leukemia."

If that's true, I feel like a dick for how I treated the guy. Although, I'm not convinced this isn't all some wild fabrication crafted by my brother. I'd be a fool to believe it without evidence.

"She's endured intense treatments since she was a child. They thought things were going well until this past year, but then it came back a few months after her eighteenth birthday. Unfortunately, the center where she was being treated can't continue to work with her now that she's not a minor anymore. But if you really want, I'll demand he leave at once, and he, his aunt, and his sickly sister can go back to fending for themselves."

He brushes my shoulder as he walks by me like he's on his way to dismiss Jonas immediately.

"Wait," I say, hating myself for even considering this BS might be true.

I struggle with my thoughts, but Simon's footsteps stopped before I even spoke, surely knowing how I'd react.

"Why did you mention an aunt?"

"Because they lost their parents. Their father when they were younger, and their mother a few years ago."

The news knots in my chest, and I don't doubt Simon brought this up as a final blow. I'm tempted to ask for specifics but stop myself. What good could come of knowing the sordid details of this poor man's past?

"Do you have proof that what you're saying about his sister is true?" I turn to him, and Simon winces.

"You mean, you don't believe me? You don't trust me?"

No, I don't. "I want to make sure *you* haven't been deceived," is my wise reply, which I doubt he believes, but it satisfies him enough to retrieve his cell from his back pocket. He approaches and displays a Facebook profile.

I peruse it, seeing that face—that goddamn face. There are multiple images of this guy with a girl in the hospital. Even an attached GoFundMe page that hasn't raised more than two grand to cover insurance or out-of-pocket expenses.

I wouldn't put it past Simon to go to all the trouble to fabricate a story, but it's plausible enough to keep me from standing my ground, which I'm sure is exactly what Simon hoped for.

If I'm wrong, I can't find out I've deprived this guy and his family of the help they need.

"Maybe you could just give him the money," I suggest. "You have more than enough."

"You think I'm not being charitable? Why don't you ask Morgan and Forsyth how much they're making this summer? Certainly not ten grand. I'm sorry if you disagree with how I choose to help the guy, but that's not my problem."

I hate how good Simon is at dancing around the issue.

"You know why I don't want him here. And you know why you asked that man here, and it has nothing to do with his sick sister."

Simon's gaze meets mine, and he approaches, stopping just inches away. I can feel his breath against my lips.

"If he's a problem or just not any good at yard work, say the word, Ryan, and I'll fire and evict him from Hawthorne Heights. How does that sound?"

I know better than to trust Simon. Even if that came to pass, he'd make up an excuse, a new reason that Jonas must stay, because clearly, he has something on his mind.

"So he can stay?" Simon asks, maybe to give the impression that I have some say in this. That once I concede, this is now something I'm doing to myself. It reminds me of when we were kids and he would slap me with my own hand and shout, "Stop hitting yourself! Stop hitting yourself!"

God, he's loving this.

I should tell him no. I should insist—demand—that Jonas leave immediately and that Simon give the guy the cash. Hell, if I had access to all the useless money in our estate, I'd give Jonas what he needed to take care of his sister for life.

But Simon has other plans, and as much as I don't want that ghost in this house, a part of me wants to know what this is all about.

"He can stay." My words are a whisper, which makes the corners of Simon's mouth perk up.

"I think you'll like working with him, big bro," he says, leaning toward me and offering a gentle kiss against my lips, the sort that stirs fury within me.

I surrender, dashing off into the hall.

As I head back through the manor, my mind goes wild as I speculate on Simon's intentions. Why the hell would he have hired a man who looks so much like our deceased brother?

2

JONAS

THE BEDROOM IS bigger than I expected. Maybe twice as big as the primary bedroom in my aunt's place.

I only brought enough luggage to get me through the week—that's how long this job should take, I figure. Although, after meeting Ryan Hawthorne, I'm wondering if I underestimated the task ahead of me.

I FaceTime my aunt to let her know I arrived safely.

"What did they say you had to do?" Aunt Amy whispers.

"Some yard work."

"Jonas Finley, I've lived long enough to know that no one tracks someone down so they can offer them ten grand to do some yard work."

"Aunt Amy, if you saw this place, you might reconsider. When I was coming up the drive, it was like a palace…maybe only small compared to the Biltmore. There's a fountain out front, a pool in the back. Just what's cleared out from the woods has to be ten acres, with ponds and plenty of flower beds. I'll send you photos when I get a chance. These guys are wealthy—like absurdly wealthy."

As I explain how impressive the place is, Aunt Amy's glare

suggests she's caught on that I'm evading her question.

"Still, they don't need someone from Chicago for that. I'm sure there are plenty of qualified people there—even more qualified, who have actual experience with yard work. So tell me honestly, Jonas, why do they want *you*?"

Fuck. I knew she wouldn't let me skirt around this that easily.

"I'm not supposed to say."

She sighs. "Well, I guess that makes sense. Maybe it's better if I don't know anyway, but I don't like it."

"Is Charity there?"

"She is, but she's resting. Do you mind if I get her to call you later?"

My sister's still recovering from her last round of chemo, so this is expected. We chat a bit more before we say our goodbyes, and then I get right to what I've wanted to do since I got here. The man in the bow tie who'd scouted me never told me who my employer was, and even when I landed in Hartsfield-Jackson, I didn't have an address. A driver took me to my destination, so until Simon Hawthorne introduced himself, I didn't even know whom I'd be working for.

With that bit of info, an internet search takes me to the Hawthorne family's Wikipedia page. At a quick glance, I can tell the family money came largely from oil. Very old money. Simon's great-grandparents are referred to as tycoons and industrialists, and apparently, there's some question about their involvement with the Soviet Union.

"Rich-people problems," I mutter, part resentment, part envy.

I check the time, and it's twelve thirty. Kace, the butler who escorted me to my room, said lunch would only be served until two, and I didn't have time to eat breakfast before I had to be at the airport, so I venture down to the kitchen. If only I could remember where he said that was…

I retrace my steps—or so I thought—but before I know it, I'm all turned around, wandering through this maze of a house, reflecting on the circumstances that brought me here.

"Would you like to earn some money? How about enough to help you with all these bills you've accumulated?"

"As a sign of good faith, and to show you how serious we are, by the time you get home tonight, the lien on your aunt's house will be gone."

Maybe I should've told the man in the bow tie to fuck off. Although, I did do just that, and he proved he meant business when he called and got me to check my aunt's mortgage account. Sure enough, it was done.

I'd been suspicious about what the job entailed. After all, what reason could the bow-tie man have for being so cryptic if it didn't involve drugs or money laundering…something that could put me in prison for a long time if I got caught.

"Pack your bags. We'll fly you to Georgia to our client. He'll let you know what will be expected of you. You'll have a chance to refuse, but you'll have to hear it from him directly."

Probably should have refused then.

I continue through the manor, admiring the artwork and the antique furnishings that fill the place, amused that most of this stuff is likely worth ten times as much as my car.

Still struggling to orient myself, I wish I'd gone to greater lengths to memorize the route the butler had taken me along. I'm tempted to call out for directions, but I'd rather figure it out on my own. It's maybe fifteen minutes before I find myself downstairs, heading toward the middle of the house, I assume. An aroma hits me—something savory—and I head through a few doors before I enter a large area with polished cement floors and hanging pots and pans.

This is promising.

Ryan Hawthorne stands at a large stove, scooping something from a pot into a bowl on the tray he holds. "Nell, if you can set aside some of this chili, I'll have it throughout the week."

I glance around for this person he's speaking to, when he turns, and I realize he must've mistaken me for someone else. I'm waiting for him to correct himself, but he just stares like he did when Simon and I approached him.

He can't know what his brother asked of me. Ryan seemed to buy that bullshit about yard work, but he knows there has to be more.

"My brother has a bad habit of leaving out pertinent information."

Isn't that the truth?

Even in my brief interaction with Simon, when he told me about this mystery opportunity, he hadn't mentioned that the guy he was paying me to seduce was his brother—and not just his brother, but his identical twin. I'm a fairly attractive guy, so I figured it would be easy enough, but after meeting Ryan, it's clear there's another twist: I look like someone he knows…or knew? And not in a way that's to my advantage, so this isn't going to be as easy as chumming up with the guy, getting drunk enough to do what I need to do, and then heading home the next day.

Of course, I should've figured Simon wouldn't pay ten grand for something I could manage in a night.

"I'm sorry," I say. "I was trying to find the kitchen."

He continues staring a few moments too long before he says, "Looks like you found it."

I step into the kitchen and glance around. "I don't know what I'm supposed to do. Do you know whom I could ask?"

Given our awkward introduction, I'm expecting him to be annoyed or act like I inconvenienced him in some way, but he says, "There are plates and trays at the other end of the counter. Drinks are in the fridge. Nell has everything covered and gets annoyed if you don't place the lids back. Also, don't spill anything onto the edge of the pots because she'll find out who did it and make a stink about it. There's an adjoining room where we eat."

He seems to have set aside all those frustrations from earlier, and he sounds professional, which assures me he might be a good boss to work for while I'm pretending to be here to help him with the groundskeeping.

Ryan lifts a tin lid and grabs some rolls before heading through a door I assume goes to the adjoining room.

Does he eat with the staff?

I'm having a hard time making sense of the dynamics around the house. When I arrived, Simon was dressed in a slick tailored suit, his dirty-blond hair neatly groomed, his bangs gelled to the side—the look I'd expect from a wealthy heir. Ryan, on the other hand, is in a dirty tank and khaki shorts, his hair cut similarly to his brother's but like the most he did to style it was run his fingers through his bangs, a look I might expect from a servant of this impressive estate.

After I grab some food and a drink, I head through the same door as Ryan, to a smaller room, taken up mostly by a table and a dozen chairs. He sits at the end, and I take a seat adjacent to him, leaving a seat between us.

Gonna have to get to know him sooner or later if I'm gonna get this 10K.

If he notices the bold move, he doesn't let on.

"I'm Jonas," I remind him.

He pauses mid-bite, then returns his spoon to the bowl of chili. "I remember your name," he says, then resumes eating.

He's clearly got his guard up, which will make this tricky, but it's also kind of nice. If he were too eager, we'd be off to the bedroom, and I'd have to get a clue about fucking around with a guy real fast.

I should've probably googled that along with the stuff about the Hawthornes, but really, I'm having a hard time accepting any of this is real. I keep waiting for a camera crew to pop out and reveal this has all been a part of some sick reality series.

"So where are you from?" Ryan asks before taking a sip of water.

"Chicago."

"That's where my brother found you?"

"Yeah."

"And you took a job from a random guy who asked you to come all this way to be a workhand?"

"I needed the money." That isn't a lie, and I can tell he doesn't doubt that.

"Money's one of those things that makes people do strange things, I guess."

"Tell me about it," I say, and his gaze shifts to me, like he's trying to read something into my expression. I doubt he could pick up from my face the strange thing I'm being paid to do for him. He's a lean, muscular guy with a jawline I'm a little envious of, and even as a straight man, I can tell he's what plenty of people would consider attractive—not the kind who would have problems getting laid. Although, out here in the middle of nowhere, maybe he doesn't have many options. Maybe his brother thinks a quick fuck might get him to lighten up a little.

Maybe this guy I look like is an ex…or maybe even weirder, a deceased partner.

I try not to entertain this kind of speculation since it doesn't change what I have to do.

I take a bite of my chili, and it's hard to tell if I'm just that hungry or if it's really that good, but I'm a few spoonfuls into it before Ryan says, "Sorry. I was caught off guard earlier. Simon didn't tell me he'd hired someone. But we start at six a.m. tomorrow. There are only four of us—including you—so it's going to be hard labor, and we'll go until four in the afternoon. You'll get an hour break for lunch and two additional fifteen-minute breaks. We don't work weekends, unless there's a big project or we're on a deadline. I don't handle the money stuff, so if you feel like you deserve overtime or something, that's for you to handle with Simon. Any questions?"

Again, this suggests the guy's a good boss. I like that he doesn't beat around the bush.

"I don't think I have any right now."

"You will. Just make sure to ask them because I'd rather you ask a dumb question than do a dumb thing."

I chuckle. "Okay, will do."

As he continues eating, I study his face. His body. What will his lips feel like? This guy seems like he could be really bossy in the bedroom. What if we get in and I'm not able to perform? Is it wrong to deceive this guy and act like I'm into him?

I shake those thoughts from my head.

I've got to do this.

Regardless of what I feel is right or wrong or whom I'm sexually attracted to, I have to put all that aside.

I'll do anything for my sis. Even this.

3

RYAN

It's only been two days since he arrived, but the extra pair of hands has already helped us make progress on the yard. This morning, we're working on the flower beds on the west wing, getting in new flowers, shrubs, and foliage.

Forsyth removes the tiller from the bed. "I'm gonna head to the next one. This noob gonna be okay if I leave him with you?" He winks at Jonas, who smiles.

Jonas hasn't struggled to charm my workhands, and I'm sure it's in no small part due to how he's thrown himself into the work.

Forsyth rolls the tiller alongside the house, and Jonas and I shovel the soil for the new roses. It's a particularly humid morning, and all the guys tossed their shirts off before noon, so it's hard for me not to notice Jonas's body as his shovel hits the ground. His firm, muscular physique shakes, thick meaty pecs and biceps continuing to tremble in the shock wave, which reverberates to his firm torso, impressive obliques disappearing behind the waistband of his shorts. His body assures me it's not just his face that reminds me of Kieran.

"What kind of construction did you say you did?" I ask as I sculpt a hole in the ground.

I've asked the occasional question, but mostly kept him busy. I want to see what kind of man he is, and nothing tells that story like seeing how he takes to manual labor.

"It's a tough market," he replies, wiping sweat off his brow, "so whatever needed to be done. I made some friends, and they'd call me whenever they needed something."

Guys in an industry like that call someone they know is reliable, something he's demonstrated the past couple of days.

"Simon told me about your sister. I'm sorry to hear that."

He eyes me uneasily. Is it because it's all a lie Simon fabricated? If that's the case, did Jonas and some little girl pose for those photos? No, that's too much, even for Simon.

"She's doing okay right now, but she has more treatments to get through. There's a place my aunt and I wanted to send her in New York. The best place for her to get care, but insurance denied covering the facility, so if I can get some cash, I might be able to get her in."

That sounds heartfelt, and it makes me hate myself for thinking this guy would try to con me with something like that.

"American healthcare system is fucked," I say.

He pulls up some more earth before glancing at me, and I lose track of place and time, as though I'm sucked into the past, gazing into Kieran's eyes.

"Funny thing for a rich guy to say."

That snaps me back to the present. "I'm not rich," I explain. "Simon got all the money, and I just get to stay on the property, which is fine by me, but the moment I step foot off our property, I'm probably worse off than you."

"Well, maybe not me." There's a trace of humor in his tone, but I detect the seriousness too.

"Sorry, that was insensitive. I only meant—"

"I get it. Well, actually, I don't get it at all. That sounds like a strange setup."

"Yeah," I say, but that's as much as I'm willing to share, and Jonas is wise enough not to ask questions. Who knows. Maybe Simon already told him the reason.

Jonas and I break for lunch together—again, not by mistake. I tell myself it's to interrogate him, but part of me can't deny that regardless of what happened between Kieran and me, I like being around a familiar face that reminds me of a time when Hawthorne Heights was buzzing with energy and life. Back when there was laughter and play. When we lived in the bliss of our ignorance…our innocence.

But it also reminds me of when it all went wrong.

My sin and the horror that followed.

Why it's my duty to remain here and maintain what little life our home—Simon's home—still has.

Jonas sits close to me, as he does for all our meals, like he's trying to get a read of me as much as I am of him.

"So…you seeing anyone?" he asks before taking a bite of his burrito.

"No." My reply is curter than intended, but hopefully sends the message that this isn't a subject I'm interested in getting into.

"Oh, okay. I imagine it's hard to meet anyone out here."

His use of *anyone* isn't lost on me. If Forsyth or Morgan had brought that up, they would have just said girls.

I wonder if Simon outed me. Not that it's a big secret. But like any true-blood Hawthorne, I don't like people knowing my business unless I want them to.

There's an awkward stretch of silence, something I've learned makes Jonas particularly uncomfortable, which I can't really relate to. I enjoy the quiet.

"You have any recommendations for where I might go around here if I did want to meet someone?"

Someone? Why is he being intentionally vague?

My gaze shifts to him, and he's looking right at me. I can't make eye contact with my brother's eyes for long before looking away.

"Are you asking if there are any bars or clubs around here?" I take a bite from Nell's nachos.

"Yeah, like places you'd go to really let loose. Meet people. I don't know, do you use like apps or something? Sorry to ask, but I'm used to having more access to stuff like that in Chicago."

It's suspicious that he's asking me about this when he could have just as easily asked Forsyth or Morgan.

Is this what Simon wants him to do? Check up on my dating life? Why would he need a man who looks like Kieran to do that?

"I don't think you're gonna find much on an app out here," I say. "Not unless someone is traveling at least half an hour, and I'm sure Simon mentioned you can't have visitors as long as you're staying here."

"Yeah, yeah. He did. I only meant, maybe I could get them to come pick me up or I could Uber over to them."

"Be ready for a very long wait on an Uber. Maybe you could

get Forsyth to drive you into downtown Renovere. That's about a ten-minute drive. Then you can Uber from there. It'll be cheaper."

"Thanks for the intel."

"Anytime."

Jonas is eyeing me strangely, and he hasn't touched his burrito since he started on this subject. All I know is, I feel bad for the guy if he thought coming to Hawthorne Heights was gonna be a place where he could get laid. If anything, it'd take 10K to get someone to be this isolated.

"So you don't have any apps on your phone?" he asks. "Like…I don't know, Grindr or…"

He waits, as though gauging my reaction.

"…Tinder?" he adds.

Tinder wouldn't mean much, but I don't think it's an accident that he brought up Grindr first, and as my gaze meets his, I'm starting to realize why he has this stiff jaw and he's staring like that.

Is he flirting with me?

It's so rare that I have exchanges like that anymore, I can't help but doubt it.

And the fact that he looks like Kieran only throws me that much more.

But his gaze doesn't let up, and I just sit there, staring at him.

"Apps? No, I don't do anything like that," I finally manage to say. "You know, I think this might not be an appropriate conversation for me to have with staff. Sorry, I should have interrupted it sooner. I'm technically your supervisor."

"Right, right," he says, then picks up his burrito again.

I'm trying to keep my cool, but I'm silently freaking out, my brain scrambling through everything that just happened. And one person keeps coming to the foreground. "Fuck," I mutter.

Simon put this guy up to this fucked-up task. Is that what he's here to do? Fuck me? And to get someone who looks like Kieran… The sick bastard.

I lower my hands beneath the table so Jonas doesn't see how tight they're clenched.

"What?" Jonas asks.

"Just thought of something I need to bring up to Simon," I lie. Just add it to all my other goddamn lies.

"I'm sorry. I shouldn't have asked. Just not used to being somewhere like this," Jonas says, and it's clear he's picked up on the change in my mood.

"You haven't done anything wrong," I tell him, making eye contact. I don't want him to think he's fucked up his chances at getting his money. As far as I'm concerned, whatever my brother has promised him, he's owed.

Now I just need to know why the hell Simon needs this guy to hit on me.

I push to my feet, snatch my tray, and head for the door. As I reach it, I turn back around. "Just get back to work with the guys. I might be a minute."

His wide-eyed expression tells me he knows I've figured out too much.

I could fucking kill Simon.

4

JONAS

As I FaceTime with Charity, she sits at her desk, reading off her laptop: "A beautiful, chateau-style manor hidden on three hundred acres of Georgia countryside. The Hawthorne family began construction of Hawthorne Heights in the early 1900s, a project that took nearly a decade to complete."

She made time to chat with me a few days ago, but she didn't have much energy, so I didn't get to talk with her much. She's more like her usual self today. Wearing a bandanna with a unicorns-and-rainbows print to cover where her hair's fallen out, she has dark bags under her eyes, and I can tell she's fighting to smile. She doesn't want me to worry about her, but no amount of forced cheerfulness can prevent me from worrying.

"Those photos you sent don't do the place justice," she adds. "But you're sticking to your story that this isn't a big deal?" She shoots me a pointed glare.

When I first talked with Amy and Charity after I arrived, I didn't reveal whom I was working for. I knew I couldn't keep it from them for long, and my sis finally managed to get it out of me, which is what started her internet search.

"Maybe a little bit of a big deal," I say.

She scans her laptop screen as she probes a little more about the job, asking about whom I work with and the duties I'm expected to perform. Of course, I stick to the story I told Aunt Amy, skirting around specifics, when she suddenly winces. "You said Simon was your boss, right? Have you read this about his parents?"

Tension rises within me. "You know, maybe you shouldn't look at that."

After my first day at Hawthorne Heights, I did a more thorough perusal on Google, discovering that Ryan and Simon's mom overdosed when they were kids. Then later, when they were eighteen, their dad shot himself.

"They both killed themselves. How tragic."

She's talking about Ryan and Simon, but I know she's thinking about our own loss.

She never met our father because his accident happened right before she was born. But she remembers the horror of losing Mom when she was torn from us by her own cancer—something that haunts me not just because of the hell we went through with that, but because it taught me that no matter how hard Charity fights this, I could still lose her too.

That's why I'm fucking here. Because I have to do what I can to protect her.

"Okay, well, let's not talk about it," I say. "This isn't exactly what I wanted to chat with you about."

Not today. Not ever.

She shakes her head, pulling her gaze from her screen, though the far-off look in her eyes suggests she's still thinking about the news she just discovered.

"Sorry," she says. "I should be polite and wait to google when we're not on the phone. I can't help it, though. You and Aunt Amy are being so secretive. Anyway, wild to think people could have all that money and be that unhappy."

"Money isn't everything." The words come out hollow. Even knowing that must be true, it's hard to accept. But I guess the death of the Hawthornes' parents is a reminder that if life can suck that bad for someone as well off as them, what chance do the rest of us have?

"Jonas…I know you said you're not sure how long it'll take to finish the job, but maybe you can come back for a weekend?"

I scratch at my face nervously. "I don't want to make promises I can't keep, Char, and I'm honestly not sure how long it'll be before I can come back."

Fucking impossible to tell after my fuckup.

I'd jumped the gun. After two days of working with Ryan, struggling to think of how to make something happen, I made a move, but it was the wrong one. As soon as Ryan picked up on what I was aiming at, he got the hell out of there.

It's been awkward the past few days.

"But I'm doing everything I can to get this job done so I can get back to you guys."

Charity beams, the first sincere smile I've seen on her face since we started the call. "Well, at least Aunt Amy's here to talk about *Vanderpump Rules* with me."

"I must say, I'm happy to miss that."

"Shut up. You love it too."

"All that screaming and fighting? No thank you."

She rolls her eyes. "You like talking to me about it, at the very least. I mean, you had more feelings about Scandoval than I did."

I can't help but laugh. "Fair. You've found a show that pisses me off enough to have thoughts and feelings about it."

But she's not wrong. I enjoy keeping up with the same shows as her. It's an easy thing to talk about, and the drama of other people's lives helps distract from the bullshit in our own.

The welcome subject change gets her chatting about podcasts and YouTube channels she keeps up with for the latest reality TV gossip—a much lighter conversation I'm happy to have before we end our talk for the night, and it's maybe fifteen minutes before I figure we both need to get to bed.

"Night, JoJo. I love you."

"Love you too. Tell Aunt Amy I said good night."

"I will."

Getting to talk to her again reignites my confidence in my mission. I have to find a way around my latest obstacle with Ryan. If I'm gonna make this happen, I have to be smarter than I was when we were at lunch. Because the longer this takes me, the longer I'll be away from my family, which physically hurts, especially while she's undergoing treatment.

I should be there for her.

No, I *am* being there for her by doing this.

It's something I have to remind myself of often.

I'll fucking figure this out.

Because I have to.

The following day, as I'm working, I'm running through casual ways to regain the progress I'd made with Ryan.

As we finish prepping a bed around the fountain on the east side of the house, Ryan says, "Get the wheelbarrow, and take this potting soil over to Forsyth. He needs more for that new bed. And then swing by that pile we've collected by the library and take a few loads back to the woods."

I glance up at him. He's not making eye contact—hasn't made eye contact since my failed attempt at flirting three days ago.

I obey his instructions, rolling the wheelbarrow to Forsyth, who's working in the front of the house today. I wonder if Ryan is sending me to another part of the house to keep me away from him. Maybe he just thinks I'm some kind of creep.

About fifteen minutes later, while I'm grabbing more dirt from the pile by the library, Ryan approaches me, an urgent expression on his face. He looks like he needs to chat about something, and I'm wondering if he's about to bring up my flirting fail.

"Jonas, if you could do about three more loads of this, and then get back to that bed and till it out, then you can take your lunch."

I don't imagine he said *your lunch* by mistake. Those first couple of days, he seemed to set up our lunches around the same time, but now he's made a point to stack them so we don't run into each other. I've also backed off during breakfast and dinner. Forsyth and Morgan don't stay at Hawthorne Heights like me since they live in town, but they'll eat breakfast and sometimes stay for dinner if they don't have other plans. Their presence has helped make things less awkward, and I've hoped that sitting farther down the table, giving Ryan some space, will help me win back his trust.

His hands come down on the end of the wheelbarrow, and I notice something in his right hand—a folded sheet of paper. When I look up at him, his gaze is right on me; he's making eye contact.

His irises are a much richer blue than mine. Darker too. There's something captivating about the shade that I hadn't noticed, maybe wouldn't have noticed if he hadn't deprived me of seeing them.

"I'll see you in a bit," he says before heading back toward the house.

But he's left the folded paper in the wheelbarrow.

Is this a pink slip? Simon said I'd need to cover as a workhand while I managed my actual objective, but I hadn't considered I might get let go before accomplishing it and then I'd have done all this other work for free. Come to think of it, this would be one hell of a way for the Hawthornes to get a week of free labor.

I grab the sheet and unfold it. It reads:

When you go back to dump dirt in the woods, follow the trail on the west side of the house toward the creek. I'll meet you there.

p.s. Keep this with you. Don't set it down, lose it, or destroy it.

Tension rises in me.

Maybe I've been reading Ryan all wrong. Maybe after what I told him, he does want to fuck me. What if he's asking me to meet him in the woods so he can strip me bare and take me right there?

Fuck, I'm not ready for this.

Since I arrived, I've read some articles and watched some gay porn to get an idea of what I might encounter, but what if ten minutes from now, he expects me to go down on him…or wants even more than that?

My nerves are shot as I consider the requests Ryan might have. A part of me thinks, *It's 10K, so you need to do whatever the fuck he wants you to do.* But I don't have the pill Simon gave me to help me get hard. Although, for all I know, Ryan just wants to bend me over and go to town on my ass without a condom or lube…maybe not even a little spit.

I'll figure it out. Maybe I'll be able to navigate it without a pill. And I can always stall if I need to.

I pack dirt into the wheelbarrow and head to the woods, accepting my fate. I leave the wheelbarrow by the area where we're spreading dirt, then follow the trail, and in about two minutes, I come to a creek.

As I wait for Ryan to arrive, I'm on edge.

You don't have to do anything you don't want to, I remind myself.

I finally see him coming along the trail. He approaches me without even looking at me, just like he had the past few days. He's a difficult guy to read as it is, but it's damn near impossible as he settles before me and says, "So…" There's a lengthy silence, and then he goes on, "Jonas, I know you're not here to help around the yard."

Fuck.

"I'm not sure what you mean." Makes me a liar, but part of my deal with Simon is that Ryan can't find out what I'm really here for, so I'm not surrendering until I know what Ryan thinks he knows.

Ryan hesitates, then says, "Simon brought you here for a reason, Jonas, and I don't know what it is, but you're gonna tell me."

"I…"

"Is this about some fucking money? Ten grand? Is it really worth it to you to fuck with people's lives for some cash?"

Simon told him about the 10K?

"Like I said, I'm not sure what you're talking about." Maybe if I just straight-up deny it, I'll be fine. Although, this doesn't seem like a confrontation that will lead to Ryan wanting to fuck me anytime soon.

He gets right in my face, his jaw clenched, his glare hard on me. "Bullshit. Simon hired you, and you know as well as I do, no one's getting ten grand to do this kind of labor for a few months in the summer, so cut the crap."

The red in his cheeks, the tension in his shoulders and face, all reveal his anger, but the way his chin quivers and his body trembles suggests most of his rage is buried under the surface, a wild animal about to tear through its cage.

"And I know it's not an accident that you look like Kieran, so just tell me why you're here."

"Kieran?"

It's the first time I've heard this name, but as soon as he says it, I know this is the guy I remind him of.

Ryan's penetrating gaze stays on me, probing into my mind. Something about it urges me to tell the truth, but another part of me is shouting that I need the fucking money, so I only manage: "I can't say anything. I'm sorry."

As soon as the words come out, his expression relaxes. I can tell it's soothed him to have his suspicions confirmed, but now I've put my payday at risk.

His gaze wanders for a moment, like he's thinking. "Jonas, I know you can't, but we're safe out here."

"Safe?" Am I in danger?

"Simon doesn't have any way of recording us out here."

At first, this sounds wild, but I guess it's not weird to have security around a mansion.

"I need this money," is all I can think to say, and again, his expression softens.

Though neither of us is showing our hands, it feels like a truce.

"I get that," he says. "But if you tell me why you're here, I won't blab to Simon. I can maybe even help you with whatever you're supposed to do."

When he says that, I reconsider my silence. This would be a lot easier if Ryan knew the truth and worked with me, whereas if I maintain my silence, he may want to have nothing to do with me, and I might spend my summer working my ass off for nothing…unless I can somehow talk Simon into giving me cash for the hours I've put in.

Ryan must see something in my expression, a crack in my armor, because he says, "Tell me, Jonas. It won't leave these woods. I promise."

Even in the few days I've known him, I believe Ryan's a man of his word, and after a few moments of consideration, I decide, fuck it all; if he does rat me out, then I know the kind of guy he really is, and if not, then maybe I'm closer to getting paid and back to my aunt and sister.

Besides, if he tells Simon and he sends me packing, maybe that's how this was going to end anyway.

"He wants me to…" Despite intending to follow through with the words, saying them out loud isn't easy. God, this is a fucked-up situation. "He said I could have the money if we had sex."

His eyes widen. It doesn't look like shock—it looks like horror.

He turns toward the house, then back to me, muttering under his breath, "That little shit. Of course he fucking did."

"He told me not to tell you, though," I remind him.

His gaze meets mine, and this is probably the most awkward moment I've had since I attempted to flirt with him.

Fuck, what must Ryan think of the guy his brother paid to fuck around with him? "I really need this money," I spit out. "My sister, Charity, is sick. Maybe if you just told him that we did something…"

"That's not gonna work. He's got cameras all over the house. He's not going to give you money unless he sees it for himself."

"Sees it?" That wasn't part of the deal.

"Jonas, the reason we had to meet out here is because he has cameras *everywhere* in the house. In your bedroom, in my bedroom. He's got mics all over the place too. He's just very…paranoid."

Part of me wants to brush it off as a rich-people thing, but I doubt even most rich people need to have security in their staff's bedrooms.

"My brother and I have a strange relationship. He's my twin—I don't know that it's possible for me not to love him, but there's this other side of him… It's controlling, and…"

Controlling seems a tame word for a guy who hired someone to fuck him.

Ryan looks toward the house again. "We can't stay out here much longer without him getting suspicious, so we have to make this quick."

"Okay…"

He closes his eyes and takes a breath. "I hate that I'm even having to go there, but I've been tested and I'm negative for STIs. Have you—"

"Your brother made me get tested before I accepted the job. Negative too."

"Of course he fucking did," he says with an eye roll. "In that case, continue working through today, and tonight, come by my bedroom. We'll…do what we need to do so you can satisfy the fucked-up terms of your deal, and then you'll be on your way, and we can both pretend this never happened."

I like the idea of pretending this never happened, but really, it was a lot easier when he was avoiding me and I didn't have to consider the practicalities of following through with Simon's request.

"I…um…"

"What? Do you want your money or not?"

"I do. This is just different than I'd talked about with Simon."

"That's not unusual, unfortunately. Give me the note I gave you. I need to destroy it. I'll hand you another note today in view of the house, so Simon will think this is all legit. Meet me at my room at nine thirty, and we'll get this show on the road. Good?"

"Great," I say, though Ryan's talking so fast and sounds so

certain that I just go along with him.

"In the meantime, don't slack on your work. We're behind, and I have a feeling when Simon sends you back to Chicago, we're not gonna have much help around here."

He sounds hurt, like the thought of struggling with his work is worse than what he's learned his brother did by bringing me here.

It makes me feel kind of bad that I'm not going to be able to help him out more.

That's ridiculous. Focus, Jonas.

"Back to work," he says, as though we haven't just agreed to meet and fuck later tonight.

5

RYAN

"Good evening, Ryan," I hear Simon say before looking up from my book to see a broad grin stretched across his conceited little face. I could deck him for the stunt he's pulled.

After putting in my hours for the day, I retired to the reading nook in the library, tucked in the corner on the first floor. I hoped a book might help me decompress, but given what I know I'll be doing in a few hours, it's been nearly impossible to concentrate.

Simon steps around the love seat, opposite the sofa where I'm seated. He passes the desk alongside the wall of bookcases, stopping when he gets to the sofa.

"To what do I owe this honor?" I ask, returning my attention to my book, though I'm not likely to progress on this page any more than I have for the past hour.

"Just wanted to check in and see if you're finding Jonas an acceptable employee. From what I can make out, he seems to be an impressive addition to our little *family*."

We exchange a look. Subtle as it may have been, he knows he stressed *family* just enough to grate on my nerves.

"Jonas has exceeded my expectations," I say. "Now, are you ready to tell me why, of everyone in the world who could have helped us out, you selected him?"

Despite what I've learned, I have no intention of letting on that I know and fuck up things for Jonas, which means I need to continue pushing like I'm oblivious to any part of whatever messed-up plan my brother's concocted.

His lips are still curled upward at the edges as he glances around, as though searching the bookcases for the best reply. "I thought you might like that he resembles Kieran. This house was very different when he was here. Full of life and vitality. Can you blame me for wanting to bring some of that back?"

I tighten my grip against the corner of my book, batting down words that threaten to spit out at him.

"Having some doppelgänger around isn't going to bring him back," is as much as I'm willing to say, and now he's the one who's pissed, his cheerful expression shifting into a frown as he stares me down.

"I'm fine with taking what I can get," he says.

We stare at each other, as though both of us are searching for something, attempting to use what at one time felt like telepathy to probe the other's thoughts, but once again, there's just a wall. The one Simon constructed, and I'm certain he's encountering the same obstacle.

We aren't the boys we once were.

Simon walks closer, then settles on the sofa beside me. "Does Jonas bring up anything for you?"

I ignore his question, but he scoots closer and goes on.

"He brings up things for *me*. Remember when we used to talk about what a sexy man he'd grown into, when we first started to understand those lustful feelings? When we started exploring with each other?"

"I don't want to talk about this." I shift closer to the arm of the sofa.

I know why he's bringing this up. After my chat with Jonas in the woods, once I knew Simon's intentions, I was much more calculating about my next move. I spent more time around Kieran's look-alike, openly admiring his ass, his nude torso. Standing just a little closer than I usually would. And when I gave him the second note, I made an obvious display of it in a spot in the yard where Simon has a mic and a camera—this I know because of previous conversations with him where he knew things he couldn't have otherwise known.

His salacious remarks tell me what his face won't: he's been spying on me to see if Jonas was succeeding in executing their bizarre plan, and deduced that he was. A solid conclusion, but it doesn't get me any closer to understanding Simon's intentions.

"Come on, Ryan. As you look at Jonas now, he must make you twitch a little."

My face flushes with heat, and as I turn to him, I doubt Simon has any trouble reading my expression now.

His smile returns, his eyes—the same blue as mine—sparkling under the gentle glow of the chandelier.

He pulls his gaze, looks out the window. "Anyway, I just came to say good night. I was planning on heading to bed a little early." He moves closer. "Come on. Say good night the way we used to so I know you're not mad."

If I don't, there'll be a punishment, and he can always just keep talking about Kieran if he really wants to make me suffer.

I lean toward him, attempting a quick kiss on the cheek, and when he turns, I try to move as quickly as he does, but he still manages to kiss me on the lips, then punishes me with a quick lick.

"You're disgusting," I mutter, but it's a defeat I'm willing to accept; besides, I already have my victory of the night by intercepting his plan.

He heads off, leaving me stewing in my rage. Some of it is just my head spinning, like it was after Jonas told me what Simon was paying him to do. But some of it is memories I beat down while Simon was in the room.

Kieran laughing, a big grin across his face as we all played Monopoly.

Straining during *Mario Party*, his hand gripping the controller as he aggressively moved the thumbstick to get his character paddling faster than ours.

Making all of us, even Father, laugh at the kitchen table.

I can't let myself go there for long, not without tears stirring in my eyes and a deep hatred welling up.

Damn Simon for putting me in this fucked-up situation.

Why did he have to drag this poor guy into our family business?

I toss my book on the coffee table and head to my bedroom to get ready for tonight's rendezvous. After pouring myself a healthy dose of whiskey, I scour through my nightstand for condoms and lube, checking the expiration dates since that's how long it's been. Should've checked that earlier, but I figured if I didn't, then Jonas probably would, considering what he's here for. Besides, if neither of us had protection, we could always swing by Simon's room. *You mind spotting your big bro?*

When was the last time I messed around with anyone—a year ago? I don't have many opportunities, but I've had Grindr dates and a few rendezvous with townies when the stress in the house became too much. I've even had a few nights with ex-staff members who I quickly learned wouldn't stick around long if I decided to mix business with pleasure.

I head into the bathroom next, tossing off my tee and inspecting my physique in the mirror. Even though this isn't about sex, there's this primal instinct that makes me self-conscious. I'm much leaner than Jonas, with smaller nipples. I wonder if he'll be interested in this. I consider running through the shower real quick. I took one after my workday, but it gets kind of clammy in the library, so I give myself a quick whiff. Seems fine to me, but if I see him cringe, I'll just pop into the bathroom for a minute.

I take a swig of my whiskey, savoring the sting, before there's a knock at the door. Hurrying into the bedroom, I check the antique clock on the fireplace mantel. It's only eight forty-five, but I guess he wants to get this over with.

I nearly put my shirt back on, but who the fuck am I kidding?

When I open the door, Jonas stands in the hall. His bangs are a little wet, so I figure, unlike me, he thought the extra shower might help. With his hands tucked in his pockets, he refuses to make eye contact.

Seeing that face again is a struggle—am I even going to be able to fuck him? I shake off my worry. I have to push through it.

"Now's not the time to be shy," I tell him, urging him into the bedroom.

I want to put up my middle finger and do a quick spin for Simon to see. I don't know where the cameras are. I've found them in the past, but finally just gave up. Even if I find one, he replaces it with another, and by now, I assume he has plenty in place just in case I yank one out when I'm in a mood one night.

"You like whiskey?" I ask. "Gin? Vodka?"

I guide him across my room, to the cabinet beside the mantel. "This is my medicine cabinet," I joke, but Jonas doesn't seem to be in the mood for jokes tonight. "I've been thinking I wish I'd started drinking a little earlier."

His shoulders are tense, hands still in his pockets, and he hasn't looked at me yet.

If he can't even look at me, I don't know how the hell he thinks we're gonna fuck. Although, I guess he doesn't need to look at me for that.

"I'll do a shot of just about anything right now," he says.

I pour him a whiskey and pass it to him, and as I'm topping mine off, he downs half the glass. Then keeps going, and when he's finished, pulls the glass away from his lips and takes a deep breath.

"More?" I ask.

"Yes, please."

I smile as I pour him another, and then we head to the bed and sit on the edge. He takes his time with his second round, glancing around my room.

As he turns to me, in my dim room lighting, there's a moment when I'd swear he's Kieran—those thick eyebrows, that strong jawline.

But he's not Kieran, I remind myself.

I'm fine to sit with him as long as he needs to, but regardless of what we say or do right now, I know it's just a matter of time before I have to fuck this guy who's the spitting image of my brother.

6

JONAS

Fuck, this is actually happening.

I take another sip of whiskey, savoring this round since I could throw back Ryan's whole bottle and it won't change what I've got to do.

There's a queasy feeling in my belly. Had it all the way to Ryan's bedroom. I've had so many chances to change my mind, but I've come this far. I might as well follow through.

Besides, I already took that pill Simon gave me to make sure I could get it up.

I glance his way again, taking in his body. When he first invited me in, I noticed his ass was looking real tight in those pajama bottoms. Not that I didn't have an idea of what he looked like after working with him around the yard; it just hits differently when I'm sitting next to him, knowing it won't be long before I'm intimately aware of Ryan in the way Simon expects—no, *demands*.

"Did you find the place all right?" Ryan asks.

"Huh?"

"Sorry. That was my idea of humor. Trying to lighten the mood."

"Oh." I smile and force a chuckle. This is so goddamn awkward.

My gaze shifts around his room. I'm wondering where these security cameras could be, and what kind of sick guy wants to capture video of his twin fucking around with someone. Of course, it's not a stretch for the guy who hired me to fuck said twin. And it's only one of the many questions I've had since my chat with Ryan in the woods.

I notice the condoms and lube on the nightstand.

I take another sip, then a deep breath.

Ryan pushes to his feet and extends his hand. I must be eyeing him strangely because he winces. "Your glass, Jonas. I was gonna put it up, unless you wanted more. Figure we should get to it so we can get to bed."

I hand him the glass, and he sets it on the nightstand.

He slides his pajama bottoms off, exposing the smooth, pale flesh of his ass. I force myself to look at his cock, which seems pretty big on a guy his size.

It's not a thought I'm used to having about guys…at least not until Simon proposed this job opportunity.

Ryan pulls back the covers and slides under them, sitting with his back to the pillow and headboard.

It's my turn. Just need to do this.

I take off my shirt and set it on the foot of the bed, then unfasten my belt and pull down my pants, so I'm just in my boxers.

Ryan's watching me as I hook my thumbs in the waistband of my boxers. "Hey, no. Don't do that. Just come here."

As soon as he says that, I realize I'm shaking.

This is not gonna be sexy for him.

I slip under the covers, mirroring his position, my back against the headboard beside him.

He rests his hand on my thigh, stroking. His touch is warm, and gentle in a way that surprises me. I've never felt like this when a guy touched me.

"You good?" he asks, and after I nod, he slides his hand up my leg, traveling to my crotch, his fingers probing my cock, which is starting to get hard for him.

I'm kind of stunned, but I guess I shouldn't be. That pill must be doing its job.

"Is that okay?" Ryan asks.

"More than okay."

He smiles and rolls toward me, disappearing as he crawls under the covers.

He lowers my boxers, and then there's a warm, wet touch—his tongue—along my shaft.

I moan, surprised by the sensation as he teases my cock. I'm rock hard before he engulfs it. I guess a blowjob feels like a blowjob.

He sucks and licks, taking me deep in his mouth, and I'm shaking, but now for a different reason. The guy knows how to give head.

God, it's been a long time since I was blown. So much life bullshit has taken up my every waking thought. Hardly given me a chance to get relief. Maybe I didn't even feel like I deserved to have that.

But now, under the circumstances, I give myself permission.

I roll my head back against the headboard, and as he keeps going, I reach under the covers, thread my fingers through his hair, and stroke gently. This seems to encourage him, his warm hand joining his efforts.

The pressure mounts, and my mind's spinning. This is what it feels like being with a guy?

He pulls the covers off his head and lets my wet cock fall against my stomach, then takes my boxers and guides them down my legs, helping me out of them.

I notice his thick, full erection… I already thought his cock looked big before he got into bed, but he's definitely a grower.

As he discards my boxers off the bed, he crawls up me and studies my face for a moment.

Is this about the guy I remind him of?

He straddles my leg and rubs his cock against it, mine rubbing against his hip.

"Are you okay with bottoming?" he asks.

Fuck. It's a reminder that our little conversation in the woods didn't cover everything.

"Ryan, I—" When we discussed his brother watching him, he mentioned mics, so I have to be careful how I convey this. "I need to top you," I explain, looking him directly in the eyes.

He snickers, his gaze turning down. He must've understood my meaning; that topping him is part of my agreement with Simon.

"Of course you do." He sounds disappointed, which sucks since I'm actually having a good time with him.

"I took a pill before I came over," I warn him.

"That explains why this thing is like a stone." He smiles, picking up my shaft and dropping it so it makes a *thud* against my belly. This is a very different side to my stoic, intense boss. Apparently, he can be playful, and I'm starting to think it's not just the pill that's getting me going.

He reaches over to the nightstand and grabs the condoms and lube. Then he crawls down my body, taking my cock in his mouth for a few quick pumps.

As tense as I was before going into this, Ryan's mouth has a way of setting me at ease.

He takes another lick, then readies me. He juggles the condom and lube like a fucking expert, stroking me, then releasing as he straddles my waist. "You can fuck me, but I want to be on top, okay?"

"Of course. It's your call. This is actually…my first time." I'm embarrassed to admit it, but I'm hoping with a pro like Ryan, he might be able to give me pointers.

His eyes widen and he looks bewildered, like I fucking slapped him out of nowhere. "With a guy?"

I nod.

His gaze wavers.

"Is that okay?" I ask.

He reaches behind him and feels my hard cock. "Are you okay with this? Are you sure?"

I can tell he's reconsidering. Definitely something I should've mentioned in the woods, but Jesus, with everything else we had to discuss, seems inevitable that we would've missed a few key details.

"Yeah. This is nice."

He grimaces. "But you're really sure?"

"Yes." I say the word clearly so there's no doubt in his mind.

He considers this, and I wonder if it's because he's trying to decide if he feels the same, but then he takes my cock and repositions, placing me between his cheeks. He starts to push me in but stops abruptly. Has he changed his mind? I hope not.

"Gonna need more lube than that," he says with another smile.

It's a cute smile, and as I think that, my dick pulses.

He squirts more lube into his palm before running it behind him, over my shaft.

He's still hard too, so despite the fact that this isn't something he's thrilled to participate in either, I'm relieved he's not going to be miserable through the experience, even knowing this is all a sick game contrived by his twin.

He rests his ass near my cock again, positioning the head at his hole. I feel him opening as he settles back steadily, letting the tip inside.

He looks up at the ceiling like he's bracing himself, which makes me feel like he thinks I'm a decent size, something he confirms as he carefully lowers himself onto me.

He's still looking away from me when he finally gets most of it in.

I check to see where he's looking. Does he think there might be a camera on the ceiling?

Or is he avoiding looking at me because I remind him of someone else?

"Fuck," he says, his eyes closed as he turns to me. He leans toward me and relaxes his hands on my shoulders.

"Does that feel okay?" I ask.

"Just give me a second to adjust."

"Okay."

He chuckles. "You're very sweet," he says, still not opening his eyes. And now I'm certain this must have something to do with that person I remind him of.

I wait patiently for him to make the next move, and his ass tightens around my cock as he rocks steadily, using his legs to push up before he comes back down.

"Oh, that feels good," I say, which makes him grin.

"You feel pretty good too."

I didn't think I could be more embarrassed than being in this situation, but his comment makes me blush, and I'm glad his eyes are closed.

"It's okay if you want to thrust now," he says, and I offer a few thrusts before his mouth hangs open.

"God, it's been a fucking long time," he says.

"It's been a long time for me too. I mean, not with a man, but…"

"Just shut up and fuck me." He says it in this teasing way I never would've expected from the guy who looked so pissed when Simon first introduced us.

I obey, enjoying how his ass grips my shaft, the friction our bodies create.

This is the fucking weirdest way to find out I can be attracted to a man, but as I'm balls-deep in Ryan, I'm glad it's this way because I doubt it's something I would've stumbled into on my own.

He leans back, resting his hands on the mattress as he takes my cock, his mouth open slightly as he releases a series of soft moans.

Is this a performance for his brother, or does he really enjoy taking me?

Feels like my cock takes control, and I fuck him faster. The sound of my hips slapping against his ass…that's a hot fucking sound.

He leans forward again and takes his cock into his hand, stroking. There's a warm sensation on my stomach, and I think he might be coming, but as I look, it's a little clear fluid. Just some precum.

With his eyes still sealed shut, he rides, his movements seeming as beyond his control as my own. We're all thrusts and fury, the intensity climbing.

The mattress springs squeak violently. Must be an old bed, like a lot of stuff in this place.

The pressure in my balls has a bite to it as my body decides I need release and fast.

"I think I'm gonna come," I warn him.

"It's okay. Come like this."

There's something gentle in his tone, so different from the man I'm used to seeing, and his invitation is too much for me. A wave of heat suffuses my face as the pressure becomes unbearable, and then I'm shooting inside him.

His ass grips my shaft before he calls out, "Fuck, yeah. Fuck…" And he sprays across my stomach, his cum settling around my navel as his body twitches above me, his ass still moving like his body wants to keep enjoying the sensation of my cock inside him.

He leans forward, opens his eyes, and the first expression he makes is unsettling. Like he's disappointed. I figure it doesn't have to do with me, but this other person.

Is he disappointed I'm not him?

He dismounts, removing my condom for me and taking it with him into the en suite bathroom. I wipe the sweat off my brow and take deep breaths as I recover, and he returns to the bed, eyeing me uneasily.

For a guy who seemed to be enjoying himself, he looks ashamed. Or like he regrets what we did. Maybe after the fuck, the reality of it all struck him. The fucked-up thing his brother wanted me to do.

I roll off the mattress. "I'll get out of your hair."

He doesn't respond, so I figure that's what he wants too.

I slide into my boxers and pants and toss on my shirt, and as he guides me to the door, I spin back around. "Thank you, Ryan."

I hope he knows I mean it. He could have easily told me to fuck off when he found out what I needed. He would have had every right, but it means so much to me that he gave enough shits to make sure I ended up with this money.

Ryan nods, not making eye contact.

"Thank you," I say again. "I actually…really enjoyed that. Really."

I don't know how else to get it across to him, but his expression twists up, and then he shakes his head. "Good night, Jonas."

"Night, Ryan."

7

SIMON

Jonas enters my office and approaches.

"Good morning," I say. "Please. Take a seat."

As he settles in the chair in front of my desk, I can't fight the grin on my face. It wasn't easy to watch them fuck, but it was deeply satisfying. Not because I wanted to see, but because I knew it wouldn't take long for Jonas to get in his bed. That Ryan wouldn't be able to resist someone who reminded him of Kieran. Despite all his protests, all his fucking lies, I knew what Ryan wanted in his heart.

The bastard. The liar.

"I'm very pleased with your work," I tell Jonas.

His eyes widen. "So you know I did the job?"

"Yes, and I guess that issue we discussed wasn't too much of a problem." During my initial proposal, Jonas was worried that being straight, he might have a problem performing. Clearly, that hadn't been an issue. I'd given him a sildenafil to help out, but he doesn't seem like a good enough actor to have pulled off last night without there being more to him than a straight man.

"No, it went fine," is all he says.

Well, you're not getting away that easily, Jonas.

"Fine?"

I saw my brother's face as he took his cock. I saw Jonas's fucking face, how he was enjoying his job. Maybe he's in denial about something, but that's really none of my business.

"So how was it?" I know what it fucking looked like, but I want to know what it was like when he was balls-deep in Ryan. I want to know if he enjoyed his tight hole. If he liked the rhythm he created as he rode him. I want to know fucking *everything*.

He hesitates, then says, "I'm sorry. What are you asking for?"

"Details, Jonas. I want to hear what happened. How it came about. What you felt intrigued him about you. What you said that made him want to fuck you. Think of it as a final report." A very thorough report that can give me some insight into my big brother's fucked-up head.

Jonas's gaze searches around—why does he have to think about it? He knows what happened between them. There's something suspicious about how he's acting.

"We got along fine, and one lunch, I brought up Grindr. He asked me to meet him in the woods, and there he told me he wanted to mess around and he'd leave me a note to go to his room."

Fucker set it up in private, but he sure didn't fuck him in private. Maybe Ryan wanted it to be a surprise for me. He knows me well enough to know I was pulling up the feed on my laptop. And he didn't even attempt to search for the cameras he knew damn well were in his room.

He wanted me to see.

Is that what turned the pervert on? Knowing I'm watching him and stroking myself off in tense fury as Jonas fucks him?

I could tell by how Ryan rolled his head back that he was about to come—that's how he usually came when he jerked himself off. I recognized those familiar twitches in his face, the way his body vibrated as he came down from his high.

He had his eyes closed—that one I'm still trying to make sense of. Maybe he was ashamed, just like he'd been when he fucked around with Kieran. Maybe he couldn't look because he knew he'd fall into a fit of tears over the death of the man he loved.

I suspect he feared that if he looked at Jonas, he would straddle two worlds, the past with our dear brother Kieran…and the present with this stranger. Because Jonas isn't Kieran—something that made it so fucking confusing as I was watching. There were times when my thoughts drifted back to a moment between Kieran and Ryan…lost in their passion, Ryan calling out his name in ecstasy…taking that big cock.

From what I could tell in the video feed, Jonas's cock was satisfactory, but he's no Kieran.

"And how did you fuck him?"

"I…" His gaze shifts around the room like he's thrown by the question.

"I guess I can be transparent with you now, Jonas. I obviously couldn't just take your word for it, so I had cameras set up around Ryan's room—just for last night. Someone will be reviewing the footage to verify you completed the task. I only want to make sure you're being truthful."

The way he's looking at me, I can tell he's unsettled, and that excites me. Maybe because it reminds me of how Kieran used to

TWISTED RIVALRY

look when he'd get uncomfortable.

Jonas offers a narrative of last night, detailing the events in the bedroom, giving me another chance to relive it. As he shares, I get hard, the crotch of my pants constricting my erection. There's a sting to it, reminding me of the sting in my chest when I watched him bring Ryan to climax.

"Well, Jonas, I'm pleased your heterosexual nature didn't hinder your ability to complete the job. And I'm *very* pleased with your work, so I'm ready to show you just how much." I pull out my phone and key away on it. "There. I deposited fifteen thousand dollars into your account."

I text him a confirmation of the transaction, then set my cell on the desk.

There's that pain in my chest again. I'm struggling to keep it together. As much as I wanted Jonas to provide a more thorough account, it took a toll. And I can't get their fuck session out of my head. The pleased expression on Jonas's face. Ryan moaning as he came across him. Even with his eyes shut, how could he help himself? He knew whom he really wanted inside him.

We both know.

"Fifteen?" Jonas asks. "You said ten."

Most guys would've taken it and gone on their way, but not Jonas. Such a nice man…the kind of man that men like me eat for breakfast.

"Consider it a tip." I push to my feet and start around the desk.

Jonas's gaze shifts to my crotch, surely noticing my erection. He looks away quickly.

There's an innocence about him that gives me a twisted sort of pleasure. Maybe because it feels like I'm exacting revenge against Kieran.

I'm glad we're not finished with him yet.

"So I guess I should pack my things? Will that driver take me to the airport, or do I need to Uber?"

"I can arrange for the driver to take you."

He glances around like he's waiting to be excused, and I let him sit there in confusion for a few moments longer as I settle in front of him, resting my palms behind me on the desk.

"You can walk out today… *Or* you could stay."

He gazes up at me. He's taller than me. Maybe that's why I enjoy towering over him like this. Maybe that's why I enjoy this whole arrangement where this pathetic man is at my mercy.

"Stay? I don't think… I can't stick around. I have to get back to my family."

"I meant for another job."

"Another job?" His expression twists with worry.

"Yes. I should explain. This first job was…a test. I needed to see if I could trust you, and you've earned that, Jonas. So now I have another task in mind for you. This will be more complicated, but the reward would be even greater."

His worry shifts to what looks like interest, but only for a moment before he blinks and says, "I think I should probably just go."

"Don't you want to at least hear it? I think you'd be very pleased with your compensation."

He bites his lip. "No, thank you. It's better if I just go, but I do appreciate the opportunity."

"That's fine. You've already been away from your family, and

I'm sure they want you to get back to them. So that said, you have your money, and you're excused. If you want to head upstairs and get your things together, I'll have someone arrange your flight and get you to the airport. And until your flight, feel free to enjoy the house. I'll let Ryan know."

"I can tell him."

Anger pulses through my chest, but…it also gives me hope.

Before he can head out the door, I say, "If you change your mind, I'd love to tell you about how I could make sure your sister is taken care of for the remainder of her life. Your sister and your aunt, really."

It's so satisfying to hold the cards close to your chest and then show them at just the perfect moment. I revel in the way he's halted at the door, his hand reaching for the knob.

He's a puppet, my words his strings.

"My sister?" He turns back to me. There's that worry in his expression again, and I know I've won.

Silly Jonas. I always win.

8

RYAN

I'M ENJOYING MY day off, and I have to admit, stressful as this Jonas situation has been, last night was nice.

Even knowing my brother was watching us.

Even knowing, as I sealed my eyes shut, that he looks like Kieran.

It was nice having a cock inside me. Nice to have a reminder of what it felt like to have that pressure against my prostate, urging me on to release.

Although, Jonas must have been fucking miserable.

He said he'd never done that before with a guy. It hadn't even crossed my mind that he could be straight and willing to do something like that.

I just hope Simon got what he wanted out of that and that he'll give Jonas his money so he can move on with his life and pretend this never happened.

Given how he was with me last night—careful, patient, considerate—it assures me of what I've suspected from the start: he's a kind man, a man who deserved better than to be used like a pawn by Simon.

While I'm eating my lunch, Nell brings out extra dumplings

she'd reheated for me. As she sets the bowl beside my plate, she says, "How's the new workhand coming along?"

She's convincing at sounding mildly interested, but I've known her long enough to know she's poking for intel, which I have no intention of offering.

"He's a hard worker." Like the work he put in last night. "And he's getting along well with Morgan and Forsyth."

"Suspicious that even you won't state the obvious."

"What do you mean?" I can't help but smirk as I turn to face her.

She glares at me, her forehead wrinkling. "You know what I mean. I have eyes too. And I'm the only one who's been around long enough to know what I'm looking at. I just don't know *why* I'm looking at it."

Nell is, in fact, the only person still employed with us who knows that Jonas is a Kieran look-alike, and I'm wondering why she decided to bring it up today.

She adds, "Just like I'm wondering why you're suddenly in such a good mood."

"Maybe I'm just having a good day."

"Ryan Hawthorne, I've known you and Mr. Simon since you were thirteen years old. You think I can't tell when you have a little pep in your step I haven't seen in, say, four years?"

That's why she's asking: she knows me well enough to intuit what I've been up to. Or, just as likely, Simon or his butler mentioned something to her.

"Are you insinuating something," I ask her, "or just making an observation?"

"An observation, of course. I wouldn't dare do more than that."

Sly Nell.

"I just figure it must be very difficult to have him around," she says. "I know how close you were. How much you adored him."

Kieran. Wisely, she doesn't speak his name.

Her remark takes me back to a time when all the staff were talking about Simon, Kieran, and me. Heat burns in my chest, and I struggle against memories fighting their way to the surface, threatening to pull me under.

"Nell, I'd rather not discuss it."

She raises an eyebrow. "As you wish. Just keep in mind, if you cling to the past, it just might take you with it."

"Nell, that's nonsensical. The past can't take you anywhere."

"Exactly my point."

I eye her suspiciously, curious if that was really her point or if she's trying to sound particularly clever today.

She smirks. "Be careful."

"Nell," I say sternly.

"I'll stay out of it. That's how I've kept this job all these years."

She heads back to the kitchen, but even after she leaves, I'm left stewing in uncomfortable memories and emotions.

It's fine. Now that Simon got his fucked-up wish, Jonas will be on his way, and I can pack all this away in my mind, rebuild the barrier that's held it back for so long.

Just as soon as I manage to quiet my mind, Jonas walks through the kitchen door, a tray in hand—I assume because he has to wait until later for a flight.

He settles in the seat adjacent to me. "Good afternoon," he says, forcing an awkward smile.

I wish I could get to the damn point, but I know better than to ask questions out loud, so I take a different approach. "So on Monday, I was going to put you on mowing. I'll need Forsyth and Morgan to help me with some things that require a little more expertise."

"Happy to do it," he says, making direct eye contact, as if trying to psychically implant a message. "Anything else you might have in mind for me next week?"

He's deliberate in the way he speaks, and I fucking know this isn't over. Why isn't it over?

We should have had a more thorough conversation in the woods. What if there's something else he forgot to mention—besides needing to top me in order to collect his money? Were condoms against the rules?

My mind's spinning all over again.

"Did you need help with anything today?" he asks. Guess he knows we have to discuss this.

"Not today, no. But on Monday we'll deal with the debris we've collected by the woods."

Does he understand what I'm suggesting? Do *I* understand what the fuck I'm suggesting?

"Sounds good." He lowers his hand below the table, and I feel something sharp and pointy against my thumb.

Paper? *Jonas, you clever fuck.* I grab the note and tuck it in my pocket.

I want to race out and read it, but I can imagine what that

would look like to Simon when he's reviewing the footage. I'm a creature of habit, and he knows this about me, so though it's excruciating, I take the appropriate length of time for my meal before heading to the library for a few hours. Then I take a walk around the grounds, walking along the trail for a few minutes before I pull the note out of my pocket and read it.

Simon's hired me for a bigger job. If I can form a relationship with you, he's willing to get Charity and my aunt more help. I know it's a lot to ask, but I really need this. Please talk to me when you have a chance.

Rage pulses through me. I should have anticipated this. Of course Simon wouldn't let it be as easy as a quick fuck. I'm pissed he's coerced Jonas into sticking around, yet as much as I hate Simon for this, once again, I'm reminded of the kind of man Jonas is, someone who's willing to put his family's needs before his own. It's a quality I admire in him, one I used to hold above all else. But those days are long gone.

I consider replying to his note, but it was risky for him to get it to me, and it's risky to keep going back and forth like that.

If he's staying for the next few days, we'll have a chance to chat again. And as much as it sucks, it's for the best.

It's hard to wait, but Jonas must be a patient man because he doesn't push me. Doesn't appear urgent. He's good at keeping his cool, which I'm sure is why we've managed to trick my brother this long. And these days give me a chance to consider what Jonas suggests.

Simon didn't just want to see us fuck; he wants us to form a relationship. What is he playing at?

On Monday, Jonas is working hard, busting his ass like this is the job he's here for. About midday, before our break, I ask him to dump some dirt in the woods with me, and we meet in the same spot as that first time. When we're finally on our own, he doesn't make eye contact. "I know it's a lot to ask," he says.

"Yeah. It is."

"But you remember that I wanted to get Charity into this place in New York? Simon knew about it already, and he said he can get her in there. She'll be seen by the best doctors, getting the best care for her type of leukemia. I mean, I have no reason to believe he's lying."

"I don't think he's lying. He has plenty of money, so if he wants, he can do amazing things with it. It's a shame he can only do kind things if it benefits him in some way. And I wish I knew what that is."

"Does that mean you're considering it?" He finally makes eye contact, and I can see his hope, his desperation.

"Jonas, I want to help you, but the other night, you said that was your first time. What exactly have you done with guys before?"

"Nothing."

"And you said you took a pill. I didn't even think to ask, but are you straight?"

"Yes."

Fuck.

"And no," he amends. "I don't know. I've always considered myself straight. Then the other night, I was nervous and scared, but when we got going…" He hesitates. "I enjoyed myself."

Why are my cheeks getting warm? I'm glad he's blushing too.

"You had a good time?" I don't know why I fucking asked that; he just told me he did. Maybe because it's been so long, I was worried I'd be shit at it. Or maybe because I wanted to know he enjoyed it as much as I had.

"Yeah," he says.

"I felt kind of guilty for how much I enjoyed it."

"Well, you shouldn't," he says with a subtle smirk.

This is fucking wild. As if I needed an extra layer of fucked up to all this. The guy my brother hired to fuck me turns out to be straight, but he enjoyed it? What does that even mean?

Unfortunately, we can't take our time sussing out the details. If we stay out here too long, Simon will figure out what we're really doing back here.

"What has to happen so you can fulfill your part of the deal? How far do we have to take this?"

"He'll go ahead and get my sister in the treatment program as long as we're messing around. And if we make it to September, he'll continue paying for it for as long as she needs it."

"I'm glad to hear he won't be waiting, but messing around until September? Jesus, that's, like, five months."

"I know. If it's too hard…"

"No, it's not that. It's just a real commitment for both of us. We need to know where we stand because there's no point to starting something neither of us is willing to finish."

His jaw clenches. "I'm willing to finish this. I *have* to finish this."

I see his intensity, his determination. I'm not going to be the one to deprive him of what could be life-changing for him and his family. It begs a question, one that was already on my mind, but I didn't feel it was right to push. "You mentioned your aunt, but not your mother or father. Simon told me…"

I stop myself.

That determination I saw moments earlier fades, and his gaze shifts to the ground. "Yeah, they, um, aren't with us anymore." He gulps. "They've both passed."

"Mine too." I don't even realize I spoke the words until his gaze shifts to me.

"Yes, I read that."

We know so little about one another, but as we gaze into each other's eyes, it feels like we know too much. A warmth moves through me. It feels good to be seen by someone else who knows this pain.

I break eye contact first. "Okay," I say, since I've already pried more than I should. And shown him more than I should. "If we're gonna do this, we need to have some ground rules."

"Right."

"Notes are risky. It makes sense we might pass notes to each other if we're an item, but you can't read them inside. You have to get away from the house. I don't know how good his security cameras are, but if he can zoom in and see anything we're saying, game over. Got it?"

He nods.

"And we can't meet out here too much, so again, this has to be reserved for emergency situations."

"I get that."

"As far as your phone and electronics, you can't use any of it to look up stuff he hasn't mentioned to you."

"Yeah, I assumed he might be savvy enough to get onto my history, so I've been careful."

I'm impressed. "Smart thinking. You're gonna have to think like that a lot moving forward. We should also come up with some hand signals. Like with the notes, we can't use them too much or he'll catch on, so again, just for emergencies."

"Good idea." He sounds like he's letting me call all the shots. Maybe it's because he appreciates that I'm the expert when it comes to dealing with one of Simon's mindfucks. He wouldn't be wrong there.

"And I don't want Morgan and Forsyth to know we're messing around," I go on. "It's only gonna complicate work stuff, so everything we do, we do in private, off the clock. And even though I know he's not technically paying you to work, you have to keep on with that because if you start slacking and I'm not making a big fuss about it, Simon will know something's up."

"That all makes sense. Don't worry. I'm a hard worker."

"I know. I've seen it, but I need you to understand why I'm being so specific here. Simon will be scrutinizing our every move. If we aren't careful, if we slip, he'll catch it and find a way to fuck us both over. Understand?"

"Yes. I understand."

I'm sure he thinks he does, but I wonder if anyone besides me can really understand just how calculating and manipulative Simon can be. Jonas doesn't know him like I do. Simon is clever; it won't be easy to outwit him.

"Also, if we're doing this…" I can't believe what I'm about to say. "It's not going to be believable if we're a serious item and still using condoms. But that's how serious we're gonna have to be if you want this to work. Are you comfortable with that? We can't half-ass this."

His gaze shifts before he nods. "Yeah. We've both been tested, and I don't know…could be fun." He makes eye contact again, this adorable smile slipping across his face as he shrugs.

It's fun. Flirtatious.

And now I'm chuckling.

"Maybe," is all I'm willing to concede.

I can disguise just how much fun I had the other night from him, but not myself. And since then, my mind has crafted other equally fun and fulfilling scenarios with the two of us.

Playing. Fucking.

The heat, the rising intensity.

Now that I know what our bodies feel like against each other, it's gonna be tough to keep from getting a semi around the yard.

"If there's anything else we need to discuss or that you're concerned about, bring it up now. We won't have many chances after this."

"Why is your brother doing this?"

"Still haven't figured that out." I'm being honest with him, but my answer is misleading. No, I don't understand exactly why, but I know it has to do with our brother. Some kind of twisted revenge.

But why he would set me up with a Kieran look-alike, that I'm stumped about. And intrigued.

Jonas says, "I know I look like this guy Kieran, but neither of you explained who this guy is. Or why he means so much to you."

There it is.

That hot tension in my chest returns.

"Jonas, I understand why you want to know. I do. But I can't share that with you. Not yet."

Maybe because I'm so used to keeping this family secret.

Or maybe because I fear that once I share it, the past will all come back, haunting me. Every memory, from the most pleasant to the most horrifying.

"I'm sorry, Jonas, and if that's not satisfactory to you, I understand. So, you still want to give this a go?"

"I've already made my decision," he says without hesitation.

I'm glad of that, and not just because I want to mess around with him again. I want this to unfold, if only to expose Simon's wicked plans.

9

JONAS

"THE DOCTORS SOUNDED really nice," Charity says, which makes me tear up.

Simon was true to his word, and by Wednesday morning, Aunt Amy and Charity already had a Zoom meeting with her new doctor.

"Aunt Amy says we'll be flying to New York on Saturday. We've never been there before! I wish you could come."

"I wish I could come too."

She frowns. "Jonas, I miss you."

"I miss you too." I wipe the back of my hand across the corner of my eye, where a tear nearly escapes.

"Aunt Amy wants to talk to you again."

"Okay, I love you, Cherry Berry."

She snickers. "Love you too, JoJo."

I smile at the nickname as she hands the phone to Aunt Amy, who relates more details about Charity's new arrangement. She looks around uneasily, then whispers, "Jonas, I didn't push before, but now there's no pretending you're doing yard work." Her tone is full of concern.

"Starting today," Simon says, "your sister will have the best care *money can buy, but that comes at a cost."*

"Can we not discuss this with Charity around?" I press.

"She's in the other room." She keeps her voice low. "Just tell me, is it drugs?"

"Not drugs."

"Firearms?"

"Wrong again."

Her forehead creases. "It's illegal, though, isn't it?"

Technically, I figure I'm a sex worker, which is illegal but certainly not the worst of crimes I could be committing to make all this happen. Still, it's not something I have any intention of ever revealing to my aunt or sister.

"Just helping some outrageously wealthy people, Aunt Amy. That's really all I can say."

"If you back out before September, for any reason, your sister and aunt will be sent back home, and you will have to make do with the fifteen thousand you already received."

"September just seems so far away, and I don't want anything bad to happen to you. She needs this, but she needs you back in one piece. So just be safe, okay?"

"I will. You make sure she has an easy transition. Sounds like a lot's about to happen really fast, and it'll be very different in New York. Now just give the phone back to Charity so I can say bye, and I'll call you after work tomorrow."

She finds my sis, and we say our goodbyes and hang up.

I glance out my bedroom window, at the luxurious estate it overlooks. Since arriving at Hawthorne Heights, I've felt like Alice falling down the rabbit hole, flipping and spinning, dizzy with confusion. It's like I'm not in a real place but some sort of dream.

Or maybe this is a nightmare, and I just don't realize it yet.

The following Monday, when I return to work, there's a weight off my shoulders. Charity and Amy are in New York, already scheduled with a doctor for today. Fuck, I can't even see my primary care physician that soon.

It gives me hope. Makes it easier to throw myself into work. I must admit, as intense and demanding as the job is, I enjoy manual labor. Keeps my mind and body busy.

Before Ryan and I left the woods last week, we agreed to meet up again tonight.

"We have to take it slow. Make it believable," Ryan says. "If we start hanging together right after your agreement with Simon, he'll know we're up to something."

It's a struggle to understand Ryan and Simon's relationship. They don't seem to love each other, at least not like I love Charity. It's almost like they're locked in a chess match, incited by Simon, leaving Ryan struggling to read and dissect every move, trying to work out his twin's strategy. That Ryan had considered how to go about this even more than me suggests he's spent a lot of his life trying to anticipate the maneuvers of his calculating brother.

Tonight's different than the first night we messed around. I can tell because as I walk to his room, I'm not on edge—I'm excited. And though Simon gave me a bottle of sildenafil, I don't take one. I'm curious to see how I'll do without.

I knock on the door, and Ryan opens it. Again, he's not wearing a shirt, just pajama bottoms, the waistband tight over the ridges along his V-line.

He grabs me and guides me into his room, pushing me up against the wall. He closes his eyes before his lips slam against mine. For the past few days, he's been even more professional than usual, so I was waiting for this to be as awkward as the first time. Yet now I'm frozen in place as his tongue slips between my lips, teasing mine.

The first time we met, we fucked without kissing, so this is a surprise—and it also assures me that Ryan's perfectly capable of giving me a hard-on without any assistance.

After recovering from my initial shock, I kiss him back, and his hand grips my crotch, running up and down against the fabric of my jeans.

His kisses relax before he offers two gentle kisses in quick succession like he wants to pull away but my lips keep drawing him back in.

As he finally leans back, he opens his eyes, assessing my face carefully, studying it. It's not like when Simon introduced us, when he looked like he'd seen a ghost. Or like during work initially, when he would cut a glare my way, maybe because he thought I was working with his brother against him. Or maybe because of something that went down between him and the guy he hasn't told me anything about.

He moves closer, slowly, steadily, then closes his eyes and kisses me again. It's like he's testing himself.

And I'm happy to be a part of his little test.

But I wish Ryan had shared that with me, told me about this mystery man, so I could have some idea whose memory Simon is trying to bring back.

Ryan takes my hand, guides me to the bed, and pulls me on top of him.

We're just going for this.

My hands are greedy for his body. There's no talking. I pull at his pajama bottoms, guiding them down and then stomping them to the floor. I don't let myself think too much. I allow myself to enjoy the experience as I kiss down his neck, his torso, then farther down. I'm curious now, and as I reach his cock, I hesitate for a moment before licking from the base to the head.

He moans, the sort of moan that makes me feel like I'm the first guy who'd ever licked it.

"I guess it's been a while, as you said," I tell him.

"Too fucking long." He threads his fingers through my hair as I taste him some more, try to get a feel for this. I run my tongue up and down his shaft, then assess the head before sliding it into my mouth.

It's strange to think I've never done this before—it feels like the most natural thing in the world, having his cock pushing my lips apart as I take it halfway, running my tongue along the bottom.

As I release it from my mouth, I notice some precum sliding out of the head and give it a lick. I'm surprised the taste is so good. And that I'm hungry for more.

I take him once again, pushing him farther back toward my throat.

"Jonas," he whispers as his fingers massage the back of my head.

Satisfaction swirls in my chest. Something about servicing him calms my body and encourages me along as I take him to the back of my throat, then move my head up and down. His dick expands in my mouth, which makes me eager to speed up.

I lose myself in the moment, worshipping his cock with my mouth, adding my hand to the base to stroke and suck at the same time, and I'm impressed with how quickly I'm picking this up. Ryan's intense moan makes me feel like I'm pretty damn good for an amateur.

"Jonas, I want you to fuck me. Raw."

I figure my dick can't get any harder, and then he says that, and now it's a fucking stone.

I'm reluctant to pull off his cock, wavering between my desire to continue pleasuring him like this and wanting to see him take me again.

My tongue travels back up his body, and I nibble and bite softly, surrendering to the animalistic impulses his body inspires. When I reach his face, he's got his eyes closed again, which raises so many questions, the most important being: why doesn't he look at me—what is it about this Kieran guy that makes Ryan unwilling to look at me?

I lean forward and take another kiss, appreciating his wet mouth, but I remind myself I'll have time to enjoy that. Right now, I need to get out of these damn clothes.

I slide off the bed, removing my shirt and jeans in a frenzy because I just want to get back to the man spread across the bed, eagerly waiting to receive me.

My eyes are drawn to the nightstand, where I notice only the lube is out.

Dirty Ryan really is ready to take my dick raw tonight.

As I grab the lube, with his eyes still closed, he asks, "Are you leaving?"

"Not a chance."

I crawl onto the mattress, between his legs, tossing the lube beside him as my lips gravitate back to his smooth skin, kissing up to his face, along his jawline, possessed by these animal impulses, letting the intoxicating sensation of his flesh guide my interest. And soon, I hook my arms under his thighs, tilt his ass, and give my first lick.

My eyes roll back as my tongue goes wild against his rim.

"Please, Jonas. You're killing me here. Just give it to me."

There's this feral hunger in his voice, and I have no intention of leaving him waiting any longer. I rise to my knees, grabbing the lube and spreading some over my shaft. Instinctively, I put some extra on my hands and run it between his cheeks.

I stop myself, recalling how insistent he was last time about being on top.

"Did you want to ride me again?"

He hesitates, biting his lip. "Let's try it this way. I want to see how it feels like this. I'll let you know if I change my mind."

I want him to do what he's comfortable with, but his response makes me feel like I earned his trust in that first fuck.

And I'm eager to earn even more.

I guide the head against his hole, watching intently. "I want to see my cock pushing into you."

He smiles, and I slide the head until it disappears inside him, and as I push farther, I feel his hole enveloping me, tightening around my shaft, but still welcoming me inside.

I build into him steadily, and as I feel him loosen up just enough for me, I start thrusting.

Ryan arches his back.

"Right there. Right there, Jonas."

"You keep saying my name like that, and I'm liable to blow."

I'm not fucking kidding him either, but he chuckles like it's a joke, until I'm buried to the hilt and his mouth gapes as he rolls his head back against the mattress.

"Fuck yes," he mutters. "I'm not fragile, Jonas. Fuck me hard."

I'm normally following his instructions in the yard, and now I'm following them in the bedroom. I lean forward, resting my hands on either side of him, testing out a few thrusts to really get a feel of him. His body welcomes the test hammering, so I pick up my pace.

Then I lean back, hooking my arms under his thighs again, lifting his ass off the bed as I drill his hole like my life depends on it.

His cock trembles on his abs as he tightens his cheeks around my shaft, then loosens them, moving in sync with me.

Some impulse in me, maybe because he's depriving me of it, makes me wish he would look at me. I want him to watch me pummel his ass. I want to see what the pleasure looks like in his eyes.

I lean back down, our abs pushing together, his cock against me as I take his mouth again, fucking so my hips slap against his ass.

As I nibble at his bottom lip, his arms hook around me.

"Jonas...oh, Jonas." He moans, and my hips jerk faster, like they've taken control, my balls tightening as the pressure builds up in me.

"I told you, if you keep saying my name, I'm gonna come."

"That's what I was hoping for."

Maybe it's the playfulness in his tone, or how his lips twist into that sexy smirk, but it's too late for me. Energy shoots through me, and a few quick thrusts are all I have left before I curse through my teeth, my cock swelling in him as I shoot deep.

"Keep fucking me with it," he says.

I lean back, and he grabs his shaft, jerking it. I put my hand over his. "Let me."

He releases his dick, and I stroke it as I continue my thrusts, watching his hand as he caresses across his torso while I fuck him. His ass tightens around my cock as he groans, his body tensing up, his expression locked in a cringe before he shoots, white streams streaking across his belly.

"Oh fuck yeah."

I don't know what possesses me, but before I know it, I've pulled out of him and my face is buried in the cum on his abs. I'm all tongue, trying to take it all in.

What's gotten into me?

What's Ryan done to me?

This isn't just about Simon's proposal. This is about something in me I've never had a chance to unleash. And as I lap up the last of his cum, I gaze up at him.

He's looking down at me, watching my work, and he grins.

"Maybe you should have had more dinner," he teases, which gets me laughing.

10

RYAN

Jonas doesn't leave right away, like he did last time.

I enjoyed having him on top this time.

That surprised the hell out of me.

Maybe it's his inexperience. Or his curiosity. Or his vulnerability in this fucked-up arrangement. Whatever the reason, I find it easy to let my guard down when I'm with him.

After we clean up our mess, I toss the towel into the laundry hamper in my closet and return to the bed, where he's sitting up against the headboard.

He watches me as I walk, still nude, to the liquor cabinet by the fireplace, his eyes drawn to my cock.

"For someone who's never messed around with guys before, you sure seem to know what you're doing." It's a safe comment to make, even if Simon is watching and listening.

Despite all the reasons I shouldn't enjoy letting Jonas fuck me, I'm surprised by how much I'm enjoying the experiences, even to the point of letting go of my awareness of the watchful eye we're under—something that never escaped my mind that first time.

"It's surprising *me*, that's for sure." He sounds satisfied, and I love knowing my body gave him that.

I pour myself a whiskey, and he requests rum and a mixer, so I fix one for him before returning to the bed.

For the first time since he came over tonight, I get a good look at his face.

Yes, his features are similar to Kieran's, but it's getting easier to see the differences. A tiny freckle near his ear, a sharper dip in the middle of his chin, fuller lips. And his personality is totally different—not the brash, goofy kid I grew up with. Jonas is more reserved. And he's sweet, with that hint of playfulness I discovered during our first fuck and then now.

I wonder if the change in my perspective is because we've messed around. Or maybe it's my mind's way of distinguishing between the two men, to protect me from my memories.

Jonas seems to notice my attention, and his mouth opens like he's about to ask something, but he stops himself. Maybe he's wise enough to know there are things we can't discuss, not as long as we know Simon's listening.

After Jonas takes a sip of his drink, I kiss him again, feeling a tingle of the rum as I taste the raspberry mixer. I'm about to pull away, but my tongue lingers against his bottom lip, and then I'm kissing him again, his tongue greeting mine.

Between the two fucks we've shared, I can't deny there's chemistry here. I fear, as Nell suspects, it might have some fucked-up connection to Kieran, but after being cooped up in this house, depriving myself of pleasure for so long, confining myself to a death of sorts, it's nice to finally do something that makes me feel alive.

"Sorry, just wanted to see if I mixed your drink right," I tease, which makes him laugh.

I pull away, and as I sit on the edge of the bed, I inspect his face again—now it's like a holographic image, shifting into another face if I angle in the light, which is strange since when I first saw it, I would've sworn it was Kieran, back from the dead.

I head to the other side of the bed and settle on the mattress, enjoying a sip of my drink before placing it on the nightstand.

"So…" I say. "How is Chicago?"

If we're making this believable, I have to find a way to talk to him about something. Simon wants more than fucking. He wants to see us bonding, creating a special connection between us. So I'll give it to him.

"It's nice," he says. "Not as humid as here. This heat about kills me by the afternoon."

I laugh. "Just wait until August."

"That bad, huh?"

"I don't know what kind of weather you get in Chicago, so maybe not."

"It can get pretty humid in the summer. I'm curious to see how it compares," he says. "Have you ever been?"

"No. I haven't traveled very much."

He winces. "Really? All that money, that's exactly what I'd do. I'd love to see the world."

"I did travel some when we were younger. Our father took us to London, Barcelona, Lisbon, Prague, Havana, Lima…"

"Oh…well, for someone who hasn't traveled much, you make my one Caribbean vacation sound pretty dull."

"That feels like lifetimes ago. Since Father died, we've just stayed here."

"You call your dad Father? Sounds a little dated."

I chuckle. "I've heard that before, but it's what we called him, and as kids, we didn't think anything of it, so it sounds more natural than Dad."

I don't want to talk about Father, though.

"So you don't travel much?" I ask to change the subject.

"Not really. My aunt, my sister, and I have been on our own since Mom passed. And my sister's been sick since she was a kid, so she's always needed care. I tried to go to college, but even with health insurance, you'd be surprised how much it costs to manage with something as care intensive as cancer."

Even knowing so little about him, it's the sort of story I would have expected to hear. It justifies his putting up with all this for his sister.

I want to ask more questions about his family, but for me, that topic is a landmine, so I'm cautious; I wouldn't want to feel as though he has to share anything he'd rather keep private.

"So what was it like growing up in this giant place?" he asks, and I'm relieved he's brought us back to lighter topics.

"For a kid, it's fun. So much exploring to do. So many nooks and crannies to hide in. Simon and I used to believe the place was haunted, which looking back, made our childhood exciting."

"Exciting?"

"He was afraid of these ghosts and would need to sleep in bed with me. He'd cling to me desperately, and I'd hold him tight against me until he fell asleep." Even after everything we've been through, after the rift between us, I still look back fondly on that time. Back when we felt safe in each other's arms.

"You weren't scared? You said you both believed in ghosts."

"I was always the brave one. I went exploring, searching for the ghosts. I'd look in every closet. Follow every *creak*. The idea of a little magic in the world, a little adventure, was exhilarating. I used to tell Simon we needed to pretend to be ghosts."

His eyebrow rises. "Why?"

"I figured we'd appear to them as they appear to us, and so they'd be just as scared. And I figured I was right since I never saw them." I can't help but smile, and I wonder if it's a fondness for that brave kid I used to be, or because I enjoy that Simon might hear us and hate me for sharing with Jonas—an outsider—how scared he was.

"But it was different back then," I go on. "Father kept more staff around the house. As you've noticed, it takes a lot of people to keep this place up and running, and that's not really Simon's priority. He's let the house suffer over the years by understaffing. He's more interested in how the financial affairs are handled. Investments, the trust, business things I don't have any knowledge of."

Jonas searches around the room like he figured what I'd shared might bother my brother, but really, the only thing pertaining to Simon that requires discretion is the proposal between the two of them so Jonas can get his reward and so that I could potentially uncover Simon's motives for arranging this disturbing coupling.

Besides, if Simon's going to fuck with me, then I'm going to fuck with him.

"Should I ask why it all went to Simon?"

"You can ask, but I'll choose not to answer."

Because even though Simon's proposal requires discretion, I have other secrets I choose not to share for my own reasons.

"In that case, I'll take the hint." He takes another sip of his cocktail.

"If you decide to google it, just know that it's not something the media has an answer for either. We Hawthornes do manage to keep our secrets."

My thoughts drift to those dark places where I keep mine. Hawthorne Heights carries a lot of dark secrets.

"Anyway," I say, shaking my head to bring myself back to the present, "it's getting late, and we have a busy day tomorrow."

"Can I see you again tomorrow night?"

I smile. There's an eagerness in his eyes, just like there was an eagerness to how he fucked me. Despite Simon's attempt to cause me excessive agony, I love knowing it isn't working. That Jonas and I are managing to make the best out of his shitty games.

"Same time?" I ask.

He smirks.

"For being your first, I must've left an impression for you to keep coming back for more."

"Yes, you have. I hope it's as fun for you. It seems to be."

Now I'm smiling. "Yes, Jonas, I don't have any complaints." I lean toward him, resting my hand on his waist as I get close to his face—daring myself to challenge this ghost in front of me. "Except maybe I'd like to fuck you some too."

His expression sobers.

"Sorry, Jonas. If that's not something you want to—"

"No, no. It's just…I really hadn't thought about it. Like ever in my life."

"We don't have to rush into that. I think it's best to do things like that when you know you're ready. When you want me to fuck you, I want you asking me for it. So I guess I can just deal with you pounding my ass for a while."

He laughs. "Anytime."

He moves close, and I close my eyes, accepting another kiss. His lips tingle against mine, a surge of heat rushing across my cheeks. God, what he does to my body. I'm already getting hard.

"Okay, I think I might need you to leave before I beg to have that cock again."

His hand wraps around the back of my head, keeping me close. "Why don't you start begging?" he whispers against my face.

An electric pulse radiates in my chest.

I'm eager for one more quick fuck before I kick him out of my room.

11

JONAS

"Come in me, Jonas. Come in me."

There's that familiar lust in his voice, hunger for me that seems to draw the cum right from my body, shooting up inside him.

I fall in a fit of spasms, collapsing onto his back.

Water from the showerhead splashes against my head, running down my face and neck, streaming down between our bodies.

Ryan presses his hands against the tile wall, and as he catches his breath, I kiss along the side of his neck.

The few weeks since we started fucking around have been hard labor. Hard, sweaty, manual labor, the kind that leaves my body achy and swollen. That's just during the day, before Ryan and I meet up. Messing around with him has become a fulfilling way to spend my nights, like a reward for the effort I've put into the premises. It seems that whenever we get together, Ryan just needs it, and I'm so fucking happy to give it to him.

I nibble at his ear. I've learned he enjoys when I give it a little tug between my teeth.

We dry off and head back into the bedroom. As has become our routine, Ryan fixes us drinks, and we enjoy a few sips before he slips into bed, rolling toward me, this eager expression on his face.

It's hard to tell if he's changed in the past few weeks or if he just lets me see more of him now that I'm not a stranger. And while he doesn't seem to struggle to look at my face as much, he still keeps his eyes closed whenever we fuck, which is a shame since I enjoy when we're in bed together and he looks at me with that blue gaze, his irises sparkling under the chandelier light.

"I feel greedy," he says.

"What?"

"Like that monster cock should have been shared with more people before you came here and started fucking me with your trick pelvis."

I blush. "Were you just saying that to get me red?"

"Would it be so horrible if I was?" There's a bit of Simon in that mischievous look. Funny, because I barely ever notice the similarities since I've started messing around with Ryan.

Smiling, he draws near, closing his eyes and taking my lips once again.

Our lips click as they part. I groan. "I don't wanna go."

"It's already ten. And I'm not keeping you up any later because you were useless that night when I kept you past one."

"I worked hard."

"Oh, you were trying. But you weren't up to the usual Jonas-standard."

"I like that you have some sort of Jonas-standard in your head."

"You should like that it's a really high standard too."

"I do." When he beams, I'm tempted. "Maybe I could stay the

night? We could mess around before work…" I'm not halfway through my suggestion when his expression tenses up. "Sorry. I'm fine with not. I just figured…"

"I'm not ready for that, Jonas. *Yet.*" That *yet* gives me hope that there will come a time when he is, but I won't push him to do anything he's uncomfortable with, just like he hasn't pushed me.

"In that case, I'll do my usual walk of shame back to my room," I say before taking one more kiss. As I pull away, his lips clamp back down against mine and he rolls onto me, as though, despite claiming he doesn't want me to stay, his body feels differently.

He grabs my wrists and pushes them against the mattress firmly as his tongue invades my mouth. When he pulls away, he gazes down at me, growling softly. "Okay, you'd better go before I change my mind."

I head to my room, riding that now familiar high from messing around with him, making this fucked-up mess with Simon worth it.

I came to Hawthorne Heights considering myself straight, but all these nights with Ryan make it a struggle to remember a time when I didn't want my dick buried in an ass.

The following morning, while I'm eating breakfast—cinnamon-raisin oatmeal and pancakes—Ryan's late. I'm curious why he's running behind, which is unlike him, when Simon walks in, dressed in a polo and jeans that look much nicer than anything I've seen Ryan in. Like he's flaunting the cash he inherited.

I try to keep my cool, but I assume the worst: He knows Ryan and I are faking. He knows this whole thing is a lie, and he's going to make me leave and get Charity kicked out of the treatment program he only just got her into.

"Morning, Jonas." He takes a seat at the end of the table, where Ryan usually sits.

"Good morning."

"Ryan will be a little late for breakfast. There was an emergency leak in the east wing that he's trying to fix, and I thought it's a good opportunity to catch up with you about your progress."

"It's going—"

"*Well.* Yes, I know."

He doesn't let up his eye contact, and my cheeks are getting warm.

It's been getting easier to forget that Simon's watching us in our intimate moments. Despite claiming he'd get someone to review the footage, I know better, and the way he's looking at me, studying my expression, it's like he's reviewing all the material he's watched.

"What I wanted to check in on is how Ryan's feeling about you. Would you say he's just warming up to you, or maybe something more?"

I don't want to answer. Not even sure I can, but he's technically my boss, so I should figure something out.

"Warming up to me, I'd say."

"Nothing more?"

"I was with him last night and asked if I could stay, but he told me no, so it must still be just messing around in his mind." I figure it's safest to stick with something he must already know, but speaking it out loud stings. Because I enjoy spending time with

Ryan, and I wish he'd asked me to stay.

Simon nods. "That makes sense. But how does it feel, when the two of you are together?"

My thoughts flash to the heat...the pulsing desire as I'm fucking him. His hot breath, how he moans out my name.

I wonder if Simon's piercing gaze has picked up on any of that—since he's surely watched us fucking like wolves plenty of times—and when he says, "Does it feel like he's drawn to you? Other than physically, I mean?" I realize I'd forgotten his question.

"It seems that way to me."

"What does that feel like? To have him want you like that?"

As if his questions weren't already weird enough. How am I supposed to answer that? *Honestly, Simon, it feels fucking great.* But is that what he wants to hear? I'm supposed to be working a job, not enjoying myself.

"It feels nice knowing it's getting us closer to our objective."

"And are you finding yourself drawn to him?"

He's not even looking me in the eyes. He studies my expression, inspecting my face for something—tells? Some clue as to what I'm thinking?

"He seems like a friendly, thoughtful guy."

Simon's jaw tightens like Ryan's sometimes does when his cum is about to explode out of his cock. It's a thought that emphasizes how strange it is to look at the face of the man I've been messing around with, and yet *not* to be looking at that man at all. Striking as the physical similarities may be, their personalities are so different that those similarities seem superficial. Strange that, while I know with every part of me that I find Ryan attractive, I don't feel the same about Simon. Not even slightly. There's no spark here. The only emotions, really, are rage at how he's fucking with Ryan and resentment that he holds the fate of my sister in his hands.

"He *seems* friendly and thoughtful," Simon says. "Yes, I agree."

Like so many of the cryptic things he says, it leaves me wondering what the hell he means.

"I don't want to rush you, Jonas. The pace you're moving at is fine, but as I mentioned previously, I want him to believe your relationship is real. Meaningful."

"Yes, I understood that to be the job."

Simon smiles. "Good. Now I have some stuff to tend to: investments, the trust, business things Ryan doesn't have any knowledge of."

Ryan had used those exact words when he spoke about it, and I can tell by how Simon stares into my eyes that he's not studying me anymore—he's sending a message: that I should never forget he's watching and listening.

It fucks with my head. Why say someone else was reviewing that initial footage if he was going to wind up revealing he's spying on us?

I wait for him to say more, but there's a *buzz*. Simon retrieves his cell from his pocket. "Looks like Ryan is finished with the leak, so he'll be heading over soon."

Does he have a tracker on his brother? Wouldn't surprise me if he had security cameras with AI monitoring to alert him when there's movement anywhere in the house. God only knows the kind of security this guy can afford.

What if Simon is monitoring Ryan in ways Ryan doesn't know about?

What if he's heard the conversations we've shared in private in the woods?

Fuck.

Simon says, "I hope you both have a good workday…and an even better night." A sly smirk plays across his lips. He winks, and it feels so calculating, so nefarious—a reminder of the stark contrast between these brothers. Ryan's abrasiveness can be intimidating, but he has a tenderness to him once he lets his guard down. Simon's charm is intimidating, and all I see—or all he lets me see—is something sadistic and menacing.

He pushes to his feet. "Finish your breakfast. You need your strength. I'll swing by like this for updates occasionally, so don't be surprised when that happens. In the meantime, I'm looking forward to when you're able to fuck him with his eyes open."

Why did he want to have this meeting with me?

Maybe he feels I'm not moving fast enough, despite saying the pace is fine.

Maybe he didn't like Ryan talking to me about him, and this mindfuck is my punishment.

Maybe something we've done has given away that Ryan and I have teamed up.

Or maybe—and this wouldn't be beyond the pale to a guy like Simon—it's all just a fucking power play to remind me he's in the dominant position.

12

RYAN

I APPROACH THE oaks on the east side of the property. The guys are all in helmets and safety goggles. Morgan holds the bottom of the ladder while Jonas hacks off a slender branch with the handheld chainsaw. Forsyth is supposed to be gathering the branches from the oaks they trimmed earlier, but he's chatting them up instead. It's the sort of thing I might give him hell about on another day, but he's more than earned it with how on top of shit he's been this week, so I'll excuse it.

As I draw nearer, I realize I'm tensing my jaw.

It's been two days since something in Jonas changed. He's been on edge, agitated…not like himself. I gave him the hand signal for meeting in the woods, but he blew me off, which really messed with my head. I thought he might blow me off at night too, but he showed up both nights and we fucked around—it just wasn't as hot as always. But not being able to have a conversation with him left me having to make up reasons for the change.

Did Simon find out we're conspiring against him and confront Jonas? No, surely, if he had, he would have sent Jonas home. Although, if Simon has some fucked-up revenge planned for me, I doubt it was easy to come by a Kieran look-alike. Would he be so quick to throw away his advantage?

"I'd love to go to Chicago," Forsyth says when I'm just a few yards from the tree. "Go out to bars and clubbing. What would you think of that, Morgan? You could come with me and play wingman."

Morgan grins, I'm sure because he knows he'd be a shitty wingman.

"Coming down!" Jonas announces, and starts descending the ladder.

"Oh, hey, boss," Forsyth says. "Just making sure these slackers are working."

As I snicker at his remark, Jonas glances over his shoulder, and he misses a step. He reacts fast, tossing the chainsaw away from us as he tumbles to the ground, landing on his ass.

"The fuck, Jonas?" I'm at his side in no time, kneeling beside him. "Are you all right? Are you hurt?"

"I'm fine. It was just a little fall."

I let him take his time before Morgan and I help him to his feet.

"I'm fine," Jonas insists. "I just tripped." He wipes at some dirt on his ass.

"I'm glad you're okay," I say. "But what the hell is wrong with you?"

"Boss, it's cool, really," Forsyth says. "Shit happens."

"No, it's not *cool*. Jonas, this is the second time today you've almost injured yourself from being clumsy. I can't afford for you to break your damn arm right now. Or our chainsaw."

Morgan and Forsyth look to each other like they wish they

could slip away.

I know I'm overcompensating since I just want to fucking kiss Jonas now that I know he's fine. But I have to show the guys I treat him the same as I would them. Although, I'd never bark at them like this. I need to dial it down.

"Sorry, Ryan. I was just…distracted. I wasn't thinking."

"That's the problem. Just focus. You're not the only one you could've gotten hurt just then."

But it's not just his clumsiness that's getting to me. I want to know what's got him so worked up. Made him this damn reckless.

After he recovers, the guys get back to work, and fortunately, when I suggest Jonas help me get the branches to the woods, he doesn't resist. I guide him to the spot where we first chatted about Simon's proposal. En route, I can see how stiff he is in the shoulders, how his thumbs rub at his hands uneasily.

"What the hell is going on?" I ask Jonas when I finally have him alone.

As has been his MO the past couple of days, Jonas doesn't make eye contact. He glances around, as though suspicious of our surroundings.

"Simon said something to you, didn't he?" I can feel it in my goddamn bones.

"I don't know that we should talk, even out here." He hesitates before rushing toward me. He halts inches from me, then leans closer still. His hot breath rushes against my ear, stirring a familiar desire, some innate impulse within me that's got my cock shifting in my pants. My body feels hollow with him so close but not inside me.

"You don't know that there aren't cameras out here," he whispers.

I knew it! Simon said something that's making him freak out.

"Did he tell you he heard our conversations out here? Is that it?" I keep my reply low too.

"No, no."

"Jonas, if he'd heard what we said, he would've given you the boot. Right? I'm telling you, we're fine."

He leans away, considering this.

"Now tell me what happened."

"I know you said he has cameras on us, that we're mic'd. But I guess I minimized it or didn't want to think he was watching or listening to all of it. Maybe I needed to tell myself that to be able to keep doing this. But Simon approached me the other morning, while you were fixing a leak."

I was suspicious of how Simon magically discovered a leak in his room that seemed to be caused by something cutting into his pipe. Of course, Simon breaks things occasionally to keep me busy. I hadn't even considered it was to keep me busy while he chatted with Jonas.

"He was saying word for word things we mentioned while we were in your room, and then he did this thing where he was monitoring your movements around the house on his phone. I just think I underestimated what he's capable of. After that, I was worried that if we talked in the woods, he'd be suspicious that I was meeting you to tell you what he said. Fuck, I'm still freaking out about it now. It just feels so fucking violating."

He glances around uneasily once again, and an impulse moves

through me. I rush up against him, and my hands find their way to either side of his face as I press my lips against his. Desire courses through me as my tongue greets his. Fucking around with him is different than when we first started—like we've found a natural rhythm. I wait for him to resist me, and I'm relieved when his arm hooks around me and he caves to this experience. I move one hand to the back of his head and slide the other down his neck.

When I finally pull away, I inspect his expression. The worry he wears reminds me of Kieran. But I see my plan worked, at least to some extent.

"There. Just take a deep breath."

He winces before smirking, and this expression doesn't remind me of Kieran; it's so specific to Jonas. "Thanks for that," he says.

A jolt of satisfaction ripples through me. My body seems primed to bring him relief.

"Simon's not listening in on us out here, unless you're wearing a wire or something."

"Sorry, it's all just getting to my head. If he finds out…" There's terror in his expression; it would kill him if his sister's help was ripped away from her.

"I know, but he's not a god. He just wants you to believe he's one. If he pulled out his phone to show he's monitoring me, it's because he wanted to show you that. Just like he told you things that happened in private between us because he wanted to get into your head. It's all a bluff. Maybe to gauge your reaction. Maybe to keep you on your toes. Or both."

He bites his lip. "Ryan, what is this all about? You said you weren't ready to tell me, but don't I deserve to know who I remind you of? Why haven't you told me? Why hasn't he told me?"

Tension knots in my chest. Since he arrived, it's always been this dance between pleasure and pain, but the pain is particularly acute now that he's confronted me with this.

"What's happening?" he presses.

His probing eyes are too much for me, and I turn away, worried that if I look at him too long, he might read the truth in my expression.

Flashes of moments with Kieran push to the forefront of my mind, and I put my hands against the sides of my head, wishing I could yank out those memories as hot rage radiates in my chest. It takes me a moment to recover, to push those thoughts back.

"Ryan?"

I turn back, and that face…God, that face that at times can look so different…now I see Kieran. But only for a moment before the optical illusion fades and there's Jonas again.

I understand why he wants to know. And he deserves to know. It's not right that he should have to play an unwitting pawn in Simon's perverse game. But I fear what sharing the truth will do, that it might reveal parts of my past I wish to remain hidden.

"Please talk to me, Ryan."

You don't have to tell him everything, I remind myself.

"When I was little, there was a guy named Kieran Haynes…"

Even just saying that name while looking at Jonas's face is a struggle.

"He lived with us."

I hate myself for deceiving Jonas. Makes me feel no better than Simon, since I'm not being as honest as I should be, conveniently leaving out our blood relation, but…well, that part, he might not understand.

"He was the son of a family friend," I push on through with my half-truth. "Father took him in, treated him like his own kid. Kieran, Simon, and I got along great. Did everything together. We'd head into the woods and play or go to the library and read books together. Video games in the game room. It was like childhood is supposed to be, full of laughter and excitement. But then we got older, at that juncture in adolescence when light play collides with desires and feelings you don't understand. And Father wasn't the sort to talk to us about them.

"Simon and I experimented with those feelings together—we just didn't know any other way—and as we got older, I developed feelings for Kieran. I confided in Simon about them, and he encouraged those feelings."

"Were you and Kieran together? Romantically?"

I shake my head, a tear stirring in my eye. "And then Simon grew cold. I don't know that people who don't have twins can understand… When we were young, we could complete each other's sentences, but during this time, when we were seventeen, I felt him put up a wall. Like he didn't want me to see something in his mind. Eventually, I discovered he and Kieran had been messing around together. It felt like a sick betrayal from Simon. Cruel, even, given how much I'd discussed my feelings with him."

"Whatever happened to Kieran?" Jonas asks, because he must know the story doesn't end there.

Images surge through my mind. A rock held tight in my fist as I slam it into Kieran's skull. Then Father's: *"It's Kieran. Simon found him in the woods."*

"He passed away," I say. "Our family was never the same after that."

I study Jonas's expression. He's not an idiot.

"There's more to it than that," I confess, "but that's as much as I'm willing to share. For now."

"So this is someone you cared about?"

A conflicting mix of emotions—affection, love, lust, betrayal, rage—stir in my chest. It's as confusing as my feelings tend to be whenever the subject of Kieran comes up.

"I did," I admit. "And Simon cared about him too."

Jonas's expression twists up. "So why does he want me to be in a relationship with you?"

"I haven't been able to piece that one together."

"Could it be a peace offering, like if he brings you a look-alike to mess around with, then it makes up for what he did?"

I sincerely doubt that, but I'd rather not speculate. Not with Jonas. "Who's to say? But there's some insight for you into the fucked-up history of the Hawthornes."

He approaches me and takes my hand. It's a struggle to look at him, especially with all the fresh memories he's brought up. "So I remind you of a guy you cared about? Who you loved?"

My gaze meets his briefly before trailing around his face, spying all those things that remind me of Kieran. I confess, "Yes. I loved him."

A tear escapes my eye.

Jonas moves close, and seeing Kieran's ghost moving toward me makes me want to pull away, but I stop myself as Jonas wraps his arms around me, pulling me in for a hug.

I relax into his hold.

It's kind. Gentle.

I hook my arms around him and tug him close, appreciating his sympathy.

But I also feel guilty for those pieces of our history I didn't share. Not only because it would be confusing to him, but it confuses me too.

I still love Kieran, but I hate him too, and the two parts of my being are constantly at war as I struggle with how he betrayed me so cruelly. And with this rift he caused between Simon and me.

13

JONAS

Now I have his full name: Kieran Haynes.

I want to google him, but since my chat with Simon, my paranoia has intensified. What if he's tracking my phone, or what if he were to get ahold of it and look through my search history? This guy could effortlessly hire someone to hack my phone and get any info he wanted.

No, an internet search was too great a risk.

Still, that didn't mean I couldn't come across the name another way, one that wouldn't rouse suspicion. So I google Hawthorne Heights once again, scouring the search results for that name.

But it's a dead end.

I'm getting used to dead ends when it comes to the Hawthornes, so I accept I'll have to wait until Ryan's comfortable sharing more.

I choose to focus on the things that matter. As far as work is concerned, I'm good at this, and Forsyth and Morgan are reliable coworkers I get along with. As for Charity and Aunt Amy, they're situated at the hospital in NY, and after some rushed testing and analysis that I figure Simon's money played a large part in, they've already got her on a chemo regimen tailored specifically for her.

Everything Simon has promised has come to fruition, which makes it easier for me to enjoy nights with Ryan.

On one of these incredible nights, I thrust into Ryan, his eyes sealed shut as I serve his ass. He grips my pec with one hand and cups my side with the other.

"Harder. Destroy my hole with that fucking battering ram."

I obey, staring at his open mouth as his body trembles on the mattress beneath me, my sweat dripping onto his cheek as I think, *Please open your eyes. Look at me.*

It's moments like these when I can forget, for just a few moments, that I'm his hired cock. About all the messed-up shit that's the reason I'm really here, as I drill away, the rhythmic clapping of my hips making contact with his ass combining with the squeaking of the springs in his bed.

I feel like his fucking sex toy, and I love it.

Between his moans and the intense pressure in my cock, I'm getting close.

As I watch his head roll back and hear him moan, not for the first time, I know it must feel amazing to have a cock ramming into a prostate. I imagine us in this position, with him fucking me, dominating me. There's a jolt of sensation, and the pressure in my hips climbs.

Not going to be much longer, and the thought of my cum buried in him is too much for me.

"Kiss me, Jonas. Kiss me now," he whispers.

I lean close and take his mouth, his tongue slipping past my lips, and then he pulls away and says, "Hurry and come. I'm gonna shoot."

I'm relieved because it's too fucking late for me, and my cock pulses. His ass clenches around me, keeping me tight inside him as I thrust to finish, and when I hear a familiar moan, I look down to see him spurting across his abs.

"Oh, fuck yes," I say before kissing him some more, my body urging me through a few more thrusts like it wants to make sure I get every last drop of my cum inside him.

I hook my arms under his pits and pull him close till I feel his cum on my stomach.

Licking and nibbling. It's that feeling I get with him, like we're not even human. Just stray dogs who met in an alley and started going at it, without inhibition or reservations. Hungry with lust and submitting to wild, primal impulses.

After we clean up, I rest in the bed beside Ryan, and all those things I'm able to set aside while we fuck come rushing back.

That his brother's watching us.

That I'm only in this bed because I'm being paid to be.

That I look like a man Ryan once loved.

I take a sip of the cocktail he made me, then set it on the nightstand.

Ryan rolls toward me and smiles. "That was better than usual."

"It was very hot," I say, my cheeks warming.

"You don't get to blush after giving me a pounding like that."

Now my face must be really fucking red.

"Why are you getting like that? We've been messing around for weeks. Aren't you comfortable around me?"

"Yeah. I am. I'm also comfortable being embarrassed in front of you…or as comfortable with that as I can be."

He chuckles.

God, he's so fucking sexy when he chuckles like that.

He leans toward me and closes his eyes before offering me a kiss, then another. His tongue slides out and lingers on my bottom lip before he pulls away, opening his eyes once again.

Despite his playful, open expression, I know he's holding something back.

"Why are you looking at me like that?" he asks, because I must be staring at him.

"Just thinking about some things."

"I've been thinking about some things too."

I decide to go for a subject change before I slip up and say something neither of us wants mentioned while we're under surveillance. "You know, I remember when we first started messing around, you wanted to fuck me."

He glares at me. "I've kind of been fucking you."

"No, like topping me. And I guess I've been so greedy for your hole that it's been all I can think about, but lately, I've been curious what it'd be like for you to fuck me."

One of his brows shifts slightly. "You want me to top you?"

"I mean, I'm nervous since I've never done that, but you make it look…pretty good."

"I've lured you into bottoming because of my impressive skills? That's hot." His eyes widen like he's as excited as I am to try this out. "I'd fuck you tonight if you hadn't hammered all the cum and energy out of me."

His attention is drawn to the sheets, which must've shifted because of how hard that made me. He reaches under the covers and grabs hold of my shaft, snickering in this cocky way, like he's pleased to know he did that.

"Are you some kind of AI fuckbot?" he asks.

My smile spreads into a grin. God, he knows how to make me smile.

"Yeah, I'll fuck you, Jonas," he says, my cock swelling in his grip even more. "Any other requests?"

"I'd love if you did it with your eyes open." I must be too caught up in the afterglow, or hypnotized from gazing into Ryan's eyes, because I actually say the truth, and I regret it the moment it escapes my mouth.

Ryan's playful expression is gone in an instant, his eyes no longer on me, his hand pulling away from my cock.

I fucked this up.

I know what his issue is. I fucking know that this is something that bothers him.

"I'm sorry. I—I—"

Fuck.

"That's not something I'm willing to do, Jonas." There's no apprehension, no question in his voice. It's a final judgment he's delivering to let me know that if I had a fantasy where he looked at me while we're fucking, I need to get it out of my dumb brain.

It's a reminder that there was a man who'd captured his interest, whom I happen to resemble. That's why he fucks me. That's why he can't look at me, because he knows I'm not really him, and because the pain of being fucked by a man he loved, but who loved his brother instead, terrorizes him. And now, for some fucked-up reason, Simon feels the need to torture him about this.

"Forget I said it. Please." I don't want this to change anything. I don't want it to change *us*. Or stop anything we've been doing. "I should go."

I roll toward the edge of the bed, when I feel Ryan's gentle touch on my arm. I stop and turn back, hoping that maybe he's willing to pretend I wasn't such a fucking inconsiderate asshole.

"I don't want you to go. Stay tonight."

It's the first time he's extended the invitation. The first time I see something else in his expression. Not the frustration or anger he sometimes shows while we're working together. Not the grief I sometimes catch glimpses of in moments when he's gazing off or when he shared his secret with me. Not the ecstasy and joy and laughter when we're fucking around. It's serious—this desire for me to be with him tonight.

"Please," he adds, and I relax back against the pillow. "Will you stay?"

"Yes."

Just as quickly as he blocked me, it feels like he gave me something else, something special, and I'm so intrigued by Ryan that I'm willing to accept whatever he's willing to give me.

He moves closer, puts his arm around me, then relaxes his head against my chest.

A rush of energy shoots through me as he rests, his face planted against my flesh, his hold firm.

And I'm just glad I didn't totally fuck this up.

14

RYAN

I FEEL SAFE in his hold, lying against his firm body.
Feeling his warm touch.

Tasting his body.

Smelling his scent.

My senses are coming back to life, along with a vitality like I had as a child.

"I'd love if you did it with your eyes open."

A confession, one he regretted as soon as I reacted.

I hope my hold lets him know that it's not about him. I want him here. I enjoy our time together. Much more than I should allow myself to, since I've started pretending that it's not going to end.

Of course, I know it has to.

I usually have such a hard time sleeping. It should be difficult to fall asleep with Jonas's heavy breathing and the position that's so different from on my back against a firm pillow, but my eyes grow heavy, and before I know it, it's morning, the soft light of dawn sneaking between my drapes. I only wake him briefly as I slip out of bed and brush my teeth. Then I head downstairs, where I find Nell making breakfast.

"I would have put something out if I'd known you were going to be up," she says.

"No, no. You don't need to do anything."

"I can make some waffles real quick, if you want."

"I can make them."

"Nope. Get out of my kitchen! I need my peace of mind. Just go ahead in, and I'll bring them to you in a minute."

She offers a warm smile, and I head into the adjoining dining area, settling at the table. I pull out my phone and visit Apple News, scanning the headlines until I find a promising article to occupy my mind until my waffles are ready.

When the kitchen door opens, I say, "You really didn't have to—"

"But I insist." It's not Nell's voice, but Simon's.

He pulls up the chair adjacent to mine, the legs screeching against the polished cement floor.

I hadn't fully appreciated how rested and relaxed I was from my sleep until my body stiffens up, and as I turn my head, Simon's coming right at me, and I can't react fast enough to block his firm kiss.

"Morning, Ryan." He settles in the chair beside me.

He has bags under his eyes and seems to be shaking slightly. He doesn't look like he got much sleep. "Busy night?" I ask.

"Probably not as busy as yours."

"Probably? What a fucking joke. I hope you enjoyed the show."

"I have some notes, but I think that would be rude."

"Not as rude as watching."

Simon laughs. "Ryan, I'm only teasing. You know I haven't put any cameras in your room in a long time."

Though I've given up on looking for cameras, I recall plenty of times where he said something similar and then I discovered them anyway. Besides, I don't believe for a minute that he'd go to all the trouble of bringing Jonas here and then not watch.

"I'm being serious." He looks me right in the eyes—it's how he prefers to lie.

I feel something against my shoe, and I yank it back so hard, my heel hits the leg of the chair. "Fuck," I mutter.

"Oh, come on, Ryan. Can't we still play like old times?"

He's taunting me, being deliberately cruel, and I'm wondering if it's because this twisted game he's playing is messing with him as much as it's messing with me.

"I think *you* are still playing," I snap.

"Whatever could you be talking about?"

Reminds me of how he'd react when we were kids and he hid a toy from me. I always knew when it was him, and he'd still act totally oblivious.

"So is Jonas being as…" He seems to be carefully searching for a word. "As *helpful* as I'd hoped?"

"I'm not answering that."

"I mean, I don't have a camera in your room, but obviously I have cameras in the hallways. I know who's coming and going. I don't know that it's appropriate to have this kind of relationship with someone who's technically under you. There's a power imbalance there. It's really not very woke."

As I glare at him, his mischievous smile slips across his wicked face.

"We just get together in my room to play poker," I lie, meeting his gaze.

His eye twitches, his expression twisting into a frown, as though he's offended that I would lie to him, despite how comfortable he is doing the same to me.

"I know you have," he says. "I really do have cameras in your room, and I've seen every hand. I know he's ready to get a full house, so I'm curious if you'll give it to him."

He says it so playfully, but he's clearly referring to Jonas asking me to top him.

"Maybe," he continues, "you could play a more exciting card game so that I have a little more fun watching. Just be careful you don't lead anyone on," he says between his teeth. "You know you have a tendency to do that."

My jaw tenses, and I feel the urge to lunge from my seat and deck him, when the door opens and Nell enters with two trays. She places mugs and pours coffee, then brings us each a plate of waffles, butter, and a syrup dispenser. As she asks if there's anything else we need, my tension ebbs.

She heads back into the kitchen, and Simon and I grab our syrup dispensers, preparing our waffles the same way—syrup, then butter—our movements mirroring each other. Hard to know if it's that same instinct that drew us to do this back when we were kids, or if Simon's imitating me to remind me of those days.

JONAS AND I are working by a flower garden near the pool, placing new stone tiles to replace the ones we dug out last week. He's shirtless, as usual, and my gaze keeps drifting to his ass as he bends over.

As I sneak another glance, taking liberties since Forsyth is mowing and Morgan has the day off, I lick my lips as I think about tonight, when I'll have that ass all to myself.

He peeks over his shoulder, and his eyes narrow, probably because the sun's in them. "Enjoying the show?"

"Actually, I was thinking about tonight."

He finishes placing the stone before rising back up and turning to me, and I notice his shoulders are a little pink.

"When was the last time you applied sunscreen?"

"Just a few hours ago."

"Here," I say, retrieving a mini bottle from my pocket.

"Ryan, you can't wait a few hours to get your hands all over me?"

"Nope." I slather lotion on my hands and then get to work covering his shoulders, chest, and torso, copping a feel as I slide down into his ass crack.

As he laughs, I check behind me to ensure Forsyth isn't around before leaning close and pressing my lips against his shoulder blade. My lips tingle, and my cock stirs in my shorts. I'm waiting for him to crack a joke, but he just stays still until I pull away, then turns to me.

"What was that for?"

"In case I'm too busy fucking to give you the kisses you want tonight."

"That sounds like a lie 'cause I don't think you're one to give too few kisses."

Isn't that the truth? If anything, I've been making up for all the kisses I've been deprived of these past few years.

Suddenly, I'm looking right at his face, but once again, it's not the face I was expecting.

It's Jonas's face.

Such a strange feeling. Of course it's his face, that shouldn't surprise me, but it does.

Even though I can distinguish between them in my mind, I haven't been able to open my eyes, not while we're fucking around. Or even kissing. I fear if I do, it'll be too unbearably painful. Dredge up the past in a way that will leave me in despair, like those days before and after Kieran's death.

"What is it?" he asks.

"Nothing," I lie, but I hate lying to him.

When we meet up that night, he must be as hungry to get my dick in him as I am to put it in him because we're stripped down and on the bed in no time. He rolls so I'm on top of him, our cocks stroking against each other's pelvises.

"I think you're harder than usual," Jonas says, and I feel him smiling against my face.

"Just been thinking about pounding this ass all day, seeding up inside you."

"That sounds nice."

"Does my little straight boy need to be bred?" I ask, which makes him chuckle.

"I don't know that straight's the right label for me at this point."

"Shut up. Let me enjoy the thought of getting my cum wedged deep inside a straight guy."

He laughs again. "In that case, you can call me straight all night long."

We snicker together, his breath warm against my face.

I fetch the lube and throw it beside him. Soon, I'm on my knees between his legs, and I lean down, hooking my arms around his thighs. Lifting them up, I bury my face against his hole, licking, teasing Jonas's ass. I'm a fucking animal for it, like some part of me is determined to make him ready for my cock.

I pull back and lick my forefinger, then push it against his hole, steadily making my entrance. His moan assures me he enjoys the sensation, and I circle around, exploring, before pulling back and letting my middle finger in on the fun.

Pushing back, I feel the familiar rubbery sensation, and his body vibrates, letting me know I'm right there.

"Don't torture me anymore," Jonas says. "Please, just give me your cock."

He's so fucking impatient, but so am I. So I slide my fingers out, grab the lube, ready my cock, and rise up, closing my eyes as I move over him.

I press the head of my cock up against his hole.

"I'd love if you did it with your eyes open."

I know what he wants from me, what would make this experience that much better for him.

But I'm scared what I'll see when I look.

Come on, Ryan. Don't be a coward.

You can do this.

Do I dare?

15

JONAS

Ryan is on his knees between my legs, excitement and nervousness bubbling up in my belly as I feel his cock pressing against my ass.

After having his fingers in me, God, I can't imagine what that thing's going to feel like. Given how he reacts to me fucking him, it must be good, and I know if anyone will do me right, it's him.

He leans forward, resting his hand down at my side as he guides himself in slowly with the other.

His eyes are sealed shut, and I wish he'd open them and look. Although, why would I want that if it would hurt him?

No.

I want him to take his time with that, just like he's taking his time with my body.

"You're really tight," he says.

I feel the pressure until the head of his cock is lodged in me, opening me up.

"Sorry. I'm nervous." I chuckle, then gulp.

He doesn't push farther. Just waits patiently.

And then his face tenses up—and his eyes open.

There he is.

I'm waiting for him to seal them back shut, but he tilts his head, studying my face. He's not looking at me like he did that first day. As he smiles, my body relaxes, and I feel myself loosening up.

"You ready for some more?" he asks.

I nod, and he pushes in gently. As he reaches farther in, my cock lifts off my belly slightly, clearly aroused by the subtle movement, the promise of him hitting that sweet spot again.

He lowers onto his forearms as he pushes even farther in, and there's a burst of sensation.

"Oh fuck," I say, appreciating this lesson in my prostate. "Fuck. Now I know what the big deal is," pushes from my lips as a network of nerves radiates from my pelvis.

He chuckles, those bright eyes still fixed on me. He's not just looking; he's fucking staring at me. Like he wants to see my reaction to him being inside me.

Looking him in the eyes as he fucks me is even better than I could have imagined.

He leans close and takes a kiss, then another, pushing deeper and deeper, his girth continuing to put pressure on that spot.

"How's that feel?" he whispers against my lips.

"Real good."

"You ready to know what it feels like to have your ass pounded?"

"Yes."

His movements are slow, steady, and as he gets back up on his forearms, he kisses and nibbles along my jawline. When he gets to my chin, he bites softly. Then he thrusts in big, sweeping movements, building into a faster pace.

I'm reeling in sensation, heart racing, face flushed with heat. There's a tingle in my dick before a bead of precum pushes out with one of his thrusts. I run my hand down his back, gripping his ass, encouraging his work, until he's fucking me like a machine, building up a sweat.

"I feel so fucking stupid for waiting this long," I confess.

"Don't worry. Happy to make up for lost time." He pulls back, hooks my thighs in his arms, and adjusts my ass as he rises up on his knees. The angle gets him in deep and good.

He closes his eyes again, but this time, I can tell it's because he's enjoying having his way with me. He's got that same expression he makes when I fuck him—mouth open, head rolled back.

But now he's dominating me.

As the pressure mounts, I grunt and moan, the intensity fucking killing me. I grab my cock and stroke, my rapid pace letting me know how quickly I'm climbing.

No, I have to stop.

"Please tell me you're close," I say.

"I can be."

"Come in me. Please. I need it now. Please."

He keeps his thrusts intense, slapping my ass with that *clap* that echoes around the room. I'm scared it's going to be too late, but then he hits me with a hard, deliberate thrust, his cock expanding inside me, assuring me that has to be it.

He's doing it; he's filling me up.

It's enough to end my agony as I rip out my load, grunting through my teeth as warm cum sprays my belly.

We're all pants and grunts as Ryan's body pushes against mine. His mouth mashes up against my lips, tongue probing. I hook my arms around him, clinging as if needing him to help me brace for the fall from everything we just shared.

He slides out of me, crawling down my body and stepping off the bed, and then I feel his warm mouth against my abs. He cleans me up, leaving nothing but a thin film of saliva on me.

"Fuck that was hot," I tell him as he licks his lips and turns his gaze to me.

He's still looking at me. Fuck, I love that.

I relax my head against a pillow, and he joins me, his hand sliding down to the wet flesh and resting in what he left behind.

"That's a nice ass," he tells me before licking my cheek.

I'm nervous about bringing up that he looked at me, but I can't help myself. "You looked at me."

He grins. "Yeah, I did."

"Are you okay?"

It must be a strange thing to hear because he seems to be struggling for a moment before replying, "I am. Did *you* like it?"

I laugh. "Couldn't you tell? Or did the part where I was begging you to come in me make you think I wasn't enjoying myself?"

"Do you like that? Having my cum in you right now?"

I'm blushing.

"You do. You like knowing it's jammed up inside you, don't you, you fucking perv?"

I enjoy the playfulness in his tone.

"It's weird," I tell him, "but I do have this feeling right now."

"What's it feel like?"

"Satisfied?" Because I don't get why it feels so good.

"That's what I want to hear. So your first time bottoming was a good one?"

"Yeah, like, if I'd had any idea that's what it felt like, I'm pretty confident I would have experimented with it sooner."

"Happy to have introduced you to your prostate."

Just his mention of it makes my ass twitch slightly.

He kisses my cheek. It's a gentle move, very unlike what we just shared.

"Did you get to speak with your sister today?" he asks, and when I cringe, he adds, "Sorry. I know that's totally unrelated. I just couldn't think of a way to get from fucking you to wanting to know how things were going."

I laugh, but then I feel that sting of uncertainty. "She's doing well. She really likes the doctors, but she says the treatment has made her tired. Not a big surprise, but she could barely keep her eyes open when we were talking."

"You sound sad. It must be hard to be here when you want to be there to help her."

My chest tightens. "When our mother passed, it made me realize how fragile life is, how you have to be there with the ones you love as much as you can. Because it can be gone at any moment."

"I get that." His gaze shifts to the sheets, and he has this far-off look in his eyes. Given what he's shared about his past, I don't doubt he knows this kind of pain too.

"I'm sure you do, with your mother, father, and Kieran."

His gaze meets mine again. He's eyeing me uneasily, and I'm

not sure why.

"I notice you never mention your mom." Though I read about how she died, it hasn't come up.

"Have you read about that online already?"

I nod. "Sorry if I shouldn't have."

He gets that far-off look in his eyes again. "It's all right. Those kinds of reports and obituaries never do enough. We were only nine when it happened. I'm guessing you saw that it was pills. She wasn't well for a lot of that time. Kept her distance from us. She'd been admitted to the hospital a few times, and Father had a therapist and psychiatrist come to the house to help, but obviously, that wasn't enough to get her out of the pain she was in."

"I'm sorry."

"Thank you," he whispers. "I should have probably asked you sooner, but I was worried it might be too sensitive a subject. Your parents…"

"Dad was a firefighter. He spent a lot of time working, but whenever he was home, he gave us his everything. But right before Charity was born, he went into an apartment building to rescue people trapped there, and it collapsed on top of him." I didn't think my chest could get any tighter, but it's like a rod is being driven into my heart.

"I'm so sorry, Jonas. He sounds like a hero."

I nod. "He was. And a great father. Even with as much as he worked, he was always making time for me and Mom. He'd take us camping and taught me how to fish. Read me bedtime stories. I wish he'd been home more, but I'm also glad I had any time with him. It's sad that Charity never got to meet him and feel that kind of love."

"I think maybe she did," he says. "Just not from him."

Fuck, that gets me. I don't want to start crying, so I blurt out, "That's life, right?"

"Maybe it is life, but that doesn't make it hurt any less," he says, and my eyes are drawn back to his.

He hooks his arm around me, offering a hug as tender as his touch. Like a blanket that protects me enough to let some of that tension in my chest ease up, and I tremble as tears rush down my face.

"Sorry, I'm not—" My voice cracks before I can go on.

"Jonas, you don't have to apologize."

His hand slides up to my nape, and he strokes gently before offering a kiss against the side of my head.

When he pulls away, I find myself unspooling. "Dad's death was hard, but it brought my family closer together. Mom moved in with Aunt Amy to have Charity, and they both raised us. Two of the most loving people on the goddamn planet. Just felt like, as horrible as losing Dad was, at least we still had each other. Then as Charity got older, she got sick. And that was like hell. And then Mom was diagnosed with breast cancer at the same time Charity was undergoing treatments, and that was just so overwhelming. I have a hard time even connecting to memories around that. Kind of like right after Dad died. I don't feel emotion around it. Like this hollowness in my chest."

"That's so much for a kid to go through," Ryan says.

"We've both had our share of tragedy. Mine just happened to involve a lot of oncologist offices and chemo wards." I chuckle bitterly.

"It's different, though. My parents weren't like yours. I remember desperately wanting to be close to them, but there was this distance. I don't know that they could be close to people. I'm sorry you had to experience that, but I'm glad you had your aunt to help you through it all."

"Yeah, as shitty a hand as we've been dealt, she's always been there for us."

A tear finally pushes from my eye and slides down my cheek, and Ryan moves close and kisses it. I close my eyes, enjoying the sensation that soothes the fresh wound I just cut into.

It's so wild to see this other side of Ryan. I've seen his abrasiveness and his playfulness, but the past few days, I've experienced something so much deeper, so much more profound.

As he pulls away, he says, "I'm sorry you can't be with her right now."

I nod. "It scares me. I've taken a lot of shit jobs because I knew I could figure out the hours around it, and even if they fired me, I could get work somewhere else so that I could be with her. Drop everything if she needed anything. Now here I am, stuck in this place that's so far away, and I know it's the best thing because I sure couldn't—I—"

Ryan takes my mouth, and I immediately know why. I'm not in control of my emotions or what I'm saying, and I was about to say something that would have let Simon know all that I'd shared about our agreement.

Even knowing Ryan's motive, it doesn't keep me from savoring the moment, cherishing these lips against mine. I cup my hand against the back of his head, keeping him close. I don't want to stop kissing him because it's the only thing distracting me from the pain in my fucking soul.

When he pulls away, I realize tears are running down my face.

"Dammit," I mutter, wiping at my eyes with the back of my hands.

Ryan must think I'm this fragile baby, but I feel his warm hand rest on my thigh and massage gently. "I'm so sorry. I wish you could be with her."

"Me too," is all I'm willing to say, since I fear if I say more, I might totally lose control.

He clings tight against my body, which isn't like him. As much as I've slept in his room, we both keep to our sides of the bed. He's always seemed so guarded, like he wouldn't be this affectionate.

But now that he's giving me this, I don't want him to ever take it away from me.

"Lie down," he whispers, and I obey. As if pulling my wish right from my brain, for the first time, he cuddles me. I wrap my arm around him, greedily tugging him close as he kisses my chest, again so softly, especially for a man I know can be so rough…in ways I love.

We lie in silence, his thumb stroking my torso, just beneath my chest, for a few moments before he stirs, glancing up at me. "This is nice."

"Claiming my ass? Is that what you mean?" I say, trying to lighten the mood.

He chuckles. "That obviously, but this too. I like spending time with you, Jonas. I like getting to know you."

A warmth swirls in my chest, a soothing sensation.

"Sorry," he says. "You must be able to tell I haven't dated anyone…ever, really. I don't know what I'm supposed to say or not say."

"It's actually refreshing. Just hearing you be honest. I enjoy spending time with you too." I hope he understands I also mean outside of why I came here.

He must because his eyes light up and a beautiful smile slips across his lips.

"Would you want to…" He hesitates, and I don't know what the hell he's about to say, but I find myself in suspense.

"What is it?"

"There's somewhere I'd like to take you. Out in the woods. Would you like to go there on Saturday, for lunch maybe?"

"Like a date?"

"Yeah, like a date. I can get Nell to make some sandwiches, and I'll pack a bag with food and drinks."

"A little weekend adventure? I like the sound of that."

Some of that tension still lingers in my chest, but it's mixed with a pleasant swirling sensation as a smile tugs across my lips.

Our first date.

16

RYAN

"IF YOU WANT to fucking fight, let's do this!" Forsyth says, shoving Morgan to the ground.

Their initial shouting match has me in a light jog, and when I see Morgan go down, I pick up my pace.

Morgan jumps to his feet, tackles Forsyth, and they fall together in front of the shed. By the time I get there, Forsyth has rolled on top of Morgan and is about to get a swing in, but I snatch his wrist and force him off Morgan.

Fortunately, Jonas arrives and helps Morgan to his feet, keeping him back as Forsyth shouts, "Keep my name out of your fucking mouth, you goddamn skyte!"

I've never heard Forsyth use the slur against Skyfore, the local cult Morgan was raised in before he was shunned at seventeen. Like me, Morgan keeps the past buried, and Forsyth's always respected that, so whatever's happened that led him to use that word, it's gotta be bad.

Jonas and I share a glance; he's clearly as thrown as I am by this intense exchange between my typically fun-loving, jokey workhands.

As I'm dealing with Forsyth, I notice he's got a bloody nose, so

I take him back to the house to help him clean it up.

Today's productivity has been shot.

As he holds some tissue against his nose, I offer a few words about how unacceptable their behavior was. "There's no reason to be fighting. You know I should call the cops since that was assault and battery."

Forsyth's eyes widen. "Please, boss. I can't get anything else on my record right now."

"Neither can Morgan, so I don't know why you had to take things so far. Now, I'll talk to Morgan and see where he's at, but if he wants to call the cops, then I'm gonna have to do that. And I'm gonna have to say you instigated it when you shoved him to the ground."

There's terror in his expression, his face turning a shade whiter.

"Can you talk to him, Ryan? Tell him I'm sorry?"

"Can you tell me what the fight was over first?"

His fear is quickly replaced with a tense jaw. "I don't wanna talk about it."

"Okay, I gathered from what you said outside that you think he was talking about you to people."

"I *know* he was talking about me. He brought up something private in town, something only he knew."

"Did someone say he told them something about you? You know Morgan isn't much of a talker, right?"

"All I know is, it had to come from him, since I told him something in confidence here, and now people are chatting about it, so you don't have to be a rocket scientist to put that shit together."

Goose bumps prick across my flesh. If Forsyth told Morgan something in confidence here, then he doesn't realize Morgan might not be the one responsible for the information getting out in town. He doesn't know about Simon. How he has eyes and ears all over this place. How his favorite hobby is mindfucking…something I've seen him do to plenty of the staff over the years.

I scold Forsyth some more before chatting with Morgan who, unsurprisingly, also doesn't want the cops involved. I'm relieved because I can't afford to lose the guys. If one bolts, Simon would be more than happy to leave me without any extra hands for weeks, months. Enjoying watching me sweat and toil away at the uphill battle that is keeping Hawthorne Heights up and running, knowing I'll put up with as bad as he can make it—partly because it feels like my responsibility to keep this place alive, partly because I know I deserve to suffer for my sins.

With the scuffle defused, I let Morgan and Forsyth off early. It's Friday anyway, so I figure they could use a weekend to decompress.

Jonas has let me fuck him right through the week. Now he's greedy to bottom for me, and I'm eager to please, except tonight I need his dick in my ass to help get out some of the frustration the fight has worked up. It's been a hell of a week, and between the workload during the day and the heated frenzy of our nights, it's hard to know how I have the energy to get through it all, but somehow our bodies manage. The hot sun on a rough day isn't so bad as long as I know that after it sets, it'll be just as rough a night.

But there's something else keeping me buoyed, despite the

fight. Tomorrow's the day I take Jonas on a date, and I'm not letting Morgan and Forsyth—or even Simon—get to me.

The following day, around lunchtime, Jonas and I meet in the kitchen and pack some food in my backpack—chips, some chili from a few days earlier, the sandwiches I asked Nell to make. We grab drinks from the fridge, then head on our way. I guide Jonas along the path in the woods. Every time I glance back at him, I see the curiosity in his wandering gaze, which reminds me of the expressions he made before I enjoyed his virgin ass.

I lead him off-trail, deeper into the woods, until we come to my familiar spot. It's a magical place for me—a sanctuary. The stretch of briars goes on for half an acre, enclosed in the woods.

"Um…is this a good idea?"

"Trust me." I take his hand and guide him to a space between the briars, to the little path I've created over the years, leading him on the route, briars flanking us like coils of barbed wire.

"Be careful," I tell him.

The briar barrier only lasts a few yards before we enter the clearing in the middle, where the creek runs into the little pond that pools inside this space.

As I near the pond, I spin my backpack around to the front and retrieve the blanket I packed, handing him the backpack as I place the blanket on the ground.

He glances around uneasily, as though surprised by the place I've chosen.

"Is something wrong?" I ask.

"This place doesn't seem a little eerie to you? Like something out of a horror movie?"

"Here?" I can't understand what he means. This is my place. This is a magical place. "Would you prefer we go somewhere else?"

I hope he doesn't because I want to share this with him, and fortunately, he says, "No, no. That's not it. I was just surprised this is where we stopped, but I can tell this place means something to you, so I want to share it with you."

As we set up our little picnic beside the pond, I feel safe and at ease, nestled in the warm humid air.

"So, I'm curious what draws you to this spot," he says before taking a bite of his sandwich.

There's this serenity about me as I glance around, surprised that he can't seem to appreciate it as I do. But he doesn't understand what drew me to this place; why it's played such an important role in my life. So I try to explain.

"There are parts to being a twin that I really loved as a kid. It was great having someone to play and spend time with. Nice knowing that someone could read my thoughts so effortlessly. But there was another side of it. Sometimes we were together too much. And Simon didn't let me have much privacy. I guess I needed a place to get away from his attention.

"He never liked briars because he wasn't careful enough to navigate around them. So if I wanted to be on my own, undisturbed, I would come out here. Sometimes he would shout at me from the other side and demand that I come out. He was controlling, even back then." I chuckle as I reflect on a far more innocent version of controlling. "I knew he wouldn't bother me here. I also never told him where my secret path was. It was like a doorway into another world, one where I could have some privacy. Not that

I came here a lot. Not back then. But later, I found myself trying to get away more and more frequently. After we grew apart."

"After that stuff with Kieran?"

I gaze out at some ripples on the pond.

It's the sort of comment that makes me worry I've shared too much, yet I invited him to know these things about me, just as I invited him to my secret place.

"Yes," I confess. "After that, I really needed my privacy. But it was an issue before then too. I used to keep journals. Not sure if you've ever seen the black Moleskine ones. Father would get them for me for every occasion—birthdays, Christmas. I think the Easter Bunny even brought me one." I smile at the thought. "And I didn't just talk about my days, but about my fantasies and dreams. For a long time, Simon let me have that, but when we got older, I caught him reading them. Despite how cathartic it was writing in them, I gave it up because I knew no matter where I hid them, he'd find them. That made me feel like I couldn't even have privacy in my own head. Now he's taken that to a whole other level, and it's nice to be somewhere I know he's not watching or listening. Sometimes Hawthorne Heights can feel as oppressive as an August afternoon."

"I assume you mean humid," he says with a chuckle.

"You'll see for yourself. At least, unless Simon decides to get rid of you before then." It's a fear I allow myself to voice now that we're safely away from the house.

"Do you think that's what will happen?" he asks, and fuck, I'm relieved there's concern in his voice.

"I don't know. When we agreed to help each other, I knew he

was luring me into some fucked-up labyrinth, but now that I'm in it, I'm lost. And I don't know where the next trapdoor or trip wire might be. Just hoping I'll know the way out when I find it."

As I take my sandwich out of the bag and start to unwrap it, all this talk about Simon reminds me of something else we haven't discussed, something I wasn't willing to broach until I knew we weren't under Simon's watchful eye.

"I think he did something with Morgan and Forsyth."

"What?"

"Forsyth told me he heard something around town he'd only shared with Morgan. He wouldn't tell me what it was, but it's why that fight broke out between them. They've never had a fight since they came here two years ago, but suddenly Morgan's telling his secrets in a small town. I don't buy that."

"It's Simon," he says. "But why?"

"Sometimes he likes to do that. Pit staff against each other. He's done that plenty over the years. But I worry he's going to get them to quit and then make me start training two new people all over again, which would be a fucking pain. Maybe he'll wait until he's finished with whatever he's trying to do with you. I don't know... Maybe he thinks when you leave, it'll break my heart, and then he'll snatch my workers out from under me, and I'll really be fucked."

"Break your heart?" he asks with a smirk. "Is that what my leaving would do?"

"It won't be a happy day for me," is as much as I'm willing to confess, and that makes a smile stretch across his face.

I study him as he takes another bite out of his sandwich, before

I say, "I don't see him as much anymore."

"What?" he asks around a mouthful of bread and roast beef.

"When I look at you, I don't see Kieran. It's strange how the more time I spend with you, the less and less I see him. Makes me think of something Father once told Simon and me. That we didn't even look like twins to him because he didn't just know us by our faces, but by our personalities. Like that's what he saw rather than just these faces. Obviously, that's how I see myself, but Father was the only other person who could tell us apart like that. I finally understand what he meant. I wonder, even if you were identical to Kieran, if I'd be able to tell the two of you apart. I think I could."

It's been a gradual shift over time, but I was still nervous until the night when I opened my eyes, surprised to find it was still Jonas looking up at me. The reminders of Kieran were still there, but they didn't, as I'd initially feared, take hold and drag my thoughts kicking and screaming back to the past. Now that I can see Jonas, when I'm with him, I catch myself inspecting every line and curve in his face, desperate to etch him into my memory so I'll be able to keep these good moments even after he's gone.

I'm sketching his face to memory now, when he glances around and says, "I guess I could get used to this weird spot."

I chuckle.

Maybe he'll never fully understand what I love about this place. Maybe he can't know because he's lived a different life. But my briar sanctuary has always been here for me, always kept me safe. And even if he doesn't totally understand it, I'm glad I've had the chance to share it with him.

17

JONAS

Nell stacks pastries onto a tiered tray on the kitchen island, and without looking up, says, "Morning, Jonas."

I don't question it, since the first time I did, she said, "Don't you know everyone has a distinct walk? I can hear you coming from two rooms away."

"These are fresh," she says, "so make sure to grab two or three for breakfast. I don't have enough room in the freezer right now, so I won't be able to save many."

I laugh. "I figure I should've already put on fifteen pounds with how much you feed me."

"With all that work you're doing, you could use another fifteen pounds. While I'm in the middle of this, would you mind starting the coffee? Morning's gotten away from me, and Mr. Simon will be up in half an hour."

I happily offer my assistance, which becomes more of a task than I bargained for since I've never worked a coffee urn before, but she rattles off instructions that I try to store in my brain as fast as she gives them to me. As I'm rinsing out the urn, I'm thinking about yesterday…the date with Ryan, then spending the rest of the day in his bedroom. And I still have a spare day off.

As I'm grinding beans, I hear Nell say something, so I stop and ask her to repeat herself.

She's carrying eggs from the fridge to the kitchen island as she says, "I was asking if you've been enjoying Hawthorne Heights."

"It's been really nice." This earns a second glance from her because she must know it's not trimming, tilling, or planting that's made my stay so nice.

"Really? Interesting." She sets the eggs on the island, then returns to the fridge. "I've noticed you're very chatty with Mr. Ryan. He usually keeps to himself, but he seems so calm and at ease around you."

"Uh…yeah, we get along well." I finish grinding the beans before returning to the urn and placing the grinds in the top compartment.

"I haven't mentioned it because it's none of my business," she says, "but how did you happen to get this job? I mean, how did Mr. Simon find you?"

"A recruitment company." I figure that's a safe and accurate account of what happened.

"Recruitment company. Interesting. It's hard to predict what someone with too much money will do, I guess."

She says this in a particularly pointed way, so I ask, "What do you mean?"

"If no one's mentioned it, I don't plan to."

"Is it because I remind you of someone?"

She turns and looks at me, as though surprised to hear me say it.

"As a matter of fact, you do." Despite having had other pleasant chats with her, this is the first time she's mentioned it. "When I first saw you, I thought you were a ghost wandering the halls of this old place. You're older than the young man I remember, but that face… Other than the boys, I might be the only one left to even know how much like him you look."

"How long have you worked here?"

"Since the twins were just sprouting into their teens. Was so relieved I was the cook and not the butler, because it's a messy time. He had to clean those sheets twice a week. That's what happens when you have boys, though."

It's hard to miss her insinuation, but I'm not really interested in how much Simon and Ryan used to play with themselves, so I say, "Can I ask who I remind you of?" I know who I remind her of, but I also know Simon is listening, so I have to keep up the ruse.

Nell's expression suggests she knows this isn't the sort of thing she should be speaking with me about. I'll have to navigate this very carefully if I'm going to get anything from her.

"There was another young man around here," she says. "He was a little older than the boys."

"An employee?"

"Like I told you before, it's not really my business to know these kinds of things. The most I'm willing to say is that he wasn't staff. Mr. Hawthorne treated him just like he did his sons, so he was practically family until he had that fall in the woods."

This all lines up with what Ryan shared with me.

"A fall?"

"Terrible accident. Kids shouldn't have played as much as they did back there, but it happened, and Mr. Hawthorne wasn't the same after that. Saw him acting strange, and I considered calling the police the night before, but the next day, that's when Mr. Simon found the body in the office. Bullet to the head."

Despite her cryptic telling of the story, I can tell she has her own thoughts and feelings she's dancing around.

"Why would he have done that?" I press.

"A man killing himself after the death of a kid he treated like a son, but who as far as anyone outside the family knew was just the help? That's a good question, Jonas. Only Mr. Hawthorne will ever know the answer to that. It's possible he grew to think of Kieran as a son, but the staff who worked here before me used to say it didn't seem like a coincidence that the light in Mrs. Hawthorne's eyes dimmed after Kieran arrived."

She gives me a pointed look, making it clear she believes Kieran was Ryan's father's child. Based on what Ryan told me, could that have been why Mrs. Hawthorne had gone into therapy and to a psychiatrist before her suicide? Then when his son died, was that why Mr. Hawthorne had killed himself?

Was Kieran related to Ryan?

Is that why Ryan can't speak openly about his feelings for this guy?

And then Simon hired me—Kieran's look-alike—to come here, first to fuck Ryan, and now to be in a relationship with him?

Fucked up as it sounds, given how bizarre this whole situation has been, not to mention Ryan's evasive comments about certain things from his past, I suspect there's at least some truth to the theories Nell's spun.

"How's that coffee coming along?" she asks as she starts mixing batter.

She must know that as soon as she started talking to me about Kieran, the instructions she'd given me to finish the coffee had completely escaped my mind. Fortunately, she doesn't give me too hard a time when she has to repeat herself, maybe because she understands that what she shared is pretty shocking.

I help Nell around the kitchen some more, and she doesn't broach the subject of Kieran again—I figure she already knows she's said too much. But after chatting with her, I know two things: that Kieran might've been related to the Hawthornes, and that Simon would probably listen to this recording and find out I've become aware of this information.

Although, Simon isn't an idiot. He must've known Nell would bring up the subject at some point. He could have easily given her some extra money or even just a stern warning about the consequences if she mentioned anything to me. Given how he's using me, it's even possible he instructed her to bring it up. With a guy like Simon Hawthorne, I have to play out all possible scenarios, not jump to hasty conclusions.

When Ryan joins me for breakfast, I'm a little more cautious about rubbing my foot against his, now that I know Nell picks up on a lot more than she lets on. But even without the obvious physical nudges and caresses we sometimes sneak, surely she can't miss the way I look at him, and the way he looks at me.

Maybe that's why she's so disturbed by Simon's decision to add me to the roster.

After breakfast, I head back to my room and immediately start a Google search based on the information Nell offered up. Before, I knew if Simon checked my search history, he would suspect Ryan told me about Kieran. Now I have a perfectly justifiable reason for being curious that won't tip Simon off about my allegiance, nor fuck up Charity's chance at a future.

"William Randolph Hawthorne" + "Kieran"

"Hawthorne Heights" + "Kieran"

"Renovere, GA" + "Kieran"

"Hawthorne" + "Kieran" + "obituary"

"Hawthorne" + "rumors" + "affair"

"Hawthorne" + "nonmarital child"

The more intense my search becomes, the more I start to recognize I'm not just interested in learning about Kieran so I can fill in the gaps between the stories I heard, but because I want to know what was so special about him that he earned Ryan's affection.

My search doesn't produce any social media accounts.

No obituary.

No articles about his death.

Surely at some point during the late 2010s, Kieran must've left some online footprint? Although, with as much money as the Hawthornes have, they could easily hire a company to scrub clean certain sites. But the news sites that reported on his tragic death, those would still remain.

After a disappointing hour of searching in vain, I accept that Google isn't where I'll find my answers, and I'm left spinning in Nell's comments.

The Hawthornes are a big family, probably with plenty of ancestors and history that they keep somewhere around here. I consider the various rooms I've encountered, where I might find photo albums, old documents, or news stories.

There's Simon's office…and the library…

Yes, the library could have stuff like that.

What am I thinking? Setting aside the fact that Simon might fire me if he catches me rifling through his home, I don't need to go behind Ryan's back looking for information on a guy who might have been his half brother.

No, if I'm going to try and get answers, I need to get them from him.

18

RYAN

There's something in Jonas's gaze this week—a question I can't make out.

He gave me one of the we-need-to-talk signals, the one that means not immediately. Makes me think something's happened. Maybe Simon's had another conversation with him. Maybe he changed the rules of the game. I have to be ready for whatever this could be.

As far as our work goes, we're finally finished with the rose beds around the pool. Now we're shifting focus to the debris that's accumulated, before moving back to day-to-day upkeep. Since their fight, Forsyth and Morgan have made up, a truce I'm sure they made after I impressed upon them the consequences. When Forsyth takes his lunch break, I send Morgan into town to grab supplies. Morgan's task could have waited, but I need the excuse for Jonas and me to sneak off without rousing suspicion.

This time, I take him farther back than I usually do, to the creek, where it's a little more scenic.

"Did Simon say something else?" I ask.

Is he onto us? Has he put another part of his plan into motion? Did he say something that indicates what he wants from this disturbing arrangement?

"No, nothing like that," Jonas says before pursing his lips. His gaze shifts around.

And while I'm relieved to know I don't have to navigate a new mindfuck from Simon, my worry lingers. There's something else Jonas hasn't pushed about, and I hope he hasn't decided now's his chance.

My anxiety intensifies, but I don't rush him. I let him get to his news in his own time.

"Before I say this," he begins, "I want to be clear that I believe you have a right to your privacy. I know there are some things you don't want to talk about."

Fuck. There it is. Because this thing haunts me. It stains me for life, and no matter how much I scrub at my flesh or try to push back the memories, it'll never change the past…or my soul.

Jonas says, "I have to admit, I like spending time with you."

Despite the apprehension he's stirred, there's an eagerness in my belly. Why is it so exciting to know he likes spending time with me?

"I like spending time with you too," I confess, nearly forgetting his initial statement that made me so nervous, but only nearly.

My reciprocation doesn't change the tension in his jaw and shoulders. If anything, his wandering gaze seems even more agitated, which confuses me that much more.

"Maybe I'm not being explicit enough," Jonas says. "I like you. A lot. Not just more than I've ever liked a man, but more than what I've felt for anyone I've had a romantic interest in. And I don't want to push you, but there are things I want to know about.

About you. About why I'm here."

"What kinds of things?"

But I know what's coming before he says, "I want to know the truth about Kieran. The whole truth."

Instinctively, I turn away from him. Fuck, my eyes are already watering.

I can't. I won't! No one can see the darkness in me, especially not him.

I'm ready for him to pressure me. To insist he needs to know, demand I tell him what I'm hiding, but he says, "If you tell me right now that you have to have your secrets, I'll respect that. I'm not bringing this to you because I want to cause you pain. I just… Since we started messing around, I want to understand you. Ryan, I don't think you understand how drawn to you I am. I'm infatuated with you. And I'm scared to be honest because I don't want it to scare you off, but…I'm maybe even obsessed. Your face, your cock, your touch, your kiss, your playfulness, your seriousness. Your laugh…damn, that laugh. Even when I'm not with you, I find myself thinking about all these sides you show me."

As guarded as I've become since he said my brother's name, his words again set me at ease and elicit my own confession. "You're not the only one who's obsessed, Jonas."

He moves even closer to me. A part of me wants to sprint away to protect myself, but another part wants to face him and share my feelings.

Don't tell him. He can't know anything. He'll hate you.

"I can tell this piece of your past means so much to you, and I want to know it because it's a piece of you. Because I'm greedy. I want to know everything about you—the good, the bad, the messy."

"You wouldn't say that if you knew the truth. Of what happened to Kieran. Why Simon hates me now."

Why Father's dead.

As I turn back to him, I find him at my side, his gaze on my face.

I worry that just looking at me in this vulnerable state, he's seeing more than he should. That he'll read my secrets off every slight movement, every twitch of my eyebrows.

But I don't sense any judgment or anger. And his face, it reminds me of nights when he holds me in his arms and I gaze at him, just knowing all he wants is me.

I want to give him more, but I fear if he knew the truth, he'd see me for the monster I really am.

"Nell mentioned Kieran was your brother…or half brother, I guess."

A rush of anger pulses in me. What right did Nell have to tell him that? What right does he have to know it? And why has he come here to torture me with it?

Before I can react, he says, "I just want to know the truth about who he is. Nothing else. I want to know who this man was and why he meant so much to you."

The sincerity in his tone and expression makes it difficult to cling to my knee-jerk anger. Given the time we've spent together, the things we've shared, is it so unreasonable for him to want more? But there's more to it than that.

"Don't you realize that if I start down that path, there's no turning back? It'll all come racing back. The intensity. The fun. The laughter. And then…everything else." My gaze meets his, and I'm about to snap. To tell him to fuck off. Tell him he doesn't have a right to know about these things. Tell him he can go to hell for even asking and that the agreement we've made is off. But as I try to push the words out, I betray myself and say, "Nell was telling the truth, yes. He was our half brother."

Why did I say that? I didn't have to say that!

Tears rush to my eyes. Fuck, I want to keep it together, but also, I'm so fucking tired of keeping this secret buried inside me.

Yet even confirming that simple fact, it's as I feared—the floodgates open. I can't bear to carry this anymore, and my shame possesses my lips. "I always knew Kieran as my brother. Father and Mother said it was a secret…just for the family. After Mother died, Father told us that years before we were born, she had issues conceiving. Even with IVF, it was just failure after failure. From what I understand, she took it hard, as if she had some sort of defect. The doctors tried to tell her it wasn't worth it to keep trying, but she and Father threw every cent they had at it until she finally conceived."

I catch my breath, like even just saying that much was a strain. I want to stop myself from going on, but I can't.

"We were five and Kieran was eight when he came to Hawthorne Heights. We didn't know who he was, but suddenly Mother and Father were fighting more, and she couldn't bear to be around Kieran. Not even to look at him. I instinctively understood that Father had done something wrong. This kid's features had something in common with mine and Simon's and Father's. And his age…Mom would have been trying to conceive even that far back."

"He had an affair?"

"We've never confirmed it, but it's not something I've ever needed to confirm. Kieran was grief-stricken when he came. His mother had just died in a car accident, and he was so sad without her. Even as kids, I think Simon and I pieced it all together, but as we got older, it all made so much sense. How Father had to take him in because, even though he wasn't a cousin or an uncle, he had nowhere else to go. How suddenly we stopped having birthday parties, couldn't have friends over. How Mother started unraveling. He was only here for a few years before she started drinking more, taking pills. Father pretended everything was fine. He would take us on exotic trips. When we asked about Mother, he made excuses for her strange behavior. But eventually, she refused to leave the house. No matter what Father did, she just kept screaming and crying. One night, I found her in the library. Not moving. I knew before I even approached her that she was gone, but I lied to myself that she'd just passed out, like she had in the past.

"It felt like just a few minutes, but Father and the staff said I must've been in there for at least an hour, trying to get her limp body on her feet."

"Oh God, Ryan," Jonas says, and now he's tearing up too. "You said you were nine when that happened?"

"Yes."

"That sounds horrifying. I can't even imagine what that must've felt like."

I bat at the warm tears sliding down my cheeks. "It was horrible, but that nightmare brought Simon, Kieran, and me closer together. Now Kieran wasn't alone in knowing the agony of losing a mother. Father turned cold and quiet. He couldn't be there for us, not how we needed him to be, so for many nights, we would share a bed together, just hold whoever was crying the most. It was a very deep love that we shared for each other during those dark days."

Jonas must sense the grief that's rising up because he moves closer, resting his hand on my arm. It's nice just knowing he's here. That for once in these past few years, I don't have to carry this alone.

"As we grew older, Father became even more reclusive, so Simon and I only had him, the staff, and Kieran. I was about sixteen when I developed intense feelings for him. So intense that they were all-consuming. I couldn't go a day without thinking about my brother. Simon knew this and encouraged it. But I let this go on until I was eighteen. Then one day, I went into Father's office. Simon and Kieran were… I can't even say it."

A flash of nude flesh on Father's desk…and it took me only a moment to recognize…

And now the tears are as fresh as they were that day.

There's more, but I can't fucking say it.

I can't fucking bear it.

"Farther along down the creek, there's a place where Kieran, Simon, and I used to play. It has a steep drop-off with rocks at the bottom. The day after I caught Simon and Kieran in Father's office, that's where Kieran's body was found. And Father, determined to keep anyone from knowing about his other son, made sure everyone knew he was just a workhand at Hawthorne Heights, so it wouldn't matter to anyone. Like Kieran was nothing, nobody."

Suddenly Jonas's arms are around me. He must sense my distress. I'm a child wandering back through the past, grappling with the same horrors as in those twisted days. "Oh, Ryan," he says as I embrace the safety of his hold. It reminds me of those nights with Simon and Kieran, when we would embrace each other and let our pain sear through us, knowing we were safe even in the worst of it because we had each other.

I cling to Jonas as the tears break free while rage, guilt, and shame push to the surface, seizing control of me.

"Please don't ask for more than that. I can't give any more. I'm sorry, Jonas. I'm so sorry."

There's a burning sensation in my chest, and I remind myself that as long as he keeps his arms around me, eventually, it will fade. But there's a lump in my throat, from those things I can't share with him.

"Don't be sorry, Ryan. Thank you. Thank you."

Despite his sympathy and the care of his embrace, I know he's saying it only because he's unaware of what I left out.

Jonas can't know I was the reason why Kieran's body was at the bottom of that drop-off.

No one can ever know the truth.

19

SIMON

A FIRE RAGES in me.
You did this to yourself.

It's a vain reminder when I have to sit here, watching the footage from last night.

Jonas and Ryan were as quick as ever to get into bed, kissing and struggling to get each other naked.

Jonas's body presses up against Ryan's. "Do I remind you of someone?"

"Why do you ask?"

"Nell mentioned something earlier. She made it sound like I must really resemble this person. And I figured maybe that's why you've acted how you do around me."

Goose bumps prick across my flesh before Ryan says, "Yes."

"Who?"

Don't you dare, Ryan.

"His name was Kieran. He was…our brother. Well, half brother."

How fucking dare you!

I hit the heel of my hand against my head. Then do it harder before clawing at my skull.

"Do I remind you of him in a good way?" Jonas asks, and Ryan nods.

Of course in a good way. He's fucking you, isn't he?

I can't believe he said his fucking name.

"Now come here," Ryan whispers as he kisses Jonas again. They go through the familiar dance before Ryan takes Jonas's cock once again. It's a decent size, but he's no Kieran; he'll never be Kieran.

Ryan must know this too. That's why he couldn't open his eyes when they first began fucking around. Because it would kill him to see the man he loved so fucking much, knowing it couldn't be real.

But now he's all play and smiles with Jonas.

How dare he mention his name to this stranger? How dare he desecrate our brother's memory?

He doesn't give a damn about Kieran; he never fucking did. Otherwise, he wouldn't have such an easy time screwing this impostor, the shell of the real thing.

But I guess even an impostor is better than nothing.

"You feel so good," Ryan says as Jonas takes him. How can he look at that face and say another name? How do his sins not torment him?

Does he think he deserves this?

Rage pulses through me, stinging like a hornet's nest has exploded in my chest. I clutch at my broken heart… How it burns.

Yet I can't take my eyes off his sin.

I watch how he strokes Jonas's face. How he rolls his head back as Jonas nibbles and bites at his neck.

Does it feel like it did with Kieran?

I reflect on the touch, the taste, those sensations only he could give me.

I rub my hand against the crotch of my pajama bottoms. I'm like a stone. And pissed about it. I stroke up and down as I grind my teeth.

He didn't have a right to say his fucking name!

"Fuck me harder. Harder," Ryan pleads, but I imagine him calling out Kieran's name, the moaning. The grunting as he took that cock.

"Kieran! Kieran!" He just kept begging for it. Wanting more…desperately.

There's the old shed, the knife in my chest as I stared, the horror of the sight…of the betrayal as they went at it like dogs, tearing each other's clothes off, working to reach their release.

It's etched into my goddamn brain. No matter how many times I push it back, it always resurfaces. But I don't want to forget it either. I'm pleased to know Ryan for the traitor he is, has always been. *You destroyed this family, Ry. You destroyed all our lives, and you'll fucking pay for your crimes.*

That fire in me is a goddamn inferno, scorching my body as Ryan begs for Jonas's cock.

This is the animal in him—he doesn't give a fuck about anyone else as long as he's satisfied.

My face is hot with fury.

Ryan doesn't deserve this kind of pleasure, only pain.

"I'm coming, I'm coming," Jonas breathes, and it sneaks up on me, this jolt of energy that radiates through my body, forcing a moan as I shoot inside my pajamas, staring at Ryan's face as he comes too.

It reminds me of when we were young.

Back in a time when no one had explained how bodies worked, when we were itching to explore, caressing and humping until Ryan discovered the secret first, then me. Eve's first bite in the garden, that moment when we were no longer innocent children, but lust-hungry flesh with cravings we couldn't resist. A hunger that couldn't be sated, neither of us considering what we did wrong because we were so caught up in the frenzy of these fresh chemical reactions in our brains.

Gasping as I come down from my climax, I keep stroking my hand against the wet fabric of my bottoms. Jonas collapses onto Ryan, who hooks his arms around him.

They lie there, breathing in sync. My brother's arms wrap around Jonas, who pulls back and gazes at my brother before they kiss. It's sweet, affectionate.

There's a flash of the past again.

And like it happened on so many nights of their fucking, it tortures me because I don't see Jonas—just Kieran and Ryan locked in these beautiful moments. These images that make the darkness flare up inside me.

There's an excruciating pain in my chest, and it's too powerful. As it overtakes me, I've lost control of my body, thrashing and flailing about, releasing a primal cry to the unjust universe, my hands on a mission that feels disconnected from my body. I'm panting as if in my quick blackout, I did a lap around the house, but slowly, my senses return to me. Tears drip off my jaw, and I can feel their warmth against my cheeks as I discover my computer monitor on the floor.

Not again.

<hr />

"YOU WANTED TO see me?" Ryan asks as he enters my office.

It used to be Father's, but now it's mine. Everything in this house is mine, even Ryan.

There's a rush of eagerness mixed with fury in me, but I remain seated behind the desk, typing away on my laptop as I finalize an email to my accountant about an art donation to Emory University.

"Just one moment, Ry," I say, keeping my attention on my email because I know he hates that.

The tension as he folds his arms is so powerful, I can practically smell it. Is he mad? I hope he is. Although, he doesn't know real anger, not the sort that pulses through my being.

I sense he's losing his patience, and it's likely a few seconds before he heads on his way and I'll have to chase him down and do the whole, *No, please, I'm done now.* Or, *You made your choice. Find me after I finish working.* Or, *Please, Ry. Oh, pretty please.*

I snicker at the thought just as he starts to open his mouth to excuse himself. I close my laptop and push to my feet.

As his gaze meets mine, it's clear he knows I've intentionally used up the last of his patience. *See, Ry. There are still remnants of that connection we once shared. Before you betrayed me.*

"What is it?" he asks.

"Why do you ask it like that? I figured you would have slept like a baby."

After fucking Kieran. No, fucking Jonas. But you can't convince me you weren't thinking about our brother.

"I'm sure you would know how I slept." His eyes accuse me, and it makes me laugh.

"Oh, big bro, I didn't watch you sleep last night. Now greet me. It'll make you feel better."

He leans forward, turning as much of his cheek to me as he can, waiting for me to trick him, but I offer the most appropriate of pecks against his flesh, maybe lingering just a moment longer than I should before opening my mouth and diving to his neck, taking a quick bite.

I get a good chunk, and I wish I could have had more restraint, but it's like my body can't forgive him for the torment he put me through last night, or how the images of him and Kieran behind the shed are as fresh in my mind as if it happened yesterday.

"Fuck," he says, jerking away, rubbing at the indentations I left behind. "Simon, I'm not in the mood for games. Just tell me what you want."

"We used to have time for games. And I think you still have time for them now, just not with me." I don't expect a response, so I go on. "I wanted to see how your work with Jonas has been going. Is he proving a valuable asset to your team?"

He nods, as if he fears if he says anything, he'll tell too much.

Haven't you realized I already know what you're doing? You think I haven't planned for this? How can you, of all people, not know me better than this?

"Good. I would hate to find out otherwise and need to excuse him." I look him directly in his eyes, knowing that would pain him. Knowing that he would long for his cock, his touch, his kiss now that they've spent so much time together, learning each other's bodies.

But don't worry, Ry. If only that were my plan.

"Is that all you wanted to talk to me about?" he asks, surely annoyed since it was something I could have approached him about at lunch or dinner.

"I wanted to make sure you like Jonas. I feel like you do…*like him.*"

We stare into each other's eyes.

"Am I right?" I press.

"I'm getting back to work. I don't know what you want from me, but I'm not giving it to you."

"Ryan, can't I just want to catch up with my brother?"

"Not when I have a shit ton of work to get done."

"But I'm concerned about my staff, so I want to make sure everything's running smoothly."

"I'm not your staff."

I feign confusion. "I meant Jonas, Morgan, and Forrest."

"It's Forsyth."

Of course I fucking know his name, you fucking idiot.

"You know what I meant. I wanted to make sure Morgan and Forsyth are getting along."

He winces, and this time there's knowing there, not a question. I can't help but smirk because he doesn't really know what bit of gossip I spread around town to turn them against each other.

"I figured you might have had something to do with that," he reveals.

"Do with what? Are they having issues?"

"You know what happened."

Of course I do.

"And I know you're behind it. They're humans, not pawns for you to play with because you have too much free time on your hands."

"I'm not a mind reader, Ryan, but if something's going on, you should feel comfortable sharing it with me. I just want your work to run as smoothly as possible. You must know this."

"Then hire me some more hands."

I sigh overdramatically. "It's so hard to find people we can trust to manage the property. Look at the two hands we did find from town. Both with criminal records. And they're the exception—at least they're not sex offenders or drug addicts. This is what happens in a country that doesn't give a fuck about distribution of wealth. That's why I had to bring Jonas in all the way from Chicago. Why else would I have brought him here?"

Now I'm just having fun.

And it is *so* much fun seeing Ryan's jaw clench, his hands ball into fists.

"If you're going to be in a mood today, then I'll just let you get back to your work," I say. "I actually figured you'd be in a good mood this morning."

His neck tenses, but he doesn't spit out his usual, *Stop watching me!* or *I'll tear my room apart and find every goddamn new camera you put in there.*

"Good chat," he says, starting for the door.

I take his hand gently. As he turns to me, I offer another peck on his cheek, which turns into a lick. When he pulls back, I can see the morning light reflected on the wet part of his flesh. I run my tongue across the roof of my mouth, enjoying his taste before I release his hand and he heads on his way.

Back to his work. Back into my maze.

Some of that fury has dulled, replaced with excitement. It's too soon to execute my plan, but patience, Simon. It won't be meaningful if I jump the gun.

No, like a black racer beneath a pile of leaves, I wait as this blue jay grazes on seeds around me, knowing I must strike at the right time or run the risk of him taking flight and escaping my reach.

20

JONAS

"This one he'll be in for sure," Ryan says as he pulls another photo album from a shelf.

We stand by the desk in a little office-like area set up in the library.

After our chat about his past, Ryan and I agreed upon a script to go over in the bedroom to make sure Simon believed it was the first time we'd openly discussed their brother.

"Take two," he says as he passes me the album. He hasn't been willing to look himself; it must be too painful.

I'm wildly curious, but it'd be funny if he handed it to me and I didn't see any similarity other than dark hair and maybe the shape of our heads.

The previous album was mostly photos from when Simon and Ryan were babies and toddlers. This one is of them much older, around high school age. I stop a few pages in, my gaze zeroing in on that face—*my* face. It's as if I weren't looking at the photo of someone else, but one taken of me when I was younger. Kieran, Ryan, and Simon stand in front of the pool in their bathing suits. Kieran must have been in his late teens when it was taken, and Ryan and Simon must've been fourteen or fifteen. Ryan appears distracted in the photo, while Simon and Kieran are picture-ready, flashing ear-to-ear grins.

"I guess I don't have to ask if you see it too," Ryan says, probably because my jaw is hanging open.

"It's uncanny," I admit. I pull out my phone.

"What are you doing?"

"I wanted to show you pics from when I was younger." I pull up my Facebook app. "I think I have some photos from when I was around this age. Just want to compare."

I pull up my account and scroll through my photo albums, finding the ones from high school. I click on a photo my aunt took of Charity and me when we went to Six Flags—one of the happier times in our lives because Charity was doing really well—and I show it to Ryan.

His eyes widen, and he takes my phone. He purses his lips, then takes a deep breath before coming around me to see his family's album.

"Wild," he whispers. "You'd think you must be related to him somehow. The jaw. The eyes. The hair. When you first came here, I thought you looked like he would have a few years older, but I've wondered if that was a cruel trick of my mind. Like it was making me see more of him than was really there."

"Maybe I'm your long-lost cousin," I joke. "Maybe that means Simon might have to share the wealth with me."

He chuckles softly, but it shifts to a frown as he stares at the photo, like it's taken hold of him and carried him off to some memory—and not a good one, by the looks of him.

Ryan closes the album, and as he sets it on the desk, I notice his hands trembling.

"Ryan?" I ask, moving close, but he avoids my gaze. "Are you okay?"

His chin quivers as his eyes well with tears.

"Are you okay?" I ask again.

He nods, but I know that's not true.

"I'm sorry, Ryan. I shouldn't have given you my phone. I know you didn't want to look."

"I chose to look. You didn't make me." His words are curt, and I can feel his anger in them. I imagine he's mad at himself, but I wish he wouldn't be. Or just be mad at me.

I step to him, moving slowly as I put my arm around him, and he falls against my chest, trembling before I hear him sniffle.

With one hand around him, I place the other against his cheek.

"Oh, Ryan. It's okay to miss him."

He puts his arm around me and shakes even more before he glances up into my eyes, looking at me for the first time since he saw the photo, like he's forcing himself to do it.

His breath catches, as if he'd been terrified of what he might see instead of me.

And then he lunges at me. I can hardly process the move before my back slams against the bookcase so hard, my shoulder blades take a blow from the shelf, but Ryan's lips are like an anesthetic—any pain is set aside because my body's so hungry for the pleasure another kiss from him promises. As his tongue sweeps across mine, I grab his face in my hands.

"I…need you…to fuck me," he says between kisses.

"Here? Now?"

"Fuck, Jonas, please."

It seems like we're so exposed here, yet we're never really alone in his room either, so what does it matter?

Ryan pulls away to toss off his shirt, and I see his pants are already at his ankles. How the fuck did he do that so fast? I'm in shock from how quickly he's moving, and before I know it, he's unfastening my belt.

"Lube?" It's the only word that comes to mind.

"Just spit. I don't care. I need you in me right now. Please." I'm struggling to think straight as he yanks my pants and boxers down, then strokes my cock. "Please," he whispers against my lips. "Please."

There's pain in his plea.

What did that photo do to him? And why does he want this so badly?

He licks across my bottom lip. "It's okay if it hurts. I don't mind." I feel his smile against my face as he squeezes my dick. "That got you hard, didn't it?"

As he steps out of his pants, I notice he's already kicked off his flip-flops.

There's desperation in his eyes, a plea for me to end his agony, and fuck, I can't help myself. I rest my hands on his arms and spin him around. His hands drop onto the desktop as he pushes his hungry ass out.

In no time, I'm on my knees, cupping his ass cheeks, spreading them. They're so firm in my grip as I lick him.

I can't fucking believe he wants to do it like this. But it's clear by how I'm going at it—my tongue wild, my nose buried against his flesh—that I want to give him this as much as he wants to take it.

"Get up," he says, and I push to my feet, as though I'm just a robot programmed to follow his orders.

"Are you sure I shouldn't open you up a little with my fingers or—"

He reaches back and rubs his hand across my shaft, covering it in a thick film that I realize is his precum, which makes me even harder.

"It's okay," he says. "Please, I need you now."

And I want to give him what he wants…so badly.

Get it together, Jonas.

I spit into my palm and add it to the impromptu lubricant before resting a hand on his ass cheek and pressing the head of my cock against his hole.

Feels tighter than usual. I wonder if it's because he's so tense from his pain, or if it's because we don't have the necessary lubrication to make this happen.

I just need to be careful with my movements. Nice and steady.

It's a squeeze to get the head in, and he moans, but there's more pleasure than pain to it. I massage his ass cheek, hoping I can relax his body enough to invite me in farther.

"Just keep it right there," he says.

He takes quick breaths as we wait, both of us more than a little impatient, in silence together, my cock twitching like it's ready to just get in and pound that hole.

"A little bit more," he finally says, and I obey.

What little lubrication we have helps me move in, but not as easily as we normally do; I can feel the friction of my cock against him. I move maybe a centimeter before stopping, waiting for Ryan to give me the all clear.

"Keep going," he orders.

As I push some more, his head rolls back and he grunts, which makes me stop.

"No, it's okay. It's okay," he says, but as I continue, he grunts some more. "Don't stop. I can take it. Don't worry, you've been warming me up the past few months." He snickers—I can tell he's trying to make light of it—and as I laugh, my cock pushes farther into him so that I'm about a third of the way in.

Steadily, I creep farther and farther into him, and when I'm all in, I lean forward, resting my hands beside his, kissing the back of his neck.

He's breathing hard.

"How does that feel?" I ask.

"You feel harder than usual."

Which I'm sure is true because there's something about being wedged inside him like this that's got me going, which I don't figure is making it any easier on him.

"We can stop."

"No, stay right there," he insists. "Just give me a moment."

I kiss his neck some more, his flesh distracting me as my dick throbs within him. He turns his head to look at me, his mouth near enough that I take it, my hand navigating around to feel his hard girth, which I stroke gently.

His body relaxes before he nods, and I pull out slightly, then push forward.

He moans as I give him another small thrust, then another.

His body shakes again, legs trembling. I stop before he says, "Keep going. Please."

I offer a few more subtle movements, reveling in the sensation of flesh against flesh, how tight his ass is gripping on.

Each subtle thrust loosens him up more and more, opening his body up, and gradually, his shaking subsides.

I lean back down, jerking him as I thrust.

He twists his head back and kisses me as our bodies move in a familiar rhythm. We did it. We're there, his ass opened up for my cock and his tension no longer an obstacle. When I pull away, he pushes back, our thrusts matching as we work together to end this aching tension—the pressure that's built steadily since he began tearing off our clothes.

I work up a sweat. We're all instinct and desire.

"Fuck me harder. I need it harder," he says, and I obey, his ass clapping, the desk squealing as it creeps across the floor.

We pant together, his cock leaking warm precum over my hand, which helps lube my palm as I keep jerking him.

"God, your ass feels so good," I confess.

"It's your ass. Take it."

And I do. The pressure builds until it feels unbearable, a swirling sensation in my belly, the sort that seizes control of my thrusts.

"Ryan, I'm going to—"

"Do it. Come inside me."

I pull my hand off the desk and wrap it around him, continuing to stroke his cock in my firm grip as my body erupts into a series of violent movements, as though it's trying to get my cum as far back into Ryan as I can manage.

"Yes, Jonas, yes!" he calls out as heat rushes to my face, my climax torturing me as I release inside him, the energy rippling like a shock wave through me.

I'm so lost in the high, intoxicated by my body's fight to get to the end, that I don't even realize until I come to that I'm crying out, and so is he.

His ass clamps onto my shaft suddenly, and he goes through his own fit of spams before I feel a warm rush across my fingers. I offer him the strokes he needs to get to the end, before sliding my hand through his mess, then pulling it back to me and lapping it up.

This is just that animal in me still. I'm not thinking any of it through, just trusting that whatever the hell we're doing isn't just right, but perfect.

Even though my body's settled, he keeps pushing his ass back, like his prostate is trying to maintain that stimulation, so I offer him a few more thrusts, hooking my arms around him, kissing his shoulder.

Now we're both shaking together, reeling in what remains of the experience, my cock still buried in him.

"I should probably pull out," I say.

"You don't have to just yet."

"I mean, I guess you did say it was my ass, so can I just keep it here for the rest of the day?"

His playful chuckle lets me know what we did set him at ease.

He keeps his hands on the desk, ass out, and I kiss his shoulder again, clinging to him, both of us surely knowing that despite how much we wish we could stay in this moment, at some point, like all beautiful moments, it has to end.

21

RYAN

As I throw on my clothes, I love knowing I've still got Jonas's cum deep inside me.

There's a sting to what we just did, but I'm proud of myself for my determination despite moments when I thought it might be too much.

"Funny how much longer it takes to get clothes back on," Jonas says as he pulls up his pants.

I fasten my belt. "I'm just thankful we're able to get them off that fast."

His gaze turns my way, and he doesn't even try to look cool—just with that stupid broad grin because I know he found that as hot as I did.

I toss my shirt on before passing him his off the desk.

My gaze travels across his body, and then I glance around, wondering where Simon's cameras could be, what angle he'll have of what we just shared. I'm glad thoughts like that didn't pull me from the experience, but I shouldn't have to think like that at all.

The photo album I placed on the desk catches my attention, and I eye it uneasily. I was smart enough to know better than to look at it, but when I saw Jonas's surprise at the similarity, knowing he'd pulled up an image of himself when he was younger, I had to know how much of it was real—especially now that I knew Jonas so well, I could barely see Kieran when I looked at him. Yet seeing Kieran again in that photo, it was impossible to deny the obvious physical similarities, even more so than I remembered.

But looking at the photo didn't just remind me of what he looked like—it brought back other memories too.

A memory behind the shed.

"I'm so sorry, Ryan. Simon and I were just..." He reaches out.

"Don't touch me! I saw what you were doing with him. Just go away. I don't want to talk to you." I try not to cry, but the tears keep falling.

Fuck. I don't want him to see me like this.

Kieran places his hand on my shoulder. "Ryan, please don't cry. You don't understand. I didn't mess around with Simon because I want him. I messed around with him because I want you."

For a moment, the searing pain in me eases up, and I turn to him. "What?"

"Don't you fucking get it? You're the one I love."

He loves me?

Despite everything, my heart flutters with hope. I've wanted this for so long, so desperately. And now he's saying the words, but after what I just saw...

"I've never loved Simon. I love you, Ryan."

He leans in and kisses my forehead, a kiss that soothes the discord raging inside me.

"It's always been you, Ryan."

"Ryan?" Jonas asks, and I force my eyes from the album to him, struggling to keep the memory at bay.

"Did you say something?"

"I asked if you wanted me to put that up for you."

"Oh, yes. If you could."

For all the fun we just shared, there's concern in his expression. I wish he hadn't seen my reaction, but I'm also glad he was here when it happened and that he was able to take the pain away.

It's why I needed him so desperately. He was the only thing that could help me escape the agony tearing through me.

And what a fun distraction it was.

Jonas places the photo album back in its place on the shelf, then returns to me and hooks his arms around my waist before planting a firm kiss on my lips.

It helps push the memories back, keep them behind a boundary of briars so they can't hurt me.

Jonas's hands find their way back to my ass.

"Mmm," he says, bringing to mind the passion, the intensity, the burn.

"We're gonna have to do that again soon," I tell him.

"I'm okay with that."

"You sure felt like you were okay with it. I don't know that you've ever been that hard inside me."

His smile is sort of cocky. I like flattering him.

"So..." he says, "that whole this-ass-is-yours comment—was that just something you meant in the moment?"

"Huh?" I inspect his expression, trying to make out what he means.

"Sorry, it's nothing."

"No, it's not. What do you mean?"

His cheeks turn pink, reminding me of how he gets when he's about to come. "I like you, Ryan."

"I like you too."

Why am I not following this?

"I mean I *really* like you. Like…I wouldn't mind if we were…an item?"

I'm still blanking.

He waits for me to respond, and when I don't, "Okay. Bad idea. Forget I said anything. I don't want it to be weird."

He starts to pull away, but I keep my arms around him. "Wait. Do you mean an *item* like…together? Like boyfriends?"

"Well, yeah. What else would I mean?"

I chuckle, which makes his eyes widen. "No, I'm not laughing at that," I say quickly. "I'm laughing that I was so confused by what you said. I've never had a boyfriend before, so I guess I don't know how that comes up."

"Well, I haven't either. Girlfriends, yes, but not a boyfriend."

I smile as I consider the idea. It's a lovely thought, but nearly as soon as I entertain it, I consider that Simon only plans to have him here for the summer. "But you'll have to go back to Chicago at some point."

"I like you a lot, Ryan. I like spending time with you and doing what we're doing, but I also like getting to know you. I don't know. Maybe you're right and it's a dumb idea."

"I don't think it's dumb, Jonas. I'm just not sure how we'll make it work."

"People have long-distance relationships. It's not like you couldn't come visit me in Chicago."

He must notice my expression because he says, "Or I could come here."

Which relaxes me again.

"We don't have to figure it all out right now, Ryan. And who knows? In a few months, I might drive you away, but I want to have this ass on lockdown." He offers a firm squeeze that brings some levity to his suggestion.

Between never having a boyfriend and not really knowing how this could work out, it's confusing, but I can't deny that just his suggestion excites me.

"Okay."

"Okay, you'll consider it?"

"No, I mean, we're boyfriends now. We don't need to hold a ceremony or anything, do we?"

We share a laugh. "This feels like being a kid. Kind of weird, considering we're two grown men."

Given everything we've talked about, the lives we've lived, it's funny to think there's something childish, innocent even, about our chat. Even more so since it came after something that wasn't remotely innocent. But it's a lovely feeling. Reminds me of a time when the world wasn't so dark and gray. When I believed life could be this wonderful, beautiful thing. Back when Simon and I shared a king-size bed, his arms around me, holding me close. Had we known what life had in store for us, we probably would have clung on tighter, desperate to freeze time while we were still in the bliss of our youth.

I hook my arms around Jonas. "Well, *boyfriend*, you did a good job fucking me on this desk."

"Yeah, you might need to swing by the bathroom to take care of that…*boyfriend*."

There's a rush in my chest, and my cheeks warm, my ass clenching slightly as my body viscerally responds to having Jonas use that word on me.

"Actually, I think I want to hold on to it for a little longer," I tell him before stealing a kiss.

We enjoy a few moments to make out as boyfriends, and then Jonas heads into town to get supplies so I won't have to send Forsyth or Morgan on Monday.

I grab *Tess of the d'Urbervilles* off the desk and head to the sofa. I have to sit carefully because, damn, he gave me a pounding. But I enjoy the tenderness. It makes me think of him, that I still have a piece of him inside me.

As exciting as it was to use that word…*boyfriend*…there's a knot in my gut. Some part of me knows better.

I imagine Simon sauntering into the library.

"Do you really think this can last?" he'd ask. "He'll return home, and he'll never think twice about you. Or what? Are you going to leave Hawthorne Heights?" This, of course, is followed by a maniacal laugh—not something I've ever heard from Simon, but that I expect he's done plenty of times in spirit.

With the seeds of doubt sown, it was only a moment that I could really enjoy the innocent fantasy, because even if Jonas and I manage to sustain this over the summer, I know it's not likely to become anything more. He has to get back to his life with his sister and aunt. And my life is here.

But if a summer is all I can have with him, I'll take it.

22

JONAS

Boyfriends.

Never had one of those. Never thought I'd have one.

But there's something deeply satisfying about knowing Ryan's mine.

Despite the heavy workload we've taken on, it somehow feels more manageable because of the time I know we'll spend together at night and on our days off. We're in our own little world; it's the only thing that's real. The rest is a fantasy.

"Couldn't wait to get your greedy arms around me again?" Ryan asks as I pin him against the side of the house and steal a kiss. My lips move across his cheek and down to his neck. It's a primal exploration of his body; I don't hold back, just go with what feels natural. His moan confirms he's fine with that.

His skin tastes better now that he's my boyfriend. That doesn't even make sense, but it's true. Has been for the past month since we first started using that word.

Suddenly, his body jerks and his head turns. I follow his gaze and find Forsyth, jaw dropped as he stares.

His face flushes red. "Oh, hey. I…I was coming… I mean, I was looking for you to see if you wanted me to… I don't really remember what I was looking for you for." He chuckles awkwardly.

I've never seen Forsyth so beside himself, but the smile on his face suggests he doesn't exactly find this an abomination.

After confirming our relationship status, Ryan and I agreed not to say anything to the guys. Didn't see a reason to make a fuss, but apparently our hunger for each other's bodies did the outing for us.

"I'm gonna..." He doesn't finish his sentence, just spins around and walks back around the house.

Ryan leans close, snickering against my cheek. "Cat's out of the bag," he says, then whispers in my ear, "Guess he's gonna run and tell Morgan about the naughty things you were doing to me." It's hard to even consider what Forsyth's about to do when all I can think about is how Ryan's breath tortures my ear, but I try to be serious.

"Is that going to be okay?" I ask.

His forehead creases. "Yeah. Nell's already hinted at it. And we decided that if they find out, they find out."

"I know, but it's one thing just considering it, another when it actually happens."

He shrugs. "We made it to July. That's better than I thought we'd do. And Morgan and Forsyth could probably use some work gossip to keep them from being at each other's throats."

We share a laugh, then another kiss.

"Mmmm," Ryan hums into my mouth. "I wanna keep doing this, but I really should find out what Forsyth needed."

"Okay, but just a little more tongue, and then I'll be good for the rest of the day."

"Liar," he says, knowing damn well that won't sate my appetite for him, but he gives in anyway, and fuck, I love when he gives in to me.

We get back to work. Turns out Forsyth needed some pesticides for an aphid infestation on the roses. Ryan figured they had some around the shed, but turns out we're out, so he sends Forsyth and me into town to grab some at the Feed & Seed.

Forsyth is as awkward as I figured I'd be if I'd walked in on my boss making out with another employee. So I try to address it right away. "Sorry about earlier."

In the driver's seat, he presses his lips together, then smirks. "Really, none of my business. Just…a…surprise, that's for sure."

I chuckle, and there's a stretch of uncomfortable silence before he adds, "But that was some serious tongue you were giving him there."

He sneaks a glance my way, and we laugh awkwardly together.

"To be honest, we don't have a lot of gay guys out here. I mean, there are some, but I guess they don't feel safe being out. It's kind of a backwoods place. But wait, you mentioned girlfriends…"

It's something that had come up in one of our casual, day-to-day conversations. Just chatter, so I'm surprised he was even really listening.

"That mean you're bi?" he asks. "Or like… You know, it's none of my business. I shouldn't even be asking things like this. Please don't tell Ryan. I don't want to lose my job."

"Relax. It's really not a big deal. Yes, I've had to think a lot about it recently, and I figure I am bi. Not something I ever explored or really thought about until I came here."

He smiles, then turns to me. "That's pretty cool."

"Cool?"

"Yeah, just the fact that you've done that in this town makes me think that's cool. I don't know. Not a lot happens in Renovere, so stuff like that could keep people talking for weeks."

"Like whatever you thought Morgan said about you?"

The playful expression shifts quickly, and I immediately regret mentioning it. I guess I figured since it'd been a while, he might have calmed down and been willing to discuss it, but now it's clear that was a shit idea.

"Sorry. Now I'm the one prying."

"It's all right. Everyone in town is already on to better gossip anyway. Like I said, they don't have much to talk about. And when I told Morgan this in confidence, I just wasn't expecting to overhear it when I went into town. I figured if anyone would respect my right to privacy, it'd be the guy who told me all the shit he's been through with Skyfore."

I expect him to drop it, since he's already been cryptic about whatever Morgan purportedly told others that got him so worked up, but he says, "It was just some embarrassing shit. I was chatting with a girl online and was really into her. But then I was showing her to Morgan on my phone and turned out he recognized the photo. It was some model I was being catfished with. I thought I'd spared myself the humiliation because he'd caught it before I'd shown it to anyone else I'd talked to about her, but not a week later, this guy I went to school with brought it up, so I knew Morgan had to be the one to blab. Not cool."

"No, it's not," I say, even though I have plenty of reason to doubt Morgan was the one to blab.

"I don't let a lot of people in," Forsyth says, "and I really trusted Morgan until he pulled that. He's still saying he didn't have anything to do with it getting around, but he's the only one who knew. And it's just confusing. I figured I could trust him. So…I don't know. Anyway, I guess this is more than what you thought you'd hear on the way to the Feed & Seed."

"Yeah, that's a tough one," I say, considering how I could help bridge this gap without revealing what I know and why I know it.

"I think I could forgive him," Forsyth says, "but I don't think he'll ever forgive me for calling him a skyte."

Forsyth warned me about the cult members when we first went to town together. "Dead-eyed, all-smiling drones," he called them, and I quickly understood what he meant. Fortunately, they seem harmless enough, but from the way Morgan acts, I imagine that like with most of these cults, the real harm is done within the group.

"Guy grew up with assholes calling him that all around town," Forsyth goes on. "That's why I used the word. Just wanted to get to him like he got to me, but now he's not talking to me. Like I'm the asshole. Just sucks because I really enjoyed the time we spent together."

As he stares ahead, I see grief in his expression—the loss of someone he's maybe just now realizing used to be his friend.

"Time is a good healer," I say.

"You think that's true?" His gaze shifts to me, as if he can detect the bullshit in my tone.

"Okay, maybe it's not a healer, but things get easier. Just might take twenty or thirty years."

He laughs. "Thanks for the real helpful pep talk," he says, his tone dripping with sarcasm. "Seriously, though. Thanks. I think for that, I might just give you a hot tip."

"Hot tip?"

"I mean, I don't know how serious you and Ryan are. I'm making some assumptions based on how far you had your tongue down his throat, but his birthday's next week."

"Birthday?" He hasn't mentioned anything about it to me, but Ryan doesn't seem like he would put much stock in his birthday.

"Yeah. The twenty-first. My ma's is on the twenty-fifth, so it's come up in the past. He and Simon do a dinner together every year, but I don't know…a card or something might be nice. Just tell him I gave you the tip so I can get preferential treatment, okay?"

I laugh. "Will do."

Having this special bit of information about Ryan is exciting.

What can I do to surprise my boyfriend?

23

RYAN

It's just a day like any other.
Except it's not.

As I finish stirring up the compost pile, I receive a text, and when I look, I'm not surprised it's from Simon.

> **Tonight at 7:30, your attendance is expected in the dining room.**
> **ME: Sorry. Got plans.**
> **SIMON: See you then! Xoxo**

I know there's no getting out of this. And really, I don't want to. Our birthday reminds me of happier times at Hawthorne Heights. Of sitting in the dining room with Father and Kieran as Simon and I blew out candles on the cake. They remind me of fun and laughter, and a time when I would've trusted Simon with my life.

All that's as dead as Mother, Father, and Kieran now.

While I'm sorting the supplies Morgan and Forsyth have carelessly stacked around the shed, the door swings open and Jonas enters, sporting a grin. He's been in a chipper mood all morning, since we woke up in each other's arms—something I'm getting used to.

There's dirt streaked across his forearms, the July heat has a thick film of sweat across his flesh, but this doesn't dissuade him from attacking me with a kiss.

Tasting his salty lips, I breathe in his scent.

He must be in a particularly frisky mood because he hooks an arm around me and pulls me to the wall, pinning me back against it as his tongue invades my mouth.

I'm taking it as a birthday kiss. I haven't told Jonas about today, but as tends to happen on my birthday, I tell myself I don't want any *happy birthdays* or wishes, then find myself longing for them. But if I call this my birthday kiss, then that can be enough, especially when I have a birthday fuck to look forward to after enduring a meal with Simon.

As I wrap my arms around his back, I feel something in his hand.

Smooth-textured wrapping paper?

No way.

"What do you have in your hands?" I ask, unable to disguise the suspicion in my tone.

His grin broadens, making me wonder if that's what it could be.

"Sorry, but Forsyth mentioned this to me last week, and I couldn't help myself. I was gonna wait to share during our break, but I saw you come in here, so I ran back to the house and grabbed it."

He leans back and brings his hands around, revealing a wrapped package in one hand and a gift bag in the other, both branded with confetti surrounding bold *Happy Birthday* text. His expression shifts from playful to concerned, and I'm sure it's because of how stunned I am; I can't do anything other than stand there, dumbfounded.

"Are you mad? Don't be mad."

"I'm not mad. I just wasn't expecting this. Like, at all."

"Oh, good. I wasn't sure since you didn't mention it, but I wanted to do something. Go ahead, open it."

I take the gift, giddy with an excitement that reminds me of when I was eight years old and hoping it'd be the toy I'd asked Father for. A few tears into the paper reveal a Moleskine journal—like one of those journals where I used to keep all my secrets.

As my gaze shifts to him, a tear slides down my cheek.

Fuck, where did that come from?

I turn away and bat at it quickly, and when I turn back to him, I can tell he's caught on.

"Sorry. Maybe that was a shit idea. If you'd wanted me to know about your birthday, I'm sure you would have mentioned it."

"No, no. It's not that I'm upset. It's a very thoughtful gift." I hug the journal close to my chest. "Thank you."

His smile returns. "Well, it's not over yet."

He reaches into the gift bag and takes out a cupcake with a candle on it. Setting the bag on a nearby shelf, he retrieves a gas lighter from the bottom of the bag and sparks it, lighting the wick.

"Didn't know what kind of cake you'd want, so I stuck with vanilla with chocolate frosting. Felt safe."

"Did you make this?"

"Yeah. Remember last night when I said I was gonna call my aunt and sis?"

"You sneaky devil."

He beams. "So vanilla with chocolate frosting is a win?"

I laugh. "It's perfect."

"Okay, now give me one sec." He pulls his phone from his back pocket and hits a few keys before putting it on speaker.

There's a pause before I hear two voices singing "Happy Birthday." As he displays the screen for me, I realize what's going on. It's his sister and aunt on FaceTime. He sings along with them—well, not really singing, or at least not well, but it's got me blushing. As they reach the end of the song, he says, "Make a wish."

I haven't made a birthday wish in a very long time, and I fear that even thinking my wish will jinx it, but in the shed with him, his bright eyes on me while his face is still red from singing, I brave it before blowing out the candle.

His aunt and Charity applaud.

"Yay!" Charity says. "And don't blame Jonas for this. He was telling me about you, and I told him I had to meet you!"

"It's nice meeting you too," Amy says.

"I wanted to meet you both too," I say. "And it's the perfect day for it."

"I'm just glad Jonas texted us before he gave you his present," Charity says, sounding a little annoyed, "because the plan was for later tonight, but you'll learn that my brother is terrible at surprises."

"Sorry," Jonas says. "Got a little overexcited."

"I hope I get to meet you in real life at some point, Ryan," Charity says.

"Yes, you should come visit us in Chicago," Amy adds.

Now Jonas is blushing. "Okay, okay. I think we've had enough of a distraction for now."

"For now," Charity says. "But, Ryan, give me a call, and I'll give you all the gossip on my brother."

Jonas groans. "Maybe this was a bad idea."

Of course, it's obvious he's only playing, and it means a lot to me that he introduced me to them on a special day.

As he catches up with his family, I find it difficult not to look at him in awe. He hasn't known me long, yet he couldn't have made my birthday more perfect if he tried.

When he hangs up, he says, "That might have been too much. But they really wanted to meet you since I can't shut up about you when they call."

"It was wonderful getting to meet them, Jonas. I appreciate that you care enough about me to share that part of your life. They seem as amazing as you've said."

He smiles. "Well, in that case, I hope you wished for another kiss."

Then he offers one.

But the truth is, I wished for many more.

And as fun as it was to play the childish game, it brings forth the awareness I try to hide from myself: that I have to enjoy this while it lasts.

When he starts to lean back, I grab the back of his head and press my lips tighter against his. He submits, our tongues clashing, our breath matching.

I finally release the back of his head, and he pulls away. "Okay, well, maybe I don't regret doing this after all."

We share a laugh, and then I decide we can take our break a little early to share my cupcake. While we're eating our lunch, I rub my hand gently over the cover of the journal.

I doubt I'll write in it. At least, I know if I do, I can't write as freely as I once did. But like the feelings he stirs, it reminds me of a time before all this, when this house felt like the entire world, not a prison.

"YOU GONNA TOUCH your roast beef?" Simon asks as he slices into his steak, red juice leaking onto his mashed potatoes. "Nell worked hard for two dinners. Don't be rude." He knifes some potatoes onto the piece of steak before slipping it into his mouth.

He's right. Nell bends over backward to make our birthday meal, so I can't be ungrateful.

It just sucks because I'd rather be sitting with Jonas in the little, dingy staff dining area than be sitting here in the far more opulent dining room, at Father's marble table with my brother.

Simon's updated most of the artwork to more abstract pieces, but I can still remember the landscapes Father used to keep on the walls and the iron-welded statues around the space that seemed too eerie to us as kids. But more than the pieces, I remember fragments of moments of joy. Kieran cracking playful jokes. He was so charming. So witty. So clever.

"Come on," Simon presses.

I force myself to fork a slice of the roast beef and slip it into my mouth.

His jaw tenses up as he glares at me. "That's not how you like it," he says through gritted teeth.

There's the rage in him, the monster he's become.

"Maybe I want to eat it like this tonight," I say, and knowing it bothers him encourages me to take another bite.

"Stop it, Ryan. You don't like it like that. You know I know that, and you know this is bothering me, so just do it the way you like."

"You're not Father."

I don't have to look at him. I can easily imagine the flash of rage.

He clearly took it as the assault I intended because when I go for another bite, he snatches my plate away from me. Setting it beside his, he mixes the beef and mashed potatoes before grabbing the pepper. He grinds it over my roast beef, then adds a dash of salt. The tension in his expression doesn't let up until he sets my plate back down in front of me.

"There. Now eat."

This is my favorite meal, but he's managed to spoil it.

"Just fucking eat it," Simon says, showing his teeth as he bashes his fists onto the table. He's acting like a child, but the low octave of his voice reminds me that we're not kids, and this isn't the sort of fight adults should be engaged in.

I shouldn't eat it. I should make him suffer watching me like this, but if I do that, I'm only prolonging this farce of a dinner, so I submit, hating myself as I take the roast into my mouth. But damn, he knows me, because he fixed it just right. Fuck if I don't despise him for that too.

I savor the tender roast, how the mashed potatoes move around my mouth as I chew, and when I swallow, he sighs. He wears a familiar expression, like when he's finished during more intimate moments. There's a release, and as always, I'm left wondering why he's so obsessed with my choices, my life.

We both enjoy our meal, and then he lights the candles on the cake Nell set out on the table.

It's a chocolate Oreo ice cream cake. *His* favorite. He sings "Happy Birthday," not needing my participation, since I never really sang it when we were kids, then pressures me into blowing the candles out with him. It's all part of the ritual, and I play my part, cutting our slices and placing them on dessert plates before handing one to Simon and taking the other for myself.

"You know what this means…" he says, as though there could be any suspense when we both know how the evening will play out. He retrieves a wrapped package from a bag he'd brought with him to dinner, and passes it to me.

A narrow, rectangular shape. Not sure what it could be.

I grab the present I got him and slide it to him. He takes it, grinning as he shakes it, and says, "Shoes?" He unwraps it quickly. "Oh, just like the ones on my Amazon Wish List. Wasn't that thoughtful of me to put something on there you could afford?" He winks, but then says, "Oh, come on, Ry. You know I'm only teasing. Now hurry. I want you to open yours. I want you to see how thoughtful I am."

"This definitely wasn't on my wish list," I say, eyeing my present suspiciously.

"I know," he says, his mischievous grin expanding.

Might as well get this over with, so I tear open the paper. It's a case holding a black pen that looks really nice.

As my gaze shifts to him, his eyes are right on me. He must've seen when Jonas bought me that journal…or when he was wrapping it. It's another power play, a reminder that he's always watching.

We stare each other down, communicating much more than we can with words.

"It's a Mikimoto ballpoint pen," he says. "You used to love to journal, so I thought you might like it."

"You know I don't journal anymore. I don't even have one." He winces ever so slightly, and now I'm the one smirking because we both fucking know the truth, and it must drive him wild knowing I'm looking him right in the eyes and lying my ass off.

There's a fury in my spirit, all my hate directed at him, taking my thoughts back to a moment I'll never forget: *"It's always been you, Ryan,"* Kieran says.

Always been me?

As he leans close, I think about how I could take his lips that I've always wanted, feel his familiar warmth against me. Not because I want him, but to get back at Simon. To make him suffer as he's made me suffer.

I'm so fucking mad, I can't even think straight.

All I want is revenge. Wild, sick revenge. Don't I deserve that?

Normally I would push the black part of my spirit aside, but tonight, I summon it, call upon it like a sick power lurking within me.

I lean toward Simon, fork a slice of some of the leftover steak on his dinner plate, and slide it into my mouth. He knows I hate rare steak, and if he was frustrated at the start of this meal, I can tell by how his fingers curl against the table that he's about to explode.

After I swallow, I say, "Mmm…tasty."

His nostrils flare; it's clear those words dug the knife in, so I aim for a sharp twist, adding, "Happy birthday, twinsie," before lunging toward him and kissing his cheek.

24

JONAS

The birthday sex I gave Ryan last night has me whistling throughout the day. I can't fucking help myself.

I was eager to give him that journal, but I didn't know he'd have such a powerful reaction to such a simple gift—one I was almost embarrassed to get for him, thinking he might find it stupid or corny…or much worse, insensitive. But it's clear he took it in the spirit I'd intended.

Despite how pleased I am with how it went over, I'm nervous.

Simon requested to meet with me today, and I'm worried it might have been too good of a gift. We're being too obvious. What if he picks up that this isn't fake for me?

After Forsyth saw what we were up to, I've just let my feelings hang out. There's a certain freedom in knowing we don't have anything to hide. But it's more than that. I like that it's not just our secret. Somehow, others knowing makes it feel more real, and Ryan doesn't mind me kissing him in the shed or the yard, anywhere and in front of anyone, and I don't care either.

But all these good feelings, this magic Ryan and I share, it leaves me feeling like the rug's about to be torn out from under me.

I have some time before I need to meet with Simon, and it's late enough that Charity should be finished with chemo for the day, so I try to FaceTime her. Chemo's been really tough on her recently, so I'm hoping I can cheer her up a bit, but she doesn't pick up.

I try Aunt Amy next.

"Hi," she answers, and I can tell by her tone and the tension in her expression that something's up.

"What is it? What's wrong?"

"It's not a big thing. Charity has a fever and a little cough. They're running a test now to see if it's COVID or the flu. I didn't want to call you until we had more information, but they're stopping treatment until whatever it is passes, so she can get better."

Fuck. The chemo was hard enough on her without this shit rearing its head.

"I want to talk to her."

"She's sleeping right now. She's exhausted."

"Are you able to see her?"

"They're still trying to work that out. From what they've said so far, sounds like I may just have to mask up, and then I'll be able to see her a few times a day until she's recovered."

"I should be there," I blurt out.

Aunt Amy sighs. "I'm sure she would love to see you in person, but even if you can't get off right now, maybe you can plant the seed in your boss's head? So you can come when she gets better?"

That's true. Simon would understand. He has to have a fucking heart. Although, given some of the shit Ryan told me, I have to wonder.

"I'll see what I can do," I tell her.

We chat some more before I hang up, guilt gnawing at me as daymares seize control of my thoughts, reminding me of the nightmares I had when she first got sick; when the chemo was so severe, some days I wondered if I'd walk into her room and find her stiff in bed, not breathing, her eyes wide open.

When I head to my meeting with Simon, I'm determined to work this out. There must be a way that I can see her, just for a bit. If anything were to happen to her and I wasn't with her, I couldn't fucking live with myself.

And I must convince him that Ryan and I are doing exactly what he wants.

As I open the office door, the *creak* offers what seems like an ominous warning.

"Good afternoon, Jonas," Simon says from the sofa in front of the bay window, without looking up. His laptop rests on a lap desk as he keys away. Not for the first time, I wonder if he's really doing anything important or if this is all a production. Is everything he does just part of this sick performance art he's crafting for Ryan?

As I wait for him to pull himself away from his work, I interlock my hands behind my back; it's something I didn't even think about, but now as I stand before him, I feel like a soldier awaiting his commander's orders.

I force my hands at my sides, and his typing slows to a point where the silence between us drags on at an unbearably glacial pace, made worse by the fact that I have something urgent to talk to him about.

"Simon—"

He raises a finger. "One moment."

Of fucking course.

The suspense makes me so on edge, sweat beads across my forehead.

"There we are," he says as he stops typing. He rises to his feet, his laptop in his hand so the screen flashes toward me for a moment, and I can see a paused image of what looks like night vision security footage from Ryan's bedroom. Ryan's on his knees as I bottom for him, and I assume that must've been early last night.

Simon glances at me like he's gauging my reaction, and despite a surge of rage that pulses through me at this violation of our privacy, I keep my cool. Like I would if this was still just a job for me.

Simon heads to his desk and sets his laptop down before approaching me. "Now, you were going to say something? Is it about your sister? Is everything okay there?"

After everything I've seen from Simon, I shouldn't be surprised.

"She caught a virus, and with the chemo…that can really tear a person down. And I feel good about where I'm at with Ryan, so maybe in a few days, when she shakes this, I could head up to New York? Just to check in. It doesn't have to be for long."

I'm fucking rambling, showing my desperation, though I'm hoping if he sees how much I need this, the part of him that's still fucking human will do the right thing.

His expression is stoic. Difficult to read. He winces before saying, "I don't know that I can make time for that. Not when you're making this much progress."

"Maybe the time away will make him miss me more."

A smile plays across his lips. "Jonas, I understand that your sister matters to you. That's why I made you the initial offer. But I also assumed her journey would be a rough one, and that I'd be able to rely on you even through those difficult times. Oh, but let me think…let me think… I don't want you to think I'm some kind of monster." He lets those words hang in the air before he says, "*But…*"

Now I know, whatever he's about to say, it doesn't matter. He's already made up his mind. And it's not going to involve me making a trip to see my sister. My heart sinks.

"The payment I offered is contingent upon your loyalty to me throughout this work. Surely you understand that, by being here and doing this with me, you're helping her more than you possibly could in person."

That I can't deny, but it doesn't change the absurdity of it all. Because no matter what he fucking says, I know this is little more than a power play, like everything else revolving around Simon Hawthorne.

"Your loyalty is very important to me, Jonas, and I need you to prove that you're loyal now. You've been doing a very good job. Very convincing work." He studies my face.

Is it as I feared? Does he worry I've been doing too good a job? Could he be wondering if maybe this isn't as much of an act anymore?

"I wonder how much he struggled before he finally caved," he adds. "Or if he even struggled at all. If you're too similar to Kieran for him to resist."

Our gazes meet.

"It's hard not to see what he sees," he whispers, as if to himself. "How does it feel when he looks at you? To be wanted like that?"

It feels like every moment I've lived has been so that I could get to this, share this experience with Ryan.

It feels like I've been dead all these years, but I'm finally alive.

Like there is a god, and he's making up for all the horrible shit that's happened in my life.

"What do you mean?" I ask.

Simon snickers. "Nothing. Anyway, if you want to leave to see your sister, you can keep the fifteen grand. I'm not the devil. But I can't guarantee there will still be space in their program once that happens."

A threat.

Motherfucker.

I think about Charity being ill and asking my aunt if she can see me.

About her wondering how I could be so busy that I can't make time to see her in what could potentially be her last moments.

It wrecks my heart, yet I know what I must do. "I understand," I force out. "And I'm willing to do what I have to do."

"That's good. Now that we've gotten that out of the way, let's get back to why I called you here today. Obviously, I can draw my own conclusions about you and Ryan based on what I've seen, but I figured I might as well ask the expert. How do you think he *feels* about you?"

With everything going on with Charity, fuck, this is so damn petty. How the hell can he think this is worth wasting his life over? Wasting my life over?

"He seems to like me," I say—when it's so much more than that. God, when he looks at me, it's like I'm the only thing he sees. I know that's how I feel when I look at him. And I mustn't let Simon see that.

He smirks. "You're doing yourself a disservice, Jonas. His feelings are stronger than that, but not quite there yet."

"There? Is there somewhere he's supposed to be?"

Not for the first time, I'm trying to bait him into telling me more. Maybe if I can get him to open up, it might help Ryan head off whatever Simon has in store for him.

Of course, his bastard twin won't make this easy.

He bites his bottom lip. "Yes, there is. But that's my business. I'll know when my brother's ready."

"If you tell me where I need to get him, maybe I can speed up the process."

Don't push too far.

"There's no need to speed anything up. I've been waiting a long time for this, and I don't mind waiting longer. That recruitment agency took a year to find you, even with the best, if not exactly legal, face-recognition software."

So that's how he found someone who looks so damn much like his brother.

"I would've waited ten years if I'd known they'd find such an exquisite specimen," he adds. "Just keep doing what you're doing, steady on the path. That birthday shit was a nice trick, and last night made for some great viewing."

He's still never come out and stated he's watching us, but like the other times he's danced around it, it's not by mistake.

I don't imagine he makes many mistakes.

He puts his middle and forefinger against my chest, running them down between my pecs, then my torso.

Get your fucking hands off me!

"You have a lot of energy. And you're clearly ambitious. I guess I would be too if I had someone like Charity in my life and knew they were in harm's way."

Don't fucking talk about her. I wish you didn't even know her name.

"Yes, just keep on like this." He pulls his hand back, then shrugs. "Maybe a few more dates wouldn't kill you, but I do have one concern. Like I said, maybe you're just doing a very good job, but between how easily you've warmed up to gay sex and how convincing you are when you're with him…I do worry you might have begun sympathizing with him."

Fuck.

"I…"

"Just hear me out. Ryan can be very charming. He can seem very innocent. But he's not innocent. Not at all. He's cunning. Clever. There's something dark in him that's always been there. He's a liar. I fell for the act, so I missed it. But I won't make that mistake again."

Cunning? Dark? Liar? That sounds like Simon, not Ryan.

"Is there something I need to know?" I'm proud of myself for how that came out because my instinct was to tell him, *Go fuck yourself. Ryan is a better man than you could ever dream of being.*

Simon's gaze finally pulls from me, his expression relaxing, as if releasing the facade he's put on.

"I didn't want to tell you this when you first came here. I thought it might scare you off. But Ryan is a killer."

That wasn't what I was expecting at all. He might as well have decked me.

"What?"

"Sorry. I don't mean like in cold blood. He doesn't need a knife. I shouldn't have even told you this, but I guess now that I have, I should be out with it. You deserve to know."

I also know that Simon doesn't accidentally reveal anything. Even this moment has been crafted.

"Kieran, the man you look like…Ryan killed him." His gaze meets mine again. "And then he killed our father."

My mind's spinning. What the hell is he on about? That can't be true. It's a malicious lie, given what I know not just about Ryan's character, but about the pain his memories of Kieran and his father bring him.

Tension rises in me, and I'm tempted to call Simon a fucking liar, but I bite my tongue.

As Simon watches me, I realize this could all be a test. Simon wanting to see if I'll lose it and defend Ryan. And then he'd know I'd aligned myself with Ryan, and I'd be as fucked as if I went to visit my sister.

What a piece of shit.

Simon continues staring me down, and I summon the strength to push out, "What happened?" in as measured a tone as I can muster.

"I had feelings for Kieran. Intense feelings, and so did Ryan. I guess it's no secret, I know you've discussed him with Nell and Ryan. Nell used to hint that there was something wrong with how we acted toward one another. How close we would sit. How we might kiss a little too long when we greeted each other. When one of us would make fun of the other getting aroused if we sat in each other's laps. Most of the staff back then knew we shouldn't have been that close, but no one stopped us. We fell in love with Kieran. I guess it makes sense that twins would be drawn to the same man. As Kieran and I became close, I had to learn to keep secrets from Ryan, something we'd never done before. I knew he'd be envious. I knew he'd be angry with Kieran if he found out.

"Four years ago, the summer we turned eighteen, Ryan and I were so excited about attending Emory University. We had such dreams about getting out, socializing, making friends…exploring beyond the walls of Hawthorne Heights. Kieran was intelligent, but he was never interested in schoolwork or tests, and he knew college wasn't for him. Campus isn't far, but we both knew it was going to be hell. We were so used to seeing each other constantly that we took advantage of every moment before then…until, well, let's just say Ryan discovered that Kieran and I were in love…"

Based on what Ryan told me, that sounds like a generous phrasing for what he discovered.

"Ryan decided to get back at me by taking Kieran for himself. He seduced Kieran, and I caught them in the act, behind the shed, surely staged for me to see. I was so hurt, so betrayed by what Kieran had done. I hated them both. And the next day, Ryan and

Kieran disappeared into the woods for hours. Only Ryan returned to tell us Kieran had fallen to his death at the drop-off."

Despite how calculated Simon's reveal is, as he tears up, it's difficult to tell if this is part of an act because it's more convincing than the rest. Something about this must be true.

"Are you saying Ryan pushed him?" If he thinks I'm going to believe that bullshit—

"Well, don't you have an imagination on you. No, nothing like that. We didn't know what happened at first. Ryan claimed not to know either. The lying bastard. And Father was too busy making sure it wouldn't become a scandal, fodder for the press. Father had to hide his dirty secrets, that Kieran was our half brother through an illicit affair. A few weeks later, Ryan, unable to bear the shame of his filthy secret, confessed to Father what happened that day. He told him what he and Kieran had done together, how he'd done it all to spite us for our betrayal. That the day after, he'd confronted Kieran in the woods, blamed him for the shameful thing they'd done. He wanted to make Kieran hate himself as much as Ryan hated him for what he'd done with me. And after making Kieran feel like a monster for succumbing to his desire, our brother, unable to bear the shame, threw himself from the drop-off."

He practically spits that last sentence out, so full of rage over the injustice.

"I think in Ryan's mind, it was just a game to make us pay. He didn't know how his vengeance, his desire to punish me for my feelings would hurt Kieran. And his selfish actions caused Kieran to kill himself. Father saw through his crocodile tears, and that night, he contacted his attorney. Changed his will to grant me authority over the estate. Then he took his gun and shot himself in this office, right there." He points to the desk chair, gazing at it longingly, as though he's remembering his dear father.

"That's why I call Ryan a killer. He knows he's the reason our brother and Father are dead, and it haunts him. He can't take back the consequences of his actions. He may show you his softer side, but there's something truly wicked in Ryan's heart. *Evil* is the only word that can describe it."

I'm not naive enough to believe it's the truth, but could any part of it be true?

I've sensed guilt when Ryan discusses what happened in the past, but is this the pain Ryan carries when he speaks about Kieran and his father?

"That's why I chose you," he adds. "Ryan needs to be reminded of his sins. He needs to face the darkness within him that did that to our brother. To Father. To me. He doesn't get to continue walking these halls like nothing ever happened, keeping up Hawthorne Heights like he hasn't already destroyed her heart."

As much as I want to tell myself this is all a malicious lie, it all adds up.

Why Simon's so fucking angry with his brother.

The emotion Kieran brings up in Ryan.

The reason Simon would want a look-alike to torture his twin.

But even if part of this is true, I refuse to take Simon's word for anything. Not until I know Ryan's side.

25

RYAN

"Hi, Charity, it's good to see you again," I say as Jonas turns his phone toward me.

"Hi, Ryan." In her unicorn bandanna, she smiles, though I can tell she's struggling to maintain it more than in previous conversations. Her eyelids drop for longer than they should for a blink, but she opens them as if she's just reminded herself she needed to stay awake.

"How are you?" I ask. "Jonas told me you came down with the flu."

"Yes," she says before pushing out a wet cough. "It's been a nightmare. I just wish we could have kept going with the treatment."

"I'm sorry," I say.

"It's fine. Dr. Blaire says we just need to get me to recover, and then we'll start the next round." She hacks up a few more coughs. "Sorry, just feels like if I get another few coughs out, it'll be clear, but it never is. I'm fine, though."

I can tell by how quickly she says it that it's for Jonas's benefit.

"Are you still chatting with that friend you made?" I ask. "What was his name? Ahmed?"

Her smile perks up. "Yes, before I got sick, the doctors scheduled us so we could spend more time together. We'd go to the viewing room for the aviary and talk. Now we can't even do that, but we'll text, and he's written me some notes."

"Notes? Oh really?"

"It's nothing," she says with an eye roll, then adds, "Okay, maybe not nothing, but shut up."

Jonas and I share a laugh. As she continues chatting with us about her day, Jonas is right beside me, hanging on every word. Seeing how much he cares about his sister, how much she adores him, only makes me that much more attracted to him. And I foolishly let myself imagine a world where Charity is fine and we're all together.

"It's just hard since they'll only let Aunt Amy see me a few times a day now. I miss her. And I miss you, Jonas. I know I can't see anyone right now, but please tell me you'll come visit when I get better."

"I...um..."

I can feel he wants to tell her he will with every fiber of his being, and if it wasn't for Simon, it wouldn't be an issue.

"You know I have to see this through until September, which is right around the corner, but as soon as I'm done, I'll be right there, right by your side."

Charity's frown says it all. She wants her brother to be there with her. Of course she does.

He chats with her some more before calling his aunt.

Afterward, we have another picnic planned in the woods, so we head to my place among the briars, making out before we even unpack the food. It shouldn't mean so much to me. We mess around every night, but there's something different about when we're alone—truly alone.

Jonas doesn't hold back either, so I suspect he feels the same.

"My lips are going numb," I whisper before going back for another.

It's the sort of kiss that helps me lose track of time, of where we are. Sometimes, even who the hell we are.

When I finally pull away, I lie alongside him, resting one arm on him, the other at his side as I gaze down at his beautiful face, his head resting on our picnic blanket. I lean down and nibble at his chin, which makes him laugh before I pull back and look down at his smile. This feeling—the excitement, the friskiness—I'm greedy for it because I know that as much fun as it is being his boyfriend, there's not much time left before this must end. As he pointed out earlier, we're getting so close to September.

But I don't want it to end. Ever.

Despite his playfulness, his expression sobers up quickly, assuring me there's something on his mind.

"Are you worried about her?"

After the call, he got real quiet, and I could tell he wasn't happy to see her so weak, struggling to recover not only from the last intense round of chemo, but from this flu now as well.

"You know me too well," he says as his smile twists into a frown. "She looked worse than the last time we talked, and I just wish I could go see her for a bit."

"Whatever he's doing to me isn't as important as what's going on with her. He has to know that."

"I mentioned the possibility of visiting her, but he shut that down right away."

This kind of thing…it takes me back to the Simon who used to hold me when I was sad. Who helped me nurse a sick rabbit back to health before we released him back into the wild. Who knows so much pain himself, enough that he shouldn't struggle to find empathy for others. It's a reminder of what my brother has become.

Jonas's gaze meets mine. He opens his mouth like he's about to say something, but stops himself.

"What were you about to say?"

"When I asked Simon if I could visit Charity, he started asking me questions, as if he was suspicious I might be telling you what he's been up to."

Tension knots in my chest.

"And…he said some things about Kieran and your father…"

The tension quickly drops to my belly, and I'm lightheaded.

Am I going to be sick?

I sit up, maybe a little too quickly because it only makes me feel nauseous.

"Are you okay?" he asks.

"I'm fine," I lie as I take deep breaths. "What did he say?"

"It was a pretty fucked-up story about when they passed. I think you know I don't believe anything he tells me. I don't want you to think I—"

"Please, Jonas, stop being cautious for my sake. Just tell me what he told you."

Don't I deserve to get revenge against Simon for what he's done to me?

I gaze into Kieran's blue eyes as he leans toward me, his lips craving mine.

"It's always been you, Ryan."

That should make me feel good, but why does it sear into my chest?

As his lips draw near, I can't help myself.

I'll make Simon pay for this. I'll make him suffer for all he's put me through.

"He told me," Jonas says, "that after you caught him and Kieran in the act, you seduced Kieran to make him jealous. Then you made Kieran feel terrible about it, so terrible that he…"

"That he what?" Again, there's this anger as I ask, but not at Jonas—at Simon.

"Killed himself," he forces out.

Water stirs in my eyes.

The fucking bastard. How dare he speak those vicious words to Jonas?

"And what about Father?" I have to know. "What did he say about him?"

"That a few weeks later, you told him what you'd done."

What *I'd* done?

The pain in my chest knots up as my anger rises.

"And then your dad disinherited you and…"

"And killed himself?" I say before he has a chance. I push to my feet and start for the pond. Jonas calls my name, but as the tears push from my eyes, I'm afraid to speak because I know I'll be all choked up.

My emotions are a mix of grief and rage.

I'm so pissed at Simon, but then, I'm also pissed at myself. And haunted by the past.

I grab at that spot in my chest, my breathing speeding up as I lose control, and soon I'm on my knees, sobbing into my hands as I futilely battle the flashes of memories demanding my attention.

Simon and Kieran fucking in Father's office.

Our family laughing together at the dining-room table.

Christmases in the family room.

"Ryan?" I hear before feeling a hand on my arm, pulling me out of my thoughts.

"Jonas, I wish I could say it was all a lie, but it's not."

I interlock my arms, clutching at my biceps as Jonas settles on the ground beside me, crossing his legs.

He must think I'm a monster. He must be disturbed, but as I turn, I don't see the judgment I feared.

He's listening.

"Please talk to me, Ryan."

With my lips on Kieran's, I think, Fuck Kieran and Simon. Fuck them to hell.

I keep kissing him, but it doesn't change the pain.

I'll make him pay. I'll make them both pay.

What will Jonas think when he hears the truth?

"After I caught them in the act, Kieran came to find me."

I don't want to tell him. I don't want to relive this, but I won't let Simon spread a fucking lie, and I can't do that without revealing my own sins.

"I was hiding behind the shed, crying, and Kieran sat down beside me. I was so fucking angry with them. I thought he was just going to apologize and tell me he cared for Simon. That I would have to get over him. But then he said it was me he was thinking about when he was with Simon. And he looked like he wanted to kiss me, and I wanted to kiss him too. Not because I liked him, but to get back at Simon. To get back at both of them. So I did. I kissed him. It wasn't right. It wasn't the experience I'd imagined, not for the reasons I was doing it."

I can't do this.

I pull away, and he kisses me again. "No," *I say,* "stop."

But he kisses me again, and as I pull away this time, he grabs the back of my head, pulling me back to him. I try to push him away, but he's stronger.

"Kieran!" *I grapple with him.*

"Come on, Ry. Come on. It's fine. Everything's fine." *Before I know it, we're wrestling until he rolls me onto my stomach and twists my arm behind my back. It stings, and I cry out.*

Why is he doing this?

"Please stop, Kieran. I mean it. No."

"You don't have to be afraid, Ryan. I'll be good to you. I love you."

"I kept telling him to stop, and it was like he didn't hear me. I kept thinking if I said it louder, he'd realize I didn't want this."

My jeans burn against my hips as he forces them down my legs, his hand still straining the muscles in my arm. "Please, stop! It hurts."

He had to have heard what I said. Why won't he stop?

"I love you, Ryan. I've always loved you."

"I thought it'd be like in a movie, this rage and fury in me as I scream, but it was so quiet. I felt numb. And I remember thinking that he could do what he wanted and there wouldn't be any consequences. I wouldn't feel a thing."

"Oh my God, Ryan."

The tears are still sliding down my face, but I push on because I know if I don't get this out, it'll never come out. "I know now that's not true, but at the time, it felt like my body was protecting me. And then, as he forced his way in, I remember being totally disconnected from that and just feeling claustrophobic. Like it didn't matter what he was doing to me, I just needed to get out of this position and get him off me. I had some leverage with my free arm, and I felt for a rock. I knew I only had one shot because he might grab my other arm too, so I used all my strength to hit him in the head with it. It was such an awkward angle, I didn't even know if it worked, but he released my wrist, and I was able to get out from under him. I must've gotten him good because he had his hand to his head and didn't come after me, even as I tripped on my pants before getting back up and pulling them to my waist. Then I just ran like hell back to the house."

"He raped you," Jonas says.

Even now, I want to say, *No! That's not what happened!* I want to defend my brother, even after what he did.

But I can't.

Because I know what he did to me.

"I didn't want to believe that's what it was. I just wanted to pretend it never happened."

His hand drops from my shoulder onto my thigh, his warm touch safe, and I place my hand on top of his.

"The next day, Kieran kept trying to talk to me, so I headed into the woods. I just needed to think, to make sense of what happened. But he followed me, and I hurried here to keep safe. He knew it's where I was, but he didn't know how to get in, so he just called to me from the other side. And I guess, feeling protected, I told him what he'd done, but he called me a liar. Said Father wouldn't believe me if I said anything. And as I tried to get him to just admit it, he was howling like an animal from the other side. It was this god-awful noise, echoing everywhere around me, as if the sound was coming from the briars.

"He finally left me alone, and I waited a few hours, till I felt it was safe to return home. When Simon went looking for him, he found Kieran's body at the bottom of the drop-off. So he did kill himself because of me—because he knew what he'd done to me, and I guess he couldn't stand that."

"Simon said you were the one who found him. I'm so sorry that happened to you, Ryan. I'm sure that had to be confusing and scary. And then…"

Father.

Part of me fears that when I look at Jonas, I'll see Kieran, but when I turn to him, it's just Jonas. It's a reminder that I'm safe.

"I'm guessing you told your dad what happened?"

I nod. I'm so fucking exhausted from reliving that day, but I need to finish this. I need to get it out of my head. "At first, I couldn't bear telling him what happened, not while he was grieving. And he was so busy trying to cover up his indiscretions that it was easy to stay quiet, but the secret ate away at me until I couldn't carry it alone anymore. He was sitting at his desk when I told him. I couldn't tell him I ever had feelings for Kieran. I didn't even want to believe I'd ever had feelings for the man who did that to me. And I sure as hell wasn't gonna tell him what I caught

Kieran and Simon doing. I just told him what happened by the shed, and he got quiet, couldn't even look at me. I needed something. For him to tell me I hadn't done anything wrong, or that I wasn't responsible, but he asked me to leave his office. I thought he just needed time, but then the next day he shot himself, and when I found out about the will, I knew…he didn't believe me."

As another tear trails along the path of another that came before, Jonas puts his warm hand to my face, wiping the tear. I don't feel like a man, but like that child who just wanted his father to be there for him. Needed his father to be there for him.

"That's so much trauma," Jonas says, "and in such a short span of time. None of it is your fault, though. I hope you know that."

"But it is. I've thought about it a thousand times. If I'd known the outcome, maybe I could have just taken it. Kept that secret for the rest of my life. I'd have hated Kieran forever, but at least everyone would still be alive."

"You're not responsible for how they responded to the truth."

"A part of me knows you're right. But it's one of many in the mix. Like there's a part of me that still adores Kieran, that wants to hear his laugh and see his smile again, and then there's another part that hates him for what he did, and I hate myself for wanting to remember the good times. There's the part that tells me to forget one stupid afternoon by the shed, and another that's jealous of Simon. And then there's yet another part that's asking what this is really all about, and it's all so twisted up and confusing. I always thought if someone was raped, it had to be by someone they didn't want anything to do with. Not someone I loved with all my heart.

Someone I lusted after and desired. And there are moments where I do still think about that man I lusted after, and I hate myself for that. I hate myself."

As I crumble in a fit of tears, Jonas moves close, his arms wrapping around me.

Safe in his arms, I say the thoughts I've kept to myself all these years. "Why did he do that? Why did he…" And then the sobs begin anew.

Jonas doesn't try to answer my question. Just holds me, and that's what I need right now. Just to be in his arms, for the first time sharing this story with a man who's just listening.

A man who believes me and cares, unlike Simon or Father.

26

JONAS

I HOLD RYAN close. After everything he's shared, he needs me.

Just thinking about what Kieran did and how his father treated him after he exposed his rapist brother makes my blood boil.

As his breathing steadies and the sniffles pass, I rub his back.

"I'm sorry for unloading all that on you," he says as he finally pulls back, red around his eyes, some of it from crying, some of it from wiping at the tears. "I couldn't let you only have Simon's messed-up version of the truth."

"Have you talked to him about this? I know you said you told your dad, but maybe he just doesn't understand."

His gaze sinks. "Jonas, he knows. And I think he's already found out about us."

"What?" Where the hell did that come from?

"He's not an idiot, and with how we've both been carrying on, he'd have to be an idiot not to know. And he wouldn't just tell you something like that without reason."

"Why do you think he told me?"

"I think he suspects we've gotten close, and he told you because he knew I'd have to contradict it."

I wouldn't put anything past Simon, not with everything I know, but I can't make the pieces fit. "Wouldn't he have told me the deal was off and asked me to leave?"

"He doesn't need the deal to be off. You don't know how he's using you. Neither of us does, so he can still use us like pawns, and clearly this was no different."

"But if he knows what really happened, why that story? Especially if he knew you were going to tell me the truth."

"So I'd have to replay that nightmare again. Relive it. Because he knew I couldn't bear the thought of you thinking any part of it was true. And he knew I'd have to look at you after I told it."

I rest my hand against his face once again, stroking my thumb across his cheek. "You didn't have to do that."

"I didn't want to leave you questioning…wondering if there was any truth to what Simon told you."

I'm skeptical of his conclusion that Simon knows, but at the same time, who would know Simon better than Ryan? Maybe he's picked up on something I can't because I just don't know his brother as well. Or maybe he's so used to Simon's mind games that he doesn't put anything past him.

"If he has found out about us," I say, "do you think he'll change his mind?"

"As long as you keep playing the game like he wants you to, you'll be good."

He sounds confident, but I can't imagine why. He can't know that for sure.

But my real concern right now is *him*.

"Ryan, after everything you went through, this can't be good for you, being in this place with your brother fucking with your head." I hesitate, fearing his reaction to what I'm considering, but I can't keep it to myself. "When I leave, you should come with me. You can live with me and my aunt. You're a hard worker. You'll be able to get a job in no time. It doesn't have to be anything more than that. I just don't want you to have to stay."

He smirks, but the sorrow in his expression doesn't shift. "That's a beautiful idea," he says, giving me hope, but then he goes on, "You're very kind, Jonas. But the reason I know he'll hold up his end of the deal is because Charity's gonna need more help, even after you leave. If you want his support, then you'll have to do what he wants. And I'll have to stay."

Fuck.

Maybe Ryan's right about Simon. Maybe he knows and doesn't give a fuck because he has the perfect insurance plan. I'm at his mercy, but at what price?

"No, there has to be another way. We can go back to the treatment center she was at before. We can find a way to make this work. I can't leave you here."

His lips curl into a small, sad smile. "This is where Simon's outsmarted us both. Because he knows I'd never let you do that. There aren't many people who can afford the kind of care Simon can buy, and I've researched all the doctors Charity's seeing. They're the best; of course they are. They're her chance—the chance for both of you to have a life."

Is he right? What if all this time, while we thought we've been undermining Simon's plan, we've actually been playing into his game? And now we're already in checkmate.

"No, I refuse to believe that. Ryan, I can't ask you to torture yourself to save her."

"It's not your choice to make. It's mine."

I'm torn between rage—pissed that Simon has placed us in this position—and appreciation—how willing Ryan is to sacrifice himself for this girl he's only just met. It doesn't surprise me, even from what little time I've known him, but it's not right.

"Don't worry about me, Jonas. That day Kieran attacked me, something in me died. An innocence. A hope about life. Since then, I've been a ghost, haunting the halls of Hawthorne Heights. Running through this same routine, an echo of myself, resigned to a hell I felt I deserved. Since you came here, for the first time in years, I've felt alive. You gave me a chance to live again. And when you leave, I'll still be alive because you will have left me with memories that can sustain me the rest of my life."

Oh, Ryan. My kind, compassionate, wounded Ryan. I rest my hand on the back of his head. "Until I met you, I didn't know I could feel this kind of exhilaration about life. Even with how fucked up it's been, I'm just glad I've gotten to know you."

He studies my face, his gaze gravitating to my lips before he lunges toward me and takes a kiss. I eagerly reciprocate.

There's no fixing all this in an afternoon, so we might as well enjoy each other's bodies.

He pushes me onto my back, straddling my waist, pulling away just long enough to get his shirt off.

"Fuck me here," he whispers as he moves close, until his lips are inches from mine. "I just want to forget all the bullshit, away from him. So it's just the two of us."

"I want that too."

As I probe his waist with my hands, he rocks his hips, his ass rubbing against the crotch of my shorts.

"Fuck," I mutter.

He reaches into his pocket and retrieves a bottle of lube.

"Oh, really? Someone was prepared."

"After that time in the library, I figured it was better to be prepared. Not that I had a problem with taking your dry cock."

Just his mention of that magical moment sends a warm sensation shooting through me, helping ease the ache from hearing his pain and discussing the horror of the twisted game Simon has us trapped in.

This isn't only about those things, though—it's about life. About the harsh, brutal realities we've both faced.

For a few fleeting moments, we can leave the bullshit behind.

Just the two of us, lost in each other.

In a frenzy, we struggle out of our clothes, and he lies across my shirt as I position myself between his legs. I finish lubricating my cock before I push the head against his hole.

There's still remnants of pain in his expression. The pink around his eyes. The subtlest of frowns. And something else too. Something unseen. A pain he'll always carry.

I know he can't just fuck the pain away, but it's worth a shot.

As I ease my way into him, his eyes seal shut, his mouth dropping open.

This is different than those early fucks; his ass opens up as if conditioned to accept me, his body relaxing, letting me in so I can give him this pleasure he desperately craves.

I push in until my hips touch his ass, then lean down close and reclaim his mouth. His hand settles on the back of my head, holding me, and there's something calming about it as our tongues greet each other. We kiss slowly, and as I thrust at the same pace, Ryan's free hand rests on my side. I hook an arm around his neck, keeping him tight against me as I run my tongue along his bottom lip, then lick up the middle. His hot breath hits me as I thrust some more.

"Yes, yes," he whispers as I pick up my pace. "Harder. Faster."

It's the sort of moment that makes me hate Kieran. Because this is all Ryan should have ever experienced—only receiving when he's confirming, begging, pleading for it.

I obey, speeding up, watching him moan and his eyes roll back.

"You look so hot taking me," I tell him. "You feel so good."

He trembles in my hold, a smile tugging across his face, assuring me I'm right up against his prostate.

"Jonas, I want to fuck you. Can I fuck you?"

I slow my movements, and now I'm smiling. "You can do whatever the fuck you want to me."

He smiles even bigger, the sort of smile I couldn't have expected after everything we discussed. And I'm proud to know I'm the one who's cheering him up.

I pull out of him, and we switch so I'm lying on my shirt, which is a little damp now. He takes good care of my hole, just as I did his, filling me with his cock.

"God, I hope it feels this good when I'm in you," I tell him.

"Oh, it does."

His validation makes my heart race with excitement as his dick jams up against my prostate, that familiar rush sweeping through me, stirring sensation that has me needing him that much more.

As he fucks me harder, he kisses me, our bodies pressed tight together, each thrust pounding my ass, the slapping echoing in the woods.

There's something incredible about fucking out here, like wild animals who'd stumbled upon each other once again, fucking with abandon. We're free of Simon, free of the world, free of our pasts and problems as he gets me so worked up, I can't help but call out his name.

He must know how good he's giving it because he speeds up, each thrust stimulating me that much more, taking me fucking higher. I'm all twists and gasps and moans of pleasure.

"You're so hot like that, Jonas. You're gonna make me shoot."

"Do it. Please," I beg. "I want you in me and keep fucking me when you're done so I can shoot."

He chuckles before drilling into me, and I watch as his face twists up, his mouth contorted as I feel him pulse within me, filling my greedy hole.

He obeys my request, and I grip my cock, stroking in a frenzy, because between how his dick hits that spot and knowing I'm stuffed with his cum, it's more than I can bear, and soon, I'm twitching and contorting myself, his lips smacking against mine as warmth erupts across my abs.

He lowers on top of me, his stomach spreading my cum across our bellies.

Hooking my arms around him, I pull him tight against me.

I don't want to fucking let go. If I can just hold him here, maybe we can stay like this until we're ready to go again. Maybe we won't ever have to face the world, and it can be just the two of us forever.

27

RYAN

I SIT ON the sofa in the library nook, rereading the same paragraph of *The Count of Monte Cristo* for what must be the twentieth time. It's hard to focus when the conversation I had with Jonas yesterday keeps running through my head.

Simon knows. He must. Otherwise, he wouldn't have shared that vile, distorted story. This is all part of his master plan. When Jonas and I started messing around, I wanted Simon to get it over with, reveal what this was all about. But now that we've been doing this for months and I've gotten to know this incredible man, I don't mind waiting for the inevitable. As long as that means I get to spend a few more nights with him. As long as Simon doesn't take him from me just yet. But it's cruel, since I know that's what he has in mind. What other fate could Jonas and I have?

The library door creaks open, and I don't even have to look up. I know by the sound and something in the air—a twin sense.

"Good afternoon," Simon says cheerfully.

I don't look up from my book as he draws near, walking even slower than normal, a snake sliding through the grass, stalking his prey.

The closer he gets, the more anger burns in my chest. He's

preventing Jonas from seeing his sister. And he's the reason I had to relive that hell yesterday. To go back to my darkest memories.

"*It's you I want, not Simon.*"

The words haunt me as much as the violence of Kieran's actions.

When Simon finally reaches me, he plops down on the sofa beside me, cozying up like he would have when we were kids. He closes the book enough to see the cover.

"*The Count of Monte Cristo.* Why does that make me feel like you're trying to get inside my head?"

"Feeling particularly vengeful?"

He chuckles. "Have you gotten to where Edmond Dantès begins to exact his revenge on his enemies? That's where the real fun begins."

He didn't deny feeling vengeful.

He snatches the book from me. "Oh yes, you're right at the heart of it."

I try to retrieve the book, but he pulls it out of my reach.

"I'm just trying to enjoy my day off, Simon."

"And what better way than spending time with your brother? I mean, really, Ryan, for living in the same house, I rarely ever get to see you."

"It's a big house."

He simpers. "Yes, it is. I guess I could work harder to spend time with you. I just have so many Zoom meetings. I've signed up to be on too many boards this year. I don't even know why. Maybe it just gives me something to do."

I guess he has to fill his free time with something other than tormenting me.

He rests the book at his side, away from me, then gets up. Since I'm not giving him much to work with, I'm hoping he'll leave, but he spins toward me, and before I know it, he presses his knees down into the cushion on either side of me, straddling my waist.

"Come on. Be fun. I'm bored," he says, cupping my face in his hands.

"I can't help you with that."

"Remember what we used to do whenever we got bored?" He looks me directly in the eyes, a wicked grin on his face.

"I have a feeling you're not referring to chess or *Super Mario Party*."

He rolls his head back, enjoying a laugh like a fucking supervillain before his gaze returns to mine.

"That's not what I meant, and you know it. These oppressive summer days remind me of when we first figured out what our bodies could do. Remember how I would curl up to you in bed, spooning you, and I'd just start rubbing, and it made us laugh, so I kept doing it until we found out the truth." He rocks his hips in my lap.

My cheeks warm, not for the reason they would have back then, but because he should be as embarrassed as I am about what we did.

"Stop it."

"That's not what you used to say. Our bodies were practically inseparable that summer."

"I don't want to talk about this."

"Mmmm. And that's what makes it so much more fun to talk about."

I start to push him off, but he grabs my wrists and pushes them back against the sofa, his face inches from mine. "Come on, Ryan. We could spend the day like we did back then, when we told Jada we were feeling sick." Jada was our live-in nanny up until we turned sixteen. "Then she told Father we couldn't work with the tutor, and we stayed in bed to figure out what's happening to us…trying to understand why we couldn't fucking stop. And why it felt wrong, like we couldn't share it with anyone. We knew even back then that if we told them, they'd tell us we couldn't do it anymore. And that seemed like a punishment close to death."

Still keeping my wrists against the sofa, he moves even closer to my lips, as if about to plant a kiss.

"Get. Off. Me. Simon." I'm sure he's no stranger to the contempt in my voice.

Because this isn't like those youthful days. Now there's just hot rage at his sick games.

He leans toward my ear and whispers, "Did you just say you want me to get off?"

His hot breath invades my ear. It doesn't feel like the intriguing feeling it did back when we were kids. It makes me squirm, and that pulls a laugh from him before he licks up my cheek.

"God, Simon, what the fuck?" I struggle against him, freeing my wrists, then wrap my arms around his legs and roll us over so I can pry free. Just as soon as I have him against the sofa, he hooks his legs around me, locking them together and forcing me down on top of him. "Oh, you do want to have fun," he says, a broad grin across his face. "I love lying on you, but if you want to lie on me, that's fine too."

"You're about to get a fist on you."

He rolls his eyes, but he loosens his legs and drops down onto the sofa. "You used to be more fun," he says as I push to my feet, but as soon as I think I've ended his game, he lurches off the sofa and tackles me to the floor. He's triggered my rage, and now we're wrestling. It's like when we were kids, roughhousing, getting out all our anger on each other. And feeling his crotch against me assures me that it excites him just as much as always.

Straddling his waist, I finally manage to get hold of his wrists and pin them against the rug. He huffs, still straining to get the upper hand.

"You're wasting your energy now," I tell him. "Unless your fingers are going to type me to death, I don't think you stand a chance against the muscles I've acquired over the years."

He doesn't give up easily. "Manual labor's definitely served you well. Is this what Jonas likes about you so much?"

Now he's using a different tack to win this fight. Fucker.

It makes me think about the disgusting lie he told Jonas. How he made me relive those painful memories. And how he clearly wants to torment me with them; otherwise, he never would have brought Jonas here.

"You and I both know that what you're doing to him is sick. And it's even more disgusting that you won't let him see his sister. What will you do if something terrible happens to her?"

He grins. That shouldn't make him fucking grin. "You care about him, don't you?" he asks, as though he didn't hear what I said. His gaze probes my expression.

"What?"

"I know you do. I see it in your fucking eyes when you look at him."

I can tell by how he's studying me that he doesn't just want to know if I care about him. He wants to know if I feel something more. And while a part of me wants to shout, *Yes!* another doesn't dare admit it, like if I voiced it, the universe would find some way to punish me for my feelings.

Even if the universe wouldn't punish me, I would never share that with Simon because he definitely would.

"I'm not getting into this with you."

He chuckles like some kind of demon, taunting me. Despite how we've grown apart, he can still see some things within me.

"You do. You think you can run off with him and have the life you always dreamed of with Kieran."

That blow catches me by surprise. That name. We both so rarely use that fucking name, and he seizes the moment, bucking me off him before rolling onto me and taking my wrists, pinning me as I had him.

He chuckles, his cocky expression revealing how proud he is of himself for his success.

I'm not fighting back, stunned in place by the memories that seize my mind.

"Don't ever forget that I know you, Ryan. Like no one else. Not even Jonas knows what darkness lies within you, and if he saw it, he'd hate you for it." He says that through his teeth, spit tailing behind his words and landing on my cheek.

I told Jonas my secrets, and he doesn't hate me.

He knows I didn't do anything wrong, but there's still doubt there—the kid who believed he was responsible for Kieran's and Father's deaths. And Simon's words draw those doubts out of the shadows. Those ones that will always lurk in my mind because even when I told Father the truth, he must not have believed me.

"Enjoy your little fantasy while it lasts, Ryan." A threat. But why? *What are you planning, you shit?*

Despite how much I hate him, part of me still feels I deserve whatever it is.

"Now," he adds. "I didn't mean to disturb your little read this afternoon, so I'll leave you to it. I have some shows to catch up on anyway."

He leans close, hovering near my cheek, and I'm waiting for another lick, something violating and demeaning, but he offers a peck. That's Simon, always knowing what I'm anticipating and then giving me the opposite just to fuck with my head. And just as I think he's about to lean back, he offers another before whispering, "Don't forget what I said. Enjoy it while it lasts."

That threat again. He knows I'm aware he's planning something but that I haven't figured out what just yet. And he must be loving rubbing that in.

Fucking bastard.

He finally gets off me and pushes to his feet, helping me back to mine before heading on his way, leaving my mind spinning even more than it was before he came to see me.

And I know damn well that was his plan.

Not gonna be getting any more reading in today.

28

JONAS

"She's still sleeping a lot," Aunt Amy says. "But she should be up in a few hours. I'll get her to call you back when she has the strength."

Charity's flu only took a week to pass, but the subsequent infection hasn't been as easy for her to kick. Given how much chemo she'd taken before it, the doctors aren't surprised by what a shock this has been for her system, but it's been three weeks since she first got sick. She should be doing better than this. She should be getting out of bed more, not less.

My aunt pans over to show my sister in the hospital bed.

Seeing her in that bed tears me apart.

"I should be there," I say as Aunt Amy turns the phone back so she's on-screen.

"If you could, you would be," she says, her gaze sinking, and I can tell it's because of the unspoken fear we both share that I'll spend the rest of my life regretting I wasn't there with her. If something does happen, no amount of money could ever make me whole again.

"He'll talk to Simon," Ryan finally speaks up. "Nothing we're working on here can't be picked up as soon as he gets back."

As our gazes meet, I know he's saying that for Simon's benefit, so I pick up the thread. "He was pretty adamant last time I asked."

"But this is much more serious now."

"Please ask him," Aunt Amy says. "Just see what he says. Even if you can only make it out for a day or two, don't you want to be here and see her in person…"

In case she passes.

It killed me that I never got to see my dad at the end, and I don't know what I would have done if I hadn't been there for Mom before she passed.

Fuck, I'm tearing up. I turn away because I don't want Aunt Amy to see me like this. She has enough to deal with without me being emotional too.

"I'll call you later, Aunt Amy, to let you know what he says."

"Oh, thank you, Jonas. I love you. Charity loves you too."

It's hard ending that call and knowing that Charity couldn't tell me that herself.

When I turn to Ryan, he's gazing off, clearly lost in thought. "Simon's not a monster. Tell him how bad it is. Tell him how much you love your sister. We know what it's like to lose family. Everything that needs to be finished here can be finished later."

What careful wording—a plea to Simon—to suggest that whatever torture he's planning to inflict on his brother can be finished just as easily another time. That a few days won't matter.

I just hope Simon's able to reason that himself.

And I hope for something else too. Something I know is even more impossible than Simon letting me leave. "I wish you could come with me," I whisper.

"Maybe…" he starts, like he allowed himself to consider it for just a moment, but then he closes his eyes and says, "I don't know if that will be a possibility."

Yes, even if I could persuade Simon to agree to a trip, there's no doubt in my mind hell will freeze over before he lets us both out of his sight.

He wraps his arms around me, holding me close. "Go talk to him. I'll be here when you get back."

I know he doesn't mean when I get back from talking to his brother, but from visiting my sister and aunt.

As I put my arms around him, I think how easy it would be to lift him up and carry him out of this house, take him with me. Why can't it just be Charity, my aunt, Ryan, and me? We could figure something out.

"Go," he whispers, and I pull away, pushing to my feet, when I feel his hand take mine.

I turn back, and he says, "Jonas." His warm gaze meets mine, and he says, "I love you."

He says it so effortlessly, like we've been a couple for years instead of months.

"I love you too," I say, cupping his face in my hands and taking a kiss.

It gives me much-needed relief from the anxiety coursing through me, and it provides the boost in confidence I need to stand up to his bastard of a brother.

There's power in knowing, regardless of what happens, that I have Ryan at my side.

We give ourselves this moment of peace with each other's

mouths before I pull away.

"Go find Simon."

I text Simon before heading off.

He confirms he'll meet me in his office, which takes me about ten minutes to walk to, giving me time to work myself up into a fit as I imagine the many ways he could tell me no. The sorts of arguments I could use to persuade him.

He has to understand. A few days is all I need. Although, I fear once I'm away from this place, next to my sister, I'll need so much more. The last time I mentioned it, Simon sounded like it was off the table, but this isn't just a flu.

When I find him in his office, he's grinning ear to ear; it's unsettling to my already wild emotional state.

"There you are," he says, leaning back in his chair.

Why is he smiling like that? He knows something. Was he listening in on our conversation? Is he reveling in knowing I'm ready to fucking grovel at his goddamn feet?

But I don't have too much pride for that.

"Close the door, please."

"I just got off the phone with my aunt."

"I know. I know."

He's not even trying to hide his eavesdropping. The thought that he was watching me in my vulnerable state, that he's deriving so much pleasure from my weakness, grates on me. Not that I need more reasons to fucking hate this guy.

He pushes to his feet and heads around the desk. "You need to go visit your sister. Ryan was right. We know what it's like to lose family."

He's so much more brazen than he's ever been, and it's fucking with my head.

"But regardless, you've done what I needed you to, and now I think we've come to the end."

"The end?"

"Today should be your last day."

"Are you firing me?" Is that why he's so smug?

He winces. "Firing you? No. Releasing you from your contract. We've reached the end of our work together. I'll continue supporting Charity through treatment, and I'll even throw in some money to help you with expenses so you can spend more time with her before moving on to your next job."

I'm so fucking thrown. This is not what I was expecting; not even a little.

"Once you finish the work today, that is."

Ah, a catch. Of course there's a fucking catch.

"Then you'll get this…nice severance package. Better than what I promised you to begin with because you've impressed me so much."

He's circling around something, but what? Has he found us out? Is that why he's getting rid of me? Or is it because he's bothered by how close Ryan and I have really become?

Still, I won't just leave Ryan. That's not an option.

"There's plenty of work to still be done," I object. "Ryan needs the extra hands. I can just finish out till September, like we agreed."

He snickers. "I would think you'd just thank me for not holding it against you how you betrayed my confidence. You think I couldn't make sense of what you and Ryan were doing on your little trips into the woods? Do I seem as naive as that?"

Ryan was right. Fuck.

"I don't know what you're talking about."

"So cute, you and your pathetic attempts at lies. I'm willing to forgive it all, compensate you as we agreed. But don't forget, I brought you here for a reason that doesn't have anything to do with yard work. So let's wrap this up, and you get to go back to your life. To your dear aunt and sister, and better off than you ever would have been if you hadn't taken me up on my offer."

I'm still trying to work out why he's doing this so suddenly. Is it because Ryan told me he loves me? Is that what this was all leading up to? For Ryan to fall in love and then to break his heart?

"Of course," he says, "I will need one thing before you leave. The final piece of my plan."

"Which is?"

He smiles, taking his sweet time because he's enjoying keeping his hand close to his chest. "Funny to think I'm actually nervous about saying it. Embarrassed, that is, so you don't mistake what I'm saying as interest."

"Will you just say what it is?" I've had enough of his mind-fucks.

"I like how you get right to the point." He walks back to his desk, spins to face me, and plants his palms against the edge, glancing me over. "I need you to *fuck me*, Jonas."

It's clear by how he emphasizes *fuck me* that he's trying to get a rise out of me.

And now my mind's spinning.

All this elaborate shit, and he just wants to fucking screw? What the hell?

"What? No."

"Don't be so quick, or you'll hurt my feelings," he says through his teeth. "It's not like I want to fuck you either, but this is what I need from you now. You'll fuck me right now. I have a camera up to record it, and then Ryan will stumble across it."

"Oh my God."

He said it all so calmly, as though we're talking about what I need to get from the store, which makes it even more unsettling.

"What's wrong? Don't lie and say you don't find me attractive because I obviously know better." He winks, and I know he's referring to the fact that they're identical twins, but what I feel is so beyond Ryan's flesh, and as I look at Simon, with that creepy smirk on his face, I know I could never feel for him the way I do for his brother.

"Simon…"

"What did you think you were getting all this money for? To chummy up with my brother? You knew it would lead to something. And I'm sure as you chatted it up with him, you've figured it wasn't just because he needed the fucking company. You should be thanking me. You signed up for this without any details. Aren't you glad I didn't ask you to murder him? You should be relieved, flattered even, that I just want your cock in me."

"Why are you doing this?"

"Because I have a bone to pick with him. And this will satisfy that. This will make us even, once and for all."

"Even?"

Does he really think if I fuck him, that will somehow get Ryan back for being raped by his brother?

"Come on," Simon says as he moves from the desk, approaching me. "I won't make it last longer than twenty minutes, even if you want it to." As he nears me, he reaches up to my face, grazing the back of his fingers against my cheek in a way that makes my skin crawl. "You must be good. Otherwise, he wouldn't have needed it so many goddamn times." He spits out his contempt, as if he's struggled watching all our fucks, but it's a punishment he's been inflicting upon himself by choice.

I pull away from his touch, and his gaze narrows. "Do you really want your sick sister to get booted from the treatment center she's at? While she's this fragile?"

"Don't you fucking dare," I growl.

His eyes widen. "I don't even have to enjoy it, Jonas. Just take all this anger." He grabs my fly, and as I pull away, he comes with me, unfastening it and yanking my pants down. "Just show me with your cock how much you hate me, and then you can have everything. I'll let you slap me. Fuck, if you want to punch me, I don't give a fuck. Show me your hate. Just make sure to come in me when you're finished."

This fucking psychopath. "My sister could be dying," I say as I fight to get my pants back up. "And if I don't do this, you're going to put her on the street?" I'm trying desperately to get away from his perverse desire, back to the issue at hand.

"If I were you and knew she could be dying, I'd get this over with quickly. You don't want to be responsible for her death." His gaze is fixed on me as he awaits my reply.

I'm tempted to take him up on his invitation to punch him, but I steady my temper. I have to consider this: potentially letting my sister die *or* doing this one quick, vile thing.

But how could Ryan ever look at me the same again if I did this? How could I ever look at myself? Part of me is pleading to do it for her, but another part refuses. I have morals. Principles. Standards.

"I don't know what there is to think about, Jonas. You had no issue jumping into bed with my brother for some money. First time we met, you would have fucked me stupid for hours if I'd offered you a fraction of what I did."

True. That would have been a small price to pay, but now that I know Ryan…know what a fucked-up thing that would be to do to the man who just told me he loves me, I can't bear the thought.

Simon moves closer, until his face is inches from mine. "Unlike him, I haven't had anyone in me in a very long time," he whispers. "Think of how tight I'll be."

As his gaze meets mine, I see the evil behind those eyes. The rage-filled brother ready to exact his revenge.

This is like a fucked-up moral dilemma.

I move toward him, and for the first time, he backs away. He bumps against the desk, and I lean in close, debating what to do.

"Yes, Jonas. You know you want this."

In an instant, my doubt evaporates. "Do what you have to do, Simon. I'm not helping you get revenge on Ryan. And I'm leaving. I'll figure out what's best for Charity on my own. Just know, if she dies, her blood is on your hands."

His eyes widen—a flash of rage. "Is this how it is? After everything I've done for you and your family?"

I'm not sure where my confidence is coming from. Maybe from knowing I have Ryan on my side, and that makes me feel invincible.

"More money?" Simon asks.

"If you offered all the money in the world, I wouldn't fuck you."

His jaw tightens, and despite how together he's acted, I can tell I nailed a decent blow to his ego.

"Thank you for the opportunity, Mr. Hawthorne. But no thanks. Consider this my resignation."

As I shut the door behind me, I gasp.

And suddenly, a crack in my confidence.

What have I done? Did I just kill Charity?

No. I'll figure this out. I'll do whatever has to be done. Move heaven and earth before I let Simon use me like that.

29

RYAN

Jonas throws my bedroom door open so fast, it almost pops off the hinges.

"What is it, Jonas?"

He's sweating, pale. His talk with Simon couldn't have gone well.

"He knows," he spits out, "and he just asked me to do the wildest shit. Told me to fuck him. To get back at you. He wants me to fuck him and then for you to watch a recording of it."

Despite how on edge Jonas's entrance made me, a calm sweeps over me.

Of fucking course that's what he wanted. This really was all about petty revenge.

"I obviously told him fuck no," he blurts out, which raises another concern.

"No? But what about Charity?"

His eyes widen, as if he's shocked by my response. Not that I want him to fuck my brother; I just don't want anything bad happening to his sister.

Jonas moves toward me, his breathing steadying as he takes my hands. "Ryan, I don't need him—his money, his connections, his power—if I have you. Come with me. We can figure this all out together. Help me find a place for her. Help me care for her."

"Come with you?"

So many things to process…

Simon's proposal.

His sister's health.

Leaving Hawthorne Heights.

"We can have a life, Ryan. I can help you get on your feet. I don't care how much credit I have to use to get Charity somewhere else. We'll figure it out, but together. Not with that psychopath."

As I look into those beautiful blue eyes, I struggle to think of a reason not to leave, except one: Hawthorne Heights has always been my home. It's where I've been sure I belonged.

Am I really considering giving up all I've ever known?

"You don't have to decide now. I wouldn't ask that. I'll go to Charity, and—"

"Yes, Jonas," I blurt out, almost without thinking. But as soon as I say the words, I know why I said them. Because the thought of him leaving me, traveling on his own to be with his sister… I can't bear it. Can't bear not being there for him when he needs me. Nor the thought that I might have to go back to the numb, empty life I had here before he arrived.

I told him I loved him, and I do. It might have been impulsive, but that instinct was right. And if he's willing to take this risk for his sister, I can take one to be with him.

"Really?"

"Yes. I want to go with you. But I want to talk to Simon about this fucked-up shit he just pulled. He owes me a fucking explanation."

Jonas doesn't disagree, and we take each other's hand, heading downstairs. We search for him in his office first, but he isn't there, so I start calling out his name as we head through the halls. Unsurprisingly, he's not responding to his texts either, so I suspect wherever he is, he's reveling in the fact that we're struggling to find him. Some intuition leads me to the library, and sure enough, as I burst through the dual doors, I find Simon seated on the nook sofa, my copy of *The Count of Monte Cristo* in hand.

"What the hell, Simon?" I spit out.

Our search gave me more than enough time to run through everything that's happened the past few months.

Bringing Jonas here to begin with.

This ultimate plan to wait until I told Jonas I loved him to make this perverse request.

How he plans to stop supporting Charity.

Fire sears through me.

I'm glad Jonas is at my side because Simon won't be able to deny or lie his way out of this one. Not with a witness here to contradict my backstabbing brother.

Simon doesn't seem fazed by my attitude, despite knowing I'm fuming. "Good evening, Ryan. You're right on time. I just got to my favorite part of the book." He closes it and sets it down beside him. "That's a lie. I wasn't even reading it. I just thought it would be more poetic for this moment." He wears a creepy-ass grin as he pushes to his feet. It seems that even though Jonas told him to take his offer and shove it, he thinks he's won.

"You're really gonna get Charity kicked out of the hospital?

Who the fuck *are* you that you'd do that to someone?"

Simon shrugs. "He has the fifteen thousand dollars I already gave him, which I'm not requesting back. Seems more than reasonable for the work he's done. And that stuff he's been doing with you, I think we can all chalk that up to good ole fun, don't you?"

"You piece of shit." I want to take a fucking swing at him, but I stop myself. He'd love nothing more than me stooping that low. Besides, I have a blow that'll be so much worse. "Jonas and I are leaving tonight, and I'm never coming back. That's the price you pay for your fucked-up brain. Whatever game you're playing, you can play it by yourself. Goodbye, brother." I spin around and start toward Jonas when I hear a series of claps behind me.

I should take Jonas's hand and leave, but I'm too curious not to turn around.

Simon's smug grin has not diminished even a little, as if he has something he knows will keep me here. I stay facing him, not saying a word, knowing him well enough to know he'll get to the fucking point if I stick around.

"Glorious. Just glorious. This worked out better than I imagined. Jonas, if I'd wanted you to fuck me, it would have happened the day you arrived. *This* is what I wanted."

"This?" I'm skeptical, but I know Simon, and it's clear Jonas and I were misled about the endgame.

"This declaration about leaving. Ryan, I know you better than anyone. I knew when I brought him here you wouldn't be able to resist him. Just like you couldn't resist Kieran. And I knew you would want this. Now, I didn't expect Jonas would want it back.

But this is perfect because now you're in love, which is what I was really waiting for this whole time. And you're ready to leave with someone who really cares, and I get to expose you for the liar and the monster you really are." This last part he says with a tense jaw, glaring at me, as if I were the villain and he the victim of an evil plot of my making.

"I think you've already demonstrated who the monster here is," Jonas says.

"He told you about Kieran, right? Told you you look like him, but did he tell you what he did to Kieran? What he *really* did to him?"

"Simon, stop this."

"He caught Kieran and me. And he made a plan to get back at us. A twisted plan. Fucking Kieran, then telling him he felt violated. Like it was against his will. Kieran was such a good man, he couldn't handle the thought. Couldn't bear that you would even think that about him. That's why he killed himself, and you know it. You and I both know the truth about what you did that day, and the lies you told Kieran and Father, and why you told them those lies. I, your fucking twin, who knows you better than anyone, know what you did."

Heat surges through me to the point where it feels like my cheeks are about to catch fire. "Simon, that's not true!"

"Yes, it is! You love him. Jonas, he sees you, and he's still hung up on this man he adored, yet he couldn't get over his perverse need for revenge, and he killed him because of it. Ryan, you can't change the past by being with this man. You can't undo what you did to Kieran and Father."

I stare into his eyes. Is this all part of the game, or does he really believe what he's saying right now? No, he can't.

"Don't do this, Simon. Don't lie about what happened."

"You're the liar! I'm supposed to believe Kieran raped you? But this man who came here, who's a dead ringer for him, you didn't have any problem getting fucked by him? No trauma? No torment?"

"It wasn't easy—"

"It was *too* easy."

"Jonas isn't Kieran! Jonas never did anything to hurt me."

"Kieran never did anything to hurt you either!" He raises his voice until it's booming through the library, echoing off the walls.

I'm lying beneath Kieran, wondering why he hasn't heard my cries to stop.

Am I not being loud enough?

Am I not using the right words?

"You know that's not true," I say.

"I don't know that!"

While he's expressing himself in shouts, my rage comes out as a whisper. Maybe because the truth doesn't need to cry out so desperately. "Yes. You. Do."

I don't want to say it, I *shouldn't* say it, but it seems the only way to get Simon to face a truth he can't seem to. "You were there, Simon."

As I turn toward the arm Kieran's restrained, I see Simon standing on the other side of the shed, watching.

"Simon! Simon!" I call out.

"No, it's just you, Ryan," Kieran says, which only confuses me.

And now there's a flash of terror in Simon's expression.

A knowing.

Because despite this elaborate performance, he knows.

He's always known the truth.

30

JONAS

"*You were there.*"

Goose bumps prick across my flesh.

Ryan didn't share that with me when he told me about what happened the day Kieran raped him. Not that he needed to. Fuck, with all the trauma he endured, it was painful enough just hearing the highlights, but this reveal makes Simon's fucked-up game all the more disturbing.

The way Simon freezes, his nostrils flaring, his eyes widening, his hands balling into fists, either he doesn't believe his brother, or he knows he's telling the truth. Knowing Ryan, I suspect it's the latter.

"Shut your dirty, lying mouth," Simon practically growls.

"You watched what he was doing to me. I screamed out your name."

Simon can't make eye contact with Ryan. A damning reaction.

"We were beside the shed, and he had my arm twisted behind my back. I turned and saw you watching. I called out your name, and Kieran just kept saying, 'It's okay. I don't love him. I love you.' And you heard us both."

"I said stop!" Simon calls out as he bashes a fist into his head.

Once. Twice. A third time.

Ryan rushes to him and seizes his wrist. "You heard me calling out to you for help. You had to have heard me telling him to stop."

Simon struggles against Ryan's grip. "No, that doesn't make sense. You wanted him."

"That day I didn't. And you know I didn't. Say that you remember. Say that you saw me. That you heard me."

"I don't know what you're talking about." Simon tears up as he looks behind him, as though he fears Ryan will see the truth in his expression, which I understand since I can see it from here.

"He didn't care about me, Simon. He just took what he thought he had a right to, and that was wrong."

Simon's face turns red, his head trembling as he finally forces himself to turn back to Ryan, thrashing about. "Those lies killed Kieran and Father, and now you're trying to kill me. You're killing me!"

In his fit, he manages to get his hands free and bashes them repeatedly against his face.

Ryan shouts for him to stop, but Simon persists, to the point where I approach, hoping to intervene before he seriously injures himself. When he finally stops laying blows against himself, I halt as he shouts at Ryan, "You were calling out his name. You were thrilled to have his cock inside you. You were begging for it harder."

"That's a lie!" Ryan says, his own fists balling up, like he's liable to pummel his brother if he keeps going.

"You were asking him if he loved you more than me," Simon says. "That's why he said that. Because you made him say it because you were so fucking jealous. You couldn't stand that he picked me. He. Picked. Me."

Simon gets in Ryan's face, his defense shifting back to offense. "When I came upon you at the shed, I saw you looking at me, watching me with a fucking smile on your face because you were so happy to have your revenge. You were practically cackling, you were so happy with your win." Now Simon's looking Ryan in the eyes, spit flying from his mouth as he makes his accusation. "You wanted him!"

"I was screaming for help! Why are you saying this bullshit?"

Simon slaps himself. Again. And again.

"Fuck, Simon. What is wrong with you?"

"Why are you hurting me? Can't you see you're hurting me?"

Another slap, and Ryan tries to intercede, but Simon's slaps soon become a fit as he hits his hands against his face repeatedly until Ryan finally manages to gain control of his wrists again. "You don't care who you hurt in this family!" Simon lunges at Ryan, tackling him to the floor. I rush to them, forcing Simon back to his feet. I try to restrain him, but he gets an arm free and reaches for the desk, and the next thing I know, there's a sharp sting in my arm and I release him. As he pulls away, I see fresh blood along my forearm.

"Shit," I say, and when I look up, Simon's heading behind the desk, knife in hand—no, not a knife. It's a letter opener that looks more like a fucking fillet knife than it has any right to.

Simon's now stuck in a corner, his gaze shifting about like he's an animal searching for a way out.

"Jonas." Ryan rushes to me and assesses my wound. "Simon,

put that down. Haven't you caused enough damage already?"

"Oh, you have the right to kill him, but I'm attacked by your boyfriend and a little cut is too far?"

"Just put that down," I say, which only works him up more.

"Are you so in love that you can't see the lies he's spewing? You can't see that he's putting on this whole act for you because he can't bear to think about what he did? Can't you see who the monster is between us?"

I don't think anyone walking into this scene would struggle to work that out.

Blood spews from my arm, surprisingly fast since the cut doesn't seem very deep. Ryan pulls off his shirt and wraps it around my arm.

"Tell him who you really are," Simon pleads with Ryan. "Tell him! It's not fair that he thinks he's about to run off with some kind of saint. Say it to free your own conscience of your sins!"

"Simon, we need to get the first aid kit. This conversation is over."

"It'll never be over, not until you face the truth." Simon tightens his jaw, and his eyes go wide before he slashes into his arm with the letter opener.

"Fuck!" I call out as he draws blood.

"Tell. Him. The. Truth."

"Simon, stop!" Ryan calls out, but Simon strikes his arm again and again. Ryan approaches him, and I grab him by the arm, hoping to give him a moment to consider what he's moving toward and the danger it puts him in.

"Stop cutting yourself!" Ryan pleads.

"You're the one hurting me. Why do you keep hurting me?" Simon displays the self-inflicted wounds on his arm. "Every time you utter those lies. Every time you trample on his memory. Can't you end it, after all the harm you already caused? Just tell Jonas the truth." His face twists up, tears pushing from his eyes as he makes a final plea with Ryan.

"You know the truth, Simon. He had my arm behind my back. He twisted it to keep me in place. And while I begged him to stop, you stood beside that shed and did nothing to help me. Don't blame me because the truth is too excruciating to face!"

Simon cries out, sticking the blade into his shoulder and digging it in.

"Simon! Enough!"

Simon pulls the blade from his shoulder, and blood soaks the fabric of his shirt.

"Set that down," Ryan says as he approaches.

"Ryan, don't go any closer," I warn.

"Just put the letter opener on the desk, and I'll get some bandages. We don't have to talk about this right now. It's too much for you."

"Tell him about when you decided to go to Father and tarnish Kieran's good name. Father didn't believe you either. He saw through you, just like I did."

As defensive as Ryan's been, I see the shift in his expression as he absorbs that blow, and Simon must realize how effective it was since he presses on, "Your own father, who loved you more than anyone in the world, knew better."

"Father was wrong not to believe me," Ryan says, though I can tell it's a strain for him to get out.

Simon lurches forward, like he's about to attack Ryan, but then he thrashes about, banging the side of his hand against his head once again, which doesn't seem as horrifying as when he was slicing into his own flesh.

"You fucking liar! You goddamn liar!" he calls out as he flees the library.

He continues shouting as he hurries through the halls, his screams echoing through the house until they're so far away, they sound like the ghosts of this place, shrieking from the beyond.

Ryan rushes to me and pulls back the makeshift bandage to assess my wound.

Now that the excitement is over, I feel the sting of Simon's injury.

"I'm so sorry," Ryan says.

"You're not the one who fucking stabbed me."

"This is a lot of blood."

"It's not deep. That's not what I'm worried about. Your brother's having a mental breakdown."

"Did you think I missed that memo?" His words are hostile, like the ones he assaulted Simon with, but then he takes a breath. "I'm so sorry, Jonas. That was…"

"Don't be sorry. That was beyond anything I've ever seen. I can't imagine what it was like seeing your brother react that way."

He rewraps the shirt around my wound. Seeing him in this nurturing state is just another reason why it's so impossible for me to fathom how Simon has this warped perception of his own twin. How is his perception of Ryan so far off the mark? Although, from their fight, it's apparent there are things torturing Simon's mind that are beyond my understanding.

"We need to find you some antiseptic and bandages."

"Ryan, you know I believe you, right?" I say, hoping to pull his attention back to what's more important now than a shallow wound.

"I know you do, and I know he believes me too." He holds my arm in place. "It's a conversation we should have had a long time ago, but as much as I said he couldn't bear the truth, I couldn't either. Especially after Father died, it was just…"

"You don't have to explain anything to me." I place my hand against his cheek, stroking my thumb across his flesh. "I'm just sorry he made you relive that."

He takes a breath, as though summoning strength. Then nods. "I'll be all right, but right now, let's take care of you. Then can we get out of here? Pack and get an Uber. I have enough money tucked away that I can get us a motel for the night. We can't stay here."

"After what I just saw, you were staying in this house over my dead body."

He smirks before his expression turns serious again. "Let's not use expressions like *over my dead body* tonight."

"That sounds like a reasonable request," I say.

"Since he was self-harming, I think I need to call the police. Maybe they can get someone out here to do a psych evaluation."

I can see how much the thought weighs on him, so I take him into my arms for a hug. "How about we call while you're patching me up? We can do it together. Because you're not on your own."

His face pushes against my cheek, and I feel a tear against my skin.

No, Ryan isn't alone in this, and if I have any say in it, he won't ever be alone again.

31

SIMON

I'LL SHOW HIM what a fucking liar Ryan is.

Jonas has to see. Has to know what I've known all this time.

Using my phone light to guide me, I sprint through the yard, heading for the woods.

Heart racing. Breathing frantic. Mind twisted up from the vile distortions Ryan attacked me with.

"You were there."

I was! And that's why I know the truth better than anyone else.

I thought Ryan would cave when I confronted him with the truth. But his delusion is so deeply rooted, it'll take more than a fight to end this.

Even though our confrontation didn't go as I'd hoped, everything else has gone according to plan. Just as I suspected, Jonas believed I wanted him to fuck me. Ryan's done a good job of pitting him against me, convincing him I'm the villain. Ha! When he finds out the truth, he'll know how he was misled, deceived, just as Kieran and Father were deceived. Just as I was all those years before I discovered the rot at his core.

How effortlessly he surrendered to my plan. How easy it was to fall for Jonas. To the point that now he's willing to leave the only life he's ever known so he can enjoy this perverse fantasy, pretending his dark soul didn't corrode this family from the inside out.

No, you won't get away with this, Ryan!

I won't let you disparage Kieran's name.

"Simon, do you like me?"

It's an odd question, since Kieran and I have just been skipping rocks across the creek at the bottom of the drop-off. Even odder when I feel his hand on my thigh, rubbing. It's a strange feeling, not like it is with Ryan and me. There's something unsettling about it, so I pull away.

"You don't like me?" Kieran asks.

His chin trembles, his eyes water, and I'm immediately horrified at the thought that I've done something to hurt him. He slaps his hand against his head.

Once.

Twice.

"Stop!" I beg. "What are you doing?"

"You don't like me. I knew it."

"Of course I do. You're my brother. I love *you, Kieran." I spit the words out quickly so he doesn't have to doubt.*

As he places his hand back on my thigh, tension rises within me.

"I love you too, Simon. I want to show you that I love you."

Why is he looking at me like this?

Unlike Ryan, I didn't love Kieran right away. It took me time to share his feelings, but I eventually came to love him as much as he loved me.

He pushes up against me, pinning me to a bookcase in the library before moving in for a kiss.

"Kieran." I try to push him away.

"I need you, Simon. I love you."

"I love you too, but don't—"

He doesn't hear my request. This is how he gets sometimes when his desire's too much for me. When he can't stop himself from tugging at my clothes and pressing his lips against mine.

"Don't deny me, Simon. I need you right now."

"I don't want to."

"Why are you hurting me like this? Not touching you is so painful."

Guilt rises within me.

I don't want to hurt him. I love him.

Fuck, my fight with Ryan has memories sparking, live wires tripping in places I'd long pushed back. It's more than I can manage as they battle it out for attention.

"Please, Kieran, just slow down."

He can't, though…

He never can.

I don't deny my relationship with Kieran was complex, like any brothers' relationships. There were times when I hated him. Times when I loved him. Times when we laughed. Times when he made me cry. But he couldn't make me cry more than the day I came upon the shed, seeing him on top of Ryan.

"Simon! Simon, help!"

I'm frozen. Can't move. Can't look away. Can't even think.

Shut up! Stop it! Stop it!

Ryan told me, between our sheets, how much he wanted Kieran. I lived in guilt and shame, knowing Kieran wanted me more.

I hated Kieran sometimes for how badly he wanted me.

I race along the path in the woods, filled with as much determination as when I hired that company to seek out a look-alike. When I come to the spot, I detour off the path, and it's only a few more minutes before I come to the wall of briars.

A new set of memories pushes forward.

The day after Ryan and Kieran made love.

I keep a good distance behind Kieran. I don't want him to know I'm following him.

Is he going to tell Ryan he loves him? Why does he want him now and not me?

After everything we've been through. After how much I've helped keep him from being in pain.

We finally come to Ryan's hiding spot, in the thick of those wicked briars that used to hurt me so much as a kid.

"Ryan, please, I need to talk to you!" Kieran sounds so mad, it frightens me.

"Go away!" Ryan's voice doesn't even seem to be coming from beyond the briars, but as though the briars themselves are shouting at Kieran.

"Please. Just talk to me. I'm sorry. I didn't mean to hurt you."

No, you didn't hurt him! He loves you!

"I told you to stop! I kept telling you to stop, and you never did! You know what you did!"

"Please, just don't tell Father. He'll be so mad. He might even make me leave. I don't have anywhere else to go."

As Kieran cries, I want to rush to help him, but I remain still, watching.

"Leave me alone! I never want to talk to you again!"

"Please, Ryan! I love you!"

"You wouldn't have done that if you loved me. You would have listened to me. You would have cared."

"Ryan, get over here!" Kieran's rage returns, and I'm trembling because it reminds me of other times when I've made him angry. Like those times when I would try to deny him, before I realized how much he loved me.

"There's a word for what you did to me," Ryan calls out.

Oh, why did he have to say that?

When I finally reach the briar barrier, I search for the entrance. If only I'd followed Ryan out here more. If only he hadn't done such an exquisite job of keeping this secret from me.

I search around desperately for the path, in vain, and I don't have the fucking time to find it. If I don't get proof, he and Jonas will leave, and I'll never have another chance.

I kick at the briars and use the letter opener like a machete, slicing around me to break through. I'm mad with power as I successfully carve into the bushes, but not without pain as thorns scrape against my arms and dig through my jeans.

Fuck, they burn like my other wounds, though I embrace them because I hope the pain will keep my mind from reliving the memories that won't leave me alone.

But being among these briars makes that impossible.

Ryan's words send Kieran to his knees, and he howls and covers his ears, but it's too late. He can't unhear that vicious accusation.

The memory distracts me too much, and as I lose track of my work, my wrist gets caught in a tight collection of twisted-up briars.

"Fuck!" I call out as I struggle to free myself, but it stings so sharply that I drop the letter opener.

Using my phone with my other hand, I spot it through a series of stems. Weaving my hand through, I grab at the knife but miss, losing my balance in the process and shifting my foot in just the right place to tighten the stems around my wrist. I curse out as both wrists now grapple with their restraints.

I scream, unleashing the pain, not just from the briars, but what's been chasing me through these woods.

Pressed up against me, Kieran tries to kiss my neck. I pull away, but he snatches my arm. "No, Kieran. Not now. Maybe later," I beg, but he's too hungry for me.

This memory collides with the one of Ryan pinned to the ground.

"Simon, help!"

I'm frozen.

What's happening?

Why is this happening?

My struggle with my mind and the restraints feels insurmountable, and they coalesce in a fit as I thrash about, my recklessness only causing me more agony, thorns tearing into flesh as I throw my head back and scream into the night.

I can't die like this. I can't die until I've shown Jonas.

And yet, if these briars don't tear me apart, I fear my memories might finish the job.

32

RYAN

"I just hope, wherever he is, he's not cutting himself anymore." I place a stack of folded tees into my suitcase.

Jonas hooks his arm around me, nestling his face against my cheek.

My bedroom's dimly lit, illuminated with my phone light on my nightstand and the lantern on the fireplace mantel.

After Simon fled the library, the power cut off, and we managed with our phones while Jonas contacted the police and I tended to his injury, disinfecting the wound before wrapping it with some gauze from the first aid kit. Then we searched for the cause of the outage, discovering that the cables at the power box had been severed, which confirmed our suspicion that this was Simon's handiwork. I figure he was hoping to make it difficult for us to leave. Then Nell and Kace helped us search the house for my brother for about twenty minutes before the cops arrived. And after describing Simon's erratic and harmful behavior—while leaving out the more personal details that came up during the fight—the officers agreed to search the premises, requesting that we text them if he returned.

Despite all the terrible things he said, I'm still worried about him. In all the years we've been together, I've never seen Simon snap like that. Never watched him slice into himself. Never heard him shout as he did while running through the halls.

"He needs to dress those cuts," I say, not for the first time since the outburst; although, despite my concern about his physical wounds, I'm just as concerned about the psychological ones.

As Jonas tugs me close, I lean into his hold.

"Was that the first time you two talked about that?"

With all we've had to navigate, there hasn't been much time to chat about what came up in the library. Or maybe I've been repressing.

"I assumed neither of us wanted to discuss it. And though I hated him for not helping me with Kieran, he was the only one I had left. I thought he felt guilty for not stepping in. I never would have guessed he held that wild perspective. I'm having a hard time understanding how much of it he believes and how much is some sick lie to protect himself from acknowledging who our brother really was."

Jonas kisses my forehead.

There's something nice about having him here, just listening. Being present for me in a way no one else has ever been.

"I'm almost done," I say. "Then we can get to your stuff, and book the motel, and you should call and check in about Charity. And—"

"How about I go ahead and knock some of these things out now while you finish packing?"

I appreciate that Jonas has headed off my steadily intensifying anxiety. "That's not a bad idea. Why don't you pack too?"

He cringes. "Ryan, if you think I'm leaving you alone after what I just witnessed, you are even more far gone than your brother."

For the first time since that epic meltdown, I laugh. "I'll be fine. This isn't a horror movie, Jonas. He's my brother. And you saw him; he's more interested in hurting himself than anyone else."

"I wasn't worried about you. I'm scared of the dark." He hunches beside me and leans close, kissing my neck.

His playfulness and his warm mouth are welcome distractions from everything that happened. I turn to him and kiss him a few more times. "It'll be fine."

"I'm staying right here. I'll go ahead and call the motel and Charity, and while I'm doing that, you wrap this up. Then we head over there together."

"I like the sound of that."

As I gaze into his eyes, they disarm me, enough that when I hear a knock at the door, I'm startled, and we both jump together.

The cops? No. How the hell would they know what room we're in?

The knock comes again.

"Ryan?" With the door between us, it sounds like a whisper, in a higher register than Simon usually speaks. More like him when he was seven or eight.

Neither Jonas nor I speak before the gentle knock comes again. "Ryan, it's me, open up!"

I thought I'd been overly cautious to lock my door while packing, but given the weapon he left with and how he cut the lights, I figured better safe than sorry.

"What do we do?" I whisper to Jonas.

"I'll text that cop."

As he keys away on his phone, Simon knocks again. It's the faintest of knocks, as though he's barely trying to make a sound, and there's something unsettling about it. Eerie. "Come on, Ryan. Let me in!"

I approach the door, but Jonas says, "Ryan, just stay back."

"I've got this." When I reach the door, I ask, "Simon, are you okay?"

The doorknob rattles, startling me as it shakes furiously with the door. Then it comes to an abrupt halt.

"Come on, Ryan. I have something to show you," he says in a suspiciously gentle voice, as though trying to lull me into a false sense of security.

"Why do you sound like that, Simon? What's wrong?"

He giggles—fucking giggles. What is going on?

There's a loud *thud*, followed by another, rattling the entire door, and I step back as the knob continues trembling. "I said let me in!" Simon shouts from the other side. "Let. Me. In." After each word, there's a *bang* like he's thrusting himself against the door, and considering how old these doors are, I'm not surprised when the frame snaps and it swings open.

I jump back so it doesn't hit me, and just as soon, there's a tight grip on my arm, and Jonas pulls me back to him.

Simon stumbles in, stepping into the soft room light.

"Oh my God," Jonas says.

Simon is paler than I've ever seen him. There's a patch of blood where he stabbed himself in the shoulder, and more blood around the wounds on his arm, but now there are even more punctures and dozens of deep, crimson scratches across his face and arms, as though he's spent this time slicing into his flesh. Even his jeans are ripped to reveal lengthy gashes. With dirt just as spread out across his body, particularly focused on the knees of his jeans, he looks like he crawled out of his own grave.

Wide-eyed, he searches around the room before his gaze zeroes in on me. He grins in a way that disturbs me, makes me think it would have really been a shit idea had Jonas and I split up.

Even more concerning, he has his hand behind his back as he starts toward us.

The letter opener?

"Stay where you are," Jonas warns him.

"I've just come to show you something."

I hold up my hands. "Simon, you can show us whatever it is from there."

"I think Jonas will find it very interesting, given the conversation we just had."

"Why do you look like this?" I ask, far more concerned about his appearance than anything else. "Did you cut yourself more?"

"Oh, these little things? No, no. I've been in the woods. Had to dig this up. Went to your little hiding spot in the briars. We act like we're so distant now, but how did I know that's where it'd be? There's still something tethering us together, like there'll always be."

Tension rises within me.

I have a horrible suspicion what he dug up.

No, he didn't. He wouldn't.

"I saw you head into the woods with some of them after Father killed himself," Simon says. "You didn't return with them that day. I figured you were burying the only truth that remained, and I was right. But now I have it. You marked it like you wanted it to be found—a stick cross, marking it like a grave."

"Simon, you need professional help," Jonas says. "Please let us help you."

"You're right. I think after all Ryan has put me through, I do need help. And you want to know why?"

I'm waiting for him to reveal what's in his hand—God, I already know, and I wish I didn't.

"*Some nights, I want to creep into his room,*" Simon recites, like he put the piece to memory, "*and while he's sleeping, crawl under his sheets and only let him know I'm there when he feels my mouth against his hard cock.*"

My face flushes with heat.

"What are you talking about?" Jonas asks.

"Ask your boyfriend. They're his words," Simon says as he finally reveals a black journal, raising it before him. His thumb is tucked in to keep it open to a specific page, which he begins reading from. "How about... *I dream we're in the woods, wrestling because he wants to show me how strong he is. He pins me to the ground. Before I know it, his lips are against my neck and he's tearing at my clothes. He needs me. He wants me. His wet kisses don't let up—*"

"Stop this!" I shout, his words a cruel attack on my soul.

"*I want him inside me. I want him making me call his name. I want his body pressed up against mine, thrusting. I want him to fuck me till I cry.*"

Tears rush to my eyes. "Why are you doing this?"

"*Kieran. My Kieran. My perfect, beautiful Kieran.*"

Simon looks up from my journal, and I start toward him. "Give that back!"

"This was one of the innocent bits," Simon tells Jonas. "You should read the other vile shit that's in here, the sort of stuff he should be ashamed to have even imagined."

"You didn't have a right to read that!"

"I have a right to expose you! I already read all this when we were kids. You think your twin wouldn't peer into your private journal? It was my right to see this as much as it was to know my own thoughts. I knew how you really felt. Now you see, Jonas. This was what this pervert thought about. It's all there. His constant, unwavering obsession with his brother. The vile things you made Kieran do in these fantasies, but then you dare accuse him of violating you. And the lie you told Father. He didn't believe you either."

The tears escape my eyes.

He's right.

"Because I showed him this, just like I'm showing Jonas," Simon goes on.

In an instant, my grief shifts to something dark. "You what?"

"I followed you to Father's office. Heard you tell him that lie about what Kieran did that day, and I knew I had to disprove it. To not let you taint his memory. So I took this to Father to show him your deception. Told him of your obsession with Kieran. Told him what I saw the two of you doing like animals at the shed. Told him what a liar you were and read him these filthy pages. I exposed you."

"Simon," Jonas says, "just because he fantasized about those things doesn't mean he wanted them when Kieran did that."

Simon's jaw drops. "You're still defending him? After what you just heard?"

But my grief has transformed. Now I'm fucking seething. I can barely think straight.

All these fucking years he's kept this from me. All these fucking years of self-loathing and blaming myself, thinking if I'd just said more or the right thing, only to find out this shit.

"All this time I've blamed myself for Father's death," I say, my fury so quiet.

"You *are* to blame!"

"No, I'm not. You are. For taking this to him, then lying about what you saw that day. You had Father believe in his last moments on this earth that I was a liar and deceived him about why Kieran killed himself."

"Jonas, you have to read this." He heads toward us, but Jonas throws his hand up, promptly rejecting it. "You have to see what a monster he is." He winces, his forehead creasing. "Or are you as bad as he is? Is that it?"

"Simon, I did want Kieran. I wanted him even more than what's in that journal. But the day that happened, I didn't. Don't you get that that's all that matters? And when he did that to me, I realized he wasn't the man I believed him to be; that the man in that journal didn't exist. Because the man I wrote about would have never done that to me. I buried it because I was burying the memory of the man I created in my own mind."

Simon bares his teeth like an animal as he charges me. "Stop it with your lies!" He strikes me in the face with the journal and tackles me to the bed. In my periphery, I see Jonas heading over to intervene, but our struggle ends with me on top of Simon, pinning his wrists to the mattress. He struggles in vain against my hold before screaming out, "Someone has to stop you! Someone has to fucking stop you! He loved me. He loved us."

"No, he didn't," I say as a tear escapes my eyes and falls onto his cheek.

There's a flash of something in his eyes. It's the first time I've seen this vulnerability, this pain in him, as though he's finally allowing himself to consider an unbearable reality. But then his face twists up, and he fights violently, thrusting his hips in an effort to buck me off him, but I'm too strong. And too fucking pissed.

"I'm glad you shared this with me, Simon. All these years I believed I was responsible for Father's death, but now I know that's not true. And I know he did believe me, and that's why you did this. That's why you had to turn him against me. And in doing so, *you* killed him."

His chin quivers, his cheeks tremble. "No, I didn't. No…no…"

"You don't have to take responsibility for what Father did, but you have to take responsibility for what *you* did."

He erupts into a fit of tears, giving up his struggle against me. "Why won't you stop lying?"

It's not the demand of before, but a plea.

I release him and slide off the bed, and he flies into a fit, crying out and bashing his fists against the mattress as he flails about.

It's the tantrum of a child.

I let him have this as I retrieve my phone off the nightstand and take my journal from where it landed on the foot of the bed.

Jonas rests his hand on my shoulder, and I turn to him. Without words, I know that despite Simon's attempt to turn him against me, just like he did with Father all those years ago, it didn't work. And that despite the shame I carried about these pages for so long, he understands the truth. By the time I put my journal in the suitcase and zip it up, Simon finally wears himself down, now a sobbing mess on my sheets.

"Let's go get your things," I tell Jonas. "Anything I haven't packed already can be replaced."

Taking my suitcase in one hand and Jonas's hand in the other, we start for the door.

"Ryan, you can't leave me here!" Simon calls out. "You have to pay for what you did!"

As we reach the door, I stop and turn to him.

My brother's still on his back, breathing heavily like all the events of tonight have finally caught up with him.

"Earlier today when I told Jonas I'd leave with him, I felt guilty. Like I needed to remain a ghost, suffering in this house to atone for my sins. But now that I know the truth, I realize this guilt hasn't been mine to carry. I'm done haunting this house with you, so you're going to have to haunt it alone now, Simon."

Despite my anger, there's sadness too. Just like when Kieran died, though I hated him, I couldn't escape the mental and emotional chains binding us. And it's so much stronger with Simon.

"Ryan, no," he says, all that fury a whimper now.

I close the door.

Not just to this room, but to this part of my life.

33

JONAS

I FOLLOW RYAN into our motel room. Compared to the bedrooms at Hawthorne Heights, it's a closet, struggling to accommodate twin-size beds and a media console. Cramped as it is, there's relief in knowing we're away from that place, somewhere Simon can't see.

Ryan drops his suitcase and collapses onto the bed, facing the window.

It's been a night.

Sitting beside him, I massage his side. I want to ask him how he's feeling, but on top of everything he's been through—Simon's fits and that reveal about their father—I can't imagine what it must be like to walk away from the only life he's ever known.

I don't speak; I let him work through all this at his own pace.

"You think they'll find him?" he finally asks.

Shortly after Simon confronted us in Ryan's bedroom, the cops returned to the house, but when they went to retrieve Simon, he was already gone. They assured us they would continue searching for him, which was all we needed to know before we called an Uber and left.

"I hope they do," I reply.

"After everything he's done, I'm still worried about him. He had all those injuries. He needs to treat them."

"Hopefully the cops will find him, but if they don't, I'm sure he'll take care of them, and if they get infected, he could hire nurses to watch over him twenty-four seven."

He nods. "I feel guilty for leaving like that, but I couldn't be there another minute."

"You needed to get out of that place," I assure him. "Even if we're just a few miles away and still in town. And tomorrow we'll be in New York, hundreds of miles away."

"That sounds nice. Been so long since I've been away. I spent so much time at Hawthorne Heights, only traveling here for supplies occasionally, I really was starting to wonder if I was just a ghost. Like maybe if I tried to pass the city lines, I wouldn't be able to."

"I'm eager to prove you wrong about that tomorrow."

Ryan smirks—the first time I've seen him smirk since he closed the door to his bedroom. Just as quickly, his expression turns serious again. "With all the time I spent there, the memories it holds, I doubt I can ever truly leave. That probably doesn't make any sense, but…"

"It does." Just from the shit in my own life, I know there are things you can never really escape.

His gaze meets mine. "Part of me is mad at Father for not asking me about what Simon told him, but when I told him what Kieran had done, I obviously didn't mention I'd been lusting after him for years, so I'm sure when Simon showed him my journal, that must've confused him. If I'd mentioned that, maybe none of this would have happened. I just didn't want to admit I'd ever felt anything for the guy who did that to me."

"You shouldn't have had to explain more than you did. And Simon shouldn't have shown him your private journal, nor lied about what happened to you."

"If he'd talked to me right after, maybe all this could've been prevented. He was my brother. We used to talk about everything. I would have thought that if he didn't understand, he would have confronted me then."

"Based on the things he said, I think he might have been afraid of the truth."

His eyes get this far-off look in them. "When I had him pinned to the bed, for a moment I thought I saw something in him—something in his eyes. Like the wall he'd put up to keep me out finally came down. And I felt a remnant of that connection we had. I could see all this anger, and I've always assumed it was at me, but I saw anger at himself…and I think at Kieran too. I wonder if the truth caused him so much pain because there was something I didn't know about their relationship. With how protective he always was of Kieran, I used to believe they must've been in love, but now I worry something else was happening between them."

"What do you mean?"

"I wonder if Kieran did something that fucked Simon up, and he just responded in a different way than me." His eyes well with tears. "I'll never know the truth, but it makes me wish there was a way we could have communicated, rather than both of us suffering in our own mental prisons all these years."

I rest my hand on his cheek. "Ryan, you've been through so much. And from what I saw, Simon has serious mental health issues. But some things are too big for people to sort out on their own. I think you might need a therapist for that."

He chuckles. "Yeah. I think we've both known that for a long time, but I always felt like I had to carry this with me. I don't feel that way tonight."

"I'm glad to hear it." I lean down and offer a kiss, which he eagerly embraces.

As I pull away, he says, "You should call your aunt. Give her a heads-up that we'll be there tomorrow and about what Simon might do."

"They're not gonna just dump Charity on the side of the road. Worst case, he'll refuse to pay the bill, and I'll use that money he gave me to keep her in while we sort out what to do next, once Charity recovers from her infection."

I let Ryan sit with his thoughts as I phone my aunt. She tells me Charity's been able to get up and move a bit more, but she's still sleeping most of the day. I let her know we might need a new plan, which piques her curiosity. "Why? What's going on?"

"I'll explain everything tomorrow. Our flight is at six a.m., so we'll be there bright and early."

"I'm pleased to hear that. I'm looking forward to seeing you. And I'm sure having you here in person will make all the difference to Charity."

"I hope so."

We chat a bit more before I tell her good night, and I rejoin Ryan on one of the twin-size beds, spooning him, my arm hooked around his chest. He cradles my arm as I kiss his nape. Then he rolls toward me, cupping my face with his hands and offering another kiss that starts off tender before he firms it.

I feel his desire, his need for me to be here for him right now.

"Someone's feeling frisky," I say.

"Thank you." He leans back.

"I told you already. I didn't mind getting the Uber. You can get it tomorrow to the airport."

He glares at me. "You know that's not what I mean. Thank you for coming to Hawthorne Heights. Thank you for fucking me for money. Thank you for not fucking my brother when he offered you even more. Thank you for listening and giving a fuck." He studies my face. "Thank you for falling in love with me."

"Thank *you* for falling in love with *me*," I say, moving close and stealing a kiss.

The heat between us intensifies before Ryan says, "I need you now, Jonas. Fuck tonight out of my head. Fuck me until I'm so lost in us that I forget about all the other bullshit."

I obey, and we're a clumsy mess of tearing off clothes, pulling back the comforter, and scrambling for lube from my bag until we wind up back in bed together. Even with the interruption, we've developed a rhythm we effortlessly fall back into. Soon I'm inside him, enjoying the sensation of his tight hole against my shaft as we work each other up in a frenzy.

As we're fucking, it becomes apparent the AC isn't on since I'm soaking him with my sweat, which he doesn't seem to mind. Maybe because the oppressive heat only helps distract us even more from the horrors that unfolded tonight.

As Ryan calls out my name, I kiss across his face, licking his salty flesh, the tension in me relaxing as my body seems to accept what I already know—that we're free. Truly free.

"I'm so close," he whispers into my ear, and I lean back on my knees, jerking his cock as he writhes beneath me. I want to give him this release, this escape from his pain.

"Harder. Fuck me harder," he begs, and as I obey, the shitty metal headboard rattles against the wall. Ryan reaches back and grabs hold of the metal rods along it, clinging tight as his cock pulses in my grip and he blows across his abs.

It's a sight that's too much for me, and soon I'm a mess of thrusts and shivering as I release inside him. His ass clenches around my shaft, like it doesn't want to let me out. Like he's clinging to this moment, not wanting either of us to return to reality.

This is what so many of our fucks have been like since we met. A precious escape from a cruel world and equally cruel pasts.

As his tight hole drains my cock, it's like he's draining every last bit of stress from my body.

I collapse on top of him, swapping tongue-filled kisses. By now, the room feels like a goddamn sauna, our sweat-soaked bodies clinging, our body heat making the July night that much hotter.

I need to turn on the fucking AC, but as I gaze into his eyes, a smile tugs across his lips, and I don't want to leave this moment.

I just want to keep staring at this man who's totally enchanted me. A man I'm starting to realize I might want to spend the rest of my goddamn life with.

EPILOGUE
RYAN

Five months later

WITH A PRESENT cradled under each arm, I head downstairs and tuck the presents under the tree with all the others. The sound of "I'll Be Home for Christmas" comes from the kitchen, muddled by Amy's and Jonas's chatter.

I'm about to head in and join them, but I stop and admire the tree.

The ornaments and trim glittering among strings of white lights.

Our little star topper.

It reminds me of Christmases as a kid, when Father would buy a large tree for the front bay window. The servants decorated it, not us, but it was still beautiful, and we still enjoyed lovely nights by it as a family. After Father passed, we still put up a big tree and decorated it, but it was never the same, a shadow of the past.

Standing before this little white pine Jonas and I grabbed from the tree farm, there's a warmth in my chest I haven't felt in years. It's deeper than even when I was a child because this tree means so much more to me—it's a symbol of the life Jonas and I have begun together.

"Ryan."

I turn to see my boyfriend approaching in a sweater with a pattern of reindeer running across the chest. "Will you check the pecan pie? I'm worried I'll take it out too soon or leave it in too long."

I chuckle. "Of course."

I learned this Thanksgiving that he struggles with getting a pecan pie just right; although, with Nell having cooked most of our meals, I'm only now discovering this untapped skill I apparently possess.

I head into the kitchen and check on the pie. We don't have much time before our guests arrive—a few friends we've made over the course of our brief relationship. Despite working full-time and helping Jonas navigate Charity's care, it's been nice having time for friends. Hell, even just to have any. Although, admittedly, it's something I'm still trying to navigate. Learning how to talk casually with people. How to make light conversation. How to keep from shutting down when they ask about my past. Fortunately, the friends we've made don't seem to mind that I'm a little reserved.

After Amy starts the gravy, there's a knock at the door. I walk through the front hall and wind up in the foyer at the same time as Jonas, who was setting the table in the dining room. We share a laugh before interlocking fingers, and I offer him a kiss.

As I pull away, I say, "That was a sweet one."

"Get a room," comes from behind us, and we turn to see Charity coming down the stairs, sporting a tracksuit and a blonde wig with a pink streak in her bangs.

She wears a bright smile, which seems more natural than when I was getting to know her via FaceTiming with Jonas. She received excellent care at the hospital, but I suspect Jonas being by her side was at least partly responsible for her quick and steady recovery from her infection, along with how well she tolerated her remaining rounds of chemo. Simon never followed through with his threat to have her kicked out, and he continued paying her medical bills. And fortunately for us, the doctors have been so impressed with how the treatment is going that she's been able to stay home for the past few weeks, having her follow-ups at an affiliated clinic here in downtown Chicago, only thirty minutes away from Amy's home.

Charity passes us and opens the door, greeting Ahmed with a kiss. Jonas and I exchange a glance.

"I think she was being a bit of a hypocrite," I whisper, which makes Jonas's lips expand into an ear-to-ear grin. I've been seeing a lot more of those since we left Hawthorne Heights.

Ahmed and his parents arrived from Phoenix this morning, and I'm sure Charity is thrilled to finally have her long-distance boyfriend in her arms again. We usher our guests in, and the rest of our friends arrive shortly after. There's a bit of chaos in the kitchen as we get everything finished up and everyone grabs their food, but eventually things settle down in the dining room as we eat and enjoy a friendly conversation.

"This is a beautiful home," Ahmed's mom, Shira, says. "How far do you all work from here?"

"I work the odd job online," Amy says, "so that I'm able to help around the house."

"I'm in construction," Jonas says. "It can be about thirty minutes or an hour away depending on the gig, and Ryan…"

"Right now, I'm working with a landscaping company, but I'm planning to start my own business and then poach this guy from his job."

"Starting your own business?" Shira says. "That sounds expensive."

"I've been very fortunate. I inherited some money."

It's a misleading statement, but I'd rather not get into it. Really, after Jonas and I left that night, not only did Simon continue paying for Charity's care, but he also transferred a substantial amount of money into Jonas's and my bank accounts. A drop in the ocean to him, but it's helped us set ourselves up. Rebuild a life. It reminds me that despite all our differences and the fucked-up past we share, there will always be this connection between Simon and myself.

Our relationship was complicated. Something most people wouldn't understand. Hell, even I don't fully understand, and I'm not sure I ever will.

"I guess your brother must be very well off too," Shira says. "What does he do during the holidays?"

I tense up. Not just because of our past, but because all I can think of is him alone in that giant mansion, in a losing battle against the demons of our past, the same demons he battled with as he hammered away at his head and sliced at his flesh that dark night.

About a week after Jonas and I left, Nell caught me up on the events that had transpired. The cops found Simon, and he somehow managed to convince them he was fine. Can't help but wonder if money was involved in that too. Nell assures me he's doing much better now. I can only hope it's true. Only thing I know for certain is how much better I've been since I left. Hard to tell if it was the burden I carried or the place itself that made life such a struggle, but I've noticed things don't feel so heavy here with Jonas.

And it's easier to be hopeful about the future.

My only regret is leaving Morgan and Forsyth to work the property on their own. From what I understand, it's been a struggle for them to keep up with the workload. But they're young, strong, bright men, and regardless of what Simon has planned for them, I'm sure they'll find their way.

"My brother prefers his solitude," I tell Shira. "I used to be that way too, until I met this one and he pulled me out of my shell."

Jonas smirks, and everyone's eyes light up like they caught a glimpse of that magic I've felt since I got to know him and discover how very special he is.

After dinner, our friends stick around to help us clean up before heading on their way. As lively as Charity managed to be while her boyfriend was over, she has to take a much-needed rest.

Later that night, Jonas and I get ready for bed, and when he finishes his shower, he joins me in the bed, curling up to me as I finish writing my journal entry about my day. It's a pleasure I cherish every evening, appreciating now more than ever just how precious it is to have privacy and freedom to express my mind once again.

"Almost finished," I say.

He kisses my shoulder. Then kisses it again, and as I sneak a glance at him, I decide the journal can wait until tomorrow. I tuck it in the nightstand and slip under the covers with my Jonas.

"You seemed a little shaken," he says after a kiss, "when Shira brought up Simon."

"It's hard. It's the holidays, and I don't like thinking he's all by himself in that house. I know after all he did, I shouldn't even care, but I can't help it. He'll always be my brother, and I'll always care about him. The same is true for Kieran. I hate them both, but I love them too. Multiple truths."

"What?"

I snicker. "It's what Madge says."

Madge is my therapist. She's the second therapist I've seen since the day I freed myself from the self-imposed hell I'd been living. The first therapist's eyes kept popping when I said things that weren't even the worst of it. Madge is much better. She lets me take my time. Doesn't rush anything. And always offers a bit of insight that helps me understand myself a little better.

"Multiple truths means that more than one thing can be true. I can have horrible, nightmarish memories with someone, but also really lovely memories, and I don't have to pretend one isn't true. I can let those things coexist without trying to fit them all into a story that makes more sense."

"I can see how that'd be helpful," Jonas says.

"Helpful, yes, but I think it'll be a long time before I can get my head around it all."

"Well, as long as you know I'm here in whatever way you need me."

I kiss his cheek. "Thank you, Jonas. But tonight, I just need you to fuck me."

"Well, I did say whatever way you need me," he replies with a wicked expression before he takes my mouth again. His arms pull around me, and I relax in his hold.

I feel safe here. With him.

With each kiss, each caress, I find myself more and more in the moment, and Simon, Hawthorne Heights, and Kieran slip out of my reach, taking their rightful place in my mind.

As my past.

Allowing me to embrace my future with Jonas.

THE END

Receive New Release Alerts from Devon

eepurl.com/gi1Zzn

Find Devon on Social Media

linktr.ee/devonmccormack